The Hermit of Carmel

Gregory Phipps

Learn to become quiet, still, solitary. The world will offer itself to you to be unmasked.

Franz Kafka

chapter *I*

"Damn it, Rob!...I mean Paul. I can't keep your names straight. You might have mentioned this before we drove six bloody hours to come here."

Robert Das, who wrote his bestseller under the pseudonym Paul Thebét, was having second thoughts about this very public book reading. To say he was getting cold feet would be an understatement. His agent, Murray Levitt — everyone called him by his last name — was losing his patience.

Levitt continued his rant. "What the hell am I supposed to do now? Seriously. I could have gone golfing today. And it's actually sunny back in LA. I'm here to support you instead. My acid is going through the roof. I should have brought my damn reflux pills."

"Have a coffee and some hot chili peppers," said Robert.

"You're an asshole sometimes," countered Levitt.

"I value my privacy. You know that."

"And that's why you created the pseudonym. I get it. Nobody here knows who you really are. You're Paul Thebét. Relax. By the way, are you supposed to be French-Canadian or like, French-French? You never told me."

Robert ignored his sarcastic and rhetorical question. "Just cancel it. Let's leave. Nobody paid to come here. We don't have to give anyone a refund. I suspect it's all locals anyway. We drew, what, a hundred people to the store? I'm sure folks will buy a book while they're here. The owner will be happy. Tell her I have food poisoning or something. You're a good liar."

Levitt winced and shook his head. "No. We're not going to cancel it. You made a commitment to your publisher, and to me, that you'd do some readings. These aren't easy to get, you know. This is a big deal. And you're here in Carmel. You love Carmel! Locals are going nuts for this. You should see the Twitter chatter."

"I don't do social media."

"No shit. That's another thing we need to talk about. You're expected to be active on social media, and connect with your audience, to promote the book…. to build your brand. Work with me here please, Robert. You love to write. Social media is just another form of writing. It doesn't take a lot of work to write 140 fucking characters!"

"I'm not a writer. I'm a storyteller. You can't tell a story in 140 characters."

"Bullshit! Hemingway once wrote a short story in six words. Six words! Hemingway was a businessman… and quite content to sell books, anything, to make a buck. Listen to me, Rob. I am a businessman. I represent writers who tell stories and understand that publishing is a business. Consumer buys book. Retailer makes money. Distributor makes money. Printer makes money. Publisher makes money. Writer gets paid. Agent gets paid. It's simple. Think of it as one of those circle-of-life things. Like the forest and all its adorable creatures."

"You mean the ones that kill each other?" asked Robert.

"No, the ones that live symbiotically. Like the birds who knock pine cones off trees so the squirrels can eat the seeds."

"Birds don't do that at all. The owls in those woods out there," he said, motioning with his head, "kill and eat squirrels and even other birds. You mean that circle of life?"

"Great. You're a wildlife naturalist now. Be a writer for one hour… please. Maybe your next book can be an allegory with animal characters. How about a boy and a tiger stuck together on a lifeboat? Nobody buys that shit, Robert. Look, I know you're anxious. I know you aren't into the public speaking thing. But do this one reading and we'll talk about the others. Better yet, jump on that revolutionary new social media thing and you might never have to leave the comfort of your home again."

Levitt opened the stockroom door and pointed to the throng that had gathered on this rainy Saturday afternoon.

"Look out there. There's a bunch of successful, well-known business people, artists and even a few celebs here today. Look. It's crazy… in a good way." The look on Levitt's face suggested he regretted his comment the moment he released it. His observation probably reinforced Robert's stage fright.

"I should have returned to law," Robert sighed.

Levitt attempted to redeem himself.

"People hate lawyers. Lawyers only take. You give."

"But writers can't hide anymore."

"Truth," conceded Levitt. "But don't do the delicate genius thing."

"I am neither."

Levitt motioned to the room. "He probably doesn't do social media either, but Clint-fucking-Eastwood is out there. He's incognito, but I'm sure it's him. Geez, he got old. He used to be the frickin' mayor here. He's a living legend in Carmel. If all those people tweet about this, thousands of followers — readers — will hear about the book. This is business, Robert. When we deliver the numbers, I'll get you an advance for your next book. Then, you can tell another story. Any one you want. Please, as your agent, I'm begging you to do this. This crowd came because they love you and adore the book. You're a local hero, Rob."

"I live in Los Angeles, Murray."

"Whatever. You know what I meant."

Levitt grabbed Robert by the shoulders and manhandled him out of the skunky bookstore stockroom — like a football coach might a losing quarterback onto the field for the final quarter. They had been sequestered in the cramped and stale-smelling room for the last twenty minutes. Levitt noted the time — ten minutes later than the advertised start time of the reading. He spoke into Robert's ear, so he could be heard over the background noise, as they entered the bookstore proper.

"You crafted a great story, Robert — a real story. Write yourself a convincing story now. You're not afraid. You're an entertaining and confident speaker who loves his adoring fans and is equally loved by them. Play that role for an hour — like a character in a book. Put on sunglasses and an ascot and smoke a fucking pipe if it helps you create that persona. After this, drinks are on me. Promise. You can get drunk if you like. I'll drive back. You can get drunk while I'm driving back."

Robert looked grim. The bookstore owner saw them exit the stockroom, her cue to read a prepared introduction for Thebét. The sound of restrained applause replaced the muffled sounds of a hundred private conversations. Robert's heart raced as he shuffled onto the bookstore floor.

Robert appeared uncomfortable and out of his element standing before the group of locals, all presumably devotees. The throng filled every square foot of floor space in the modest bookstore not otherwise occupied by books — waiting. The number of people likely exceeded the allowable limit defined by local fire regulations. If the storeowner cared, it didn't show. She looked ecstatic. Thebét was a local celebrity, making the event a bit of a coup. It had taken a lot of cajoling to snag him. He was known to be reclusive. This was Thebét's first and, given his demeanor, might be his last reading ever. The proprietor of the store, a tiny woman of about sixty, waited patiently, like everyone else, for him to begin.

A damned podium or lectern to hide behind would have been nice, Robert fumed silently. He considered public speaking to be the worst form of torture for an introvert. Many writers are private people at the best of times. Robert was the personification of the solitary artist. His anxiety and fear of crowds had only increased over the years. While her intentions might have been honorable, the bookstore owner had only made things worse by providing a small, raised stage for him to stand — improving the view for attendees.

He swayed nervously on the platform, dressed in grey jeans and a black cashmere sweater — head adorned by a duckbill cap he'd neglected to remove. It represented the very last barrier behind which he could hide. Shifting his weight between feet, he looked as if he might've had to pee.

The cowbells on the front door jangled, creating a welcome distraction. One last couple pushed their way in, stomped the rain off their feet, and attempted to find a space to stand. The overcrowded store was uncomfortably damp — so many warm bodies exhaling humid air. The proprietor felt it too. She pushed her way back through the throng, excusing herself profusely as she parted people with outreached arms. She swung open the top half of the Dutch door, common in entrances to retail stores in tony Carmel-by-the-Sea. A blast of fresh, cool air flooded the room. The opening also provided additional guests the opportunity of viewing from the sidewalk outside. The proprietor could offer gawking room only at this point.

Robert had no reason to be anxious, really. The crowd had come to see and hear him, the writer they so admired, read from his bestselling book. They wouldn't be here, he reasoned, if they didn't like it. You wouldn't attend an author's reading if you didn't. Who heckles an author at a book reading? Breathing deeply, he tried to calm his nerves enough to get started. A glass of anything alcoholic would have come in handy right about now. Sherry. That would calm my nerves. The crowd looked increasingly impatient as he stood there fidgeting with a copy of the book, fashioning dog ears on the cover. To the author, it felt like twenty minutes had passed. In reality, it had been a minute and a half since the introduction. If the crowd had had any idea how personal the book was, they might have empathized more. They didn't. No one could've known.

The guests also couldn't be privy to the frantic deliberation going on in Robert's head. What would I or should I reveal about what I know about the Hermit? The man deserved his privacy. While he wished to respect that, the book, he felt, needed to be written — and for so many reasons. Robert felt pride in the work, sure, but more importantly, he hoped it would speak to readers, particularly those with exposure to grief and depression — their own, or that suffered by friends or family. Writing the book had been therapeutic for him on a personal level, too.

Group psychotherapy, Robert thought, must be exactly like this. Stand; introduce yourself; tell a bunch of strangers why you're there; and bare your soul for all to judge. Few would deny that writing a book — compiling those words, paragraphs, and chapters — demands that an author render him or herself vulnerable. He felt extraordinarily so now. He was one neurotic thought away from a full-blown anxiety attack.

Robert lifted his cap, ran his hand through his thinning hair, and looked back at the crowd to gauge their level of restlessness — another stall tactic. Will the crowd all leave in another minute if I don't start? A slight smile broke onto his face at the thought, and he considered delaying further. Scanning the room, he spied a striking woman. She was slim, well kept, well dressed, and standing near the back of the store — attractive, by any measure. The two locked eyes for a moment. She looked back at Robert without blinking and gave him a warm and knowing smile, crow's feet framing her kind eyes. The innocuous gesture was the catalyst he needed. His chest rose as he gathered a breath and exhaled audibly. He began.

"Thank you all for coming here today. The weather didn't cooperate, and I'm not doing much better." His voice crackled, gaining confidence once he saw a few smiles. The attempt at self-deprecating humor proved charmingly awkward. "I am grateful that you enjoyed my book and took the time to join me here. At least, I presume you've read my book already. I also hope that you all paid for your personal copies," he teased. "If you did, then by my rough calculation, I've broken even on the cost of gas to travel up here today, from LA, to sign copies and read a little."

Subdued laughter at a volume appropriate to a library, or its retail equal, filled the bookstore.

"This is the first time I've been asked to read from The Hermit of Carmel aloud, and I'm a little apprehensive. Perhaps nervous is better word. To be honest, I've dreamed of doing this, right here in Carmel, for a while. Thank you for making my dream a reality. I'm humbled and honored."

Robert dipped his head — a deferential bow to the crowd. From the corner of his eye, he noticed Levitt grin, color returning to his face. Robert proved a convincing liar himself. He paused, took a sip of water, and glanced at his wrist without consciously noting the time — a tic he had developed some years before. More than anything, he was checking to ensure his watch was still there. He had lost it once and wouldn't allow it to happen a second time, under any circumstance. It remained the most important material item he possessed.

Levitt waved one hand for attention and mouthed the words, "Take off your hat," hoping Robert could read his lips from where he stood.

Robert could, removed his cap and continued. "I knew the Hermit well… at one point. For those who don't already know, this is a true story — a fictionalized account of sorts. Narrative non-fiction is what the publishers call it. It's always the first thing readers ask when we meet. Some folks living in the area might know parts of the story. You might have even caught a glimpse of the Hermit. I'm quite certain that none of you truly knew him, though. I'm uncertain that anyone really knew him. He was a complicated man who meant well but had been hobbled by sadness and a profound sense of loss.

"You know," he continued, gaining some confidence. "I try not to be judgmental. People process and react to grief in unpredictable and sometimes unproductive ways. The Hermit's loss triggered a deep depression, which in turn, drove him into the woods. In the forest, he battled his private demons, the physical elements, and a few locals. It's hard to say what saved him — his inner strength, or the game of golf. Perhaps a little of both."

Robert reached into his pocket, pulled out a handkerchief, and wiped the nervous sweat from his brow. Holding the copy of his book slightly aloft, as a preacher might a Bible, he spoke with equal reverence.

"This is his story."

He paused, unintentionally adding to the dramatic effect.

"I'm not sure what you folks want from this afternoon. I'd like to live up to your expectations, whatever those might be. Was there a section or chapter you'd like me to read, or would you rather hear small excerpts from a few different chapters, like you're sampling a flight of wine?"

He looked around the room, hoping for a hint or definitive response. After a moment of uncomfortable quiet, a female speaker, unseen by the author, but about mid-crowd, broke the silence.

"Just read, please," she said, in a restrained and respectful way. All heads nodded in agreement. And he did, from the start, in his best narrative voice. The room became quiet again and Robert perceived that the crowd collectively leaned in — just a bit. From her station, at the back of the store, the tall, striking woman caught his attention, again. She placed two fingers on her lips, removed a kiss and pointed it in his direction. To anyone else watching, it might have appeared an inappropriately familiar gesture. Only Robert noticed.

chapter 2

The bailiff leapt to his feet, caught off guard by the judge's unexpected entry into the courtroom. He looked embarrassed to have been unprepared. He should have been more so. There was not much more to the job, frankly.

"All rise," he stated hurriedly. "The Superior Court of California, County of Monterey, is now in session. Judge Dina Kerry presiding. Please be seated."

He issued his well-practiced script so rapidly that most in the courtroom hadn't risen to their feet before being directed to sit again. The gallery appeared to be simply shifting in their seats, trying to get more comfortable. The bailiff caught himself and slowed his pace.

"I apologize, Your Honor. Here are the docket files for this morning."

She raised her hand, accepting the stack of paperwork without looking at him.

"The court is now in session," added the bailiff. He looked at the judge, seeking forgiveness, or at least acknowledgement. He got neither. The bailiff sulked for the rest of the proceedings. To add insult to injury, he had to stand the entire time, while the judge enjoyed comfortable leather seating. At least the courtroom was air-conditioned. Dark circles, from sweat, circled the underarms of the bailiff's otherwise well-pressed uniform top. He opted to walk to work this hot, summer morning. The bailiff drew a handkerchief from his pocket and blotted his brow.

"Good morning, ladies and gentlemen, counsels," the judge said in a rather robotic monotone. "First case on this morning's docket — People of the State of California versus Das — for plea hearing. Are both sides prepared?"

The smartly-suited district attorney responded enthusiastically. "Ready for the People, Your Honor."

The defense for the plaintiff did not appear present, but the judge hadn't noticed. She seemed preoccupied with the files strewn about her substantial desk and had yet to look up. When she finally turned her attention to the court, she fixated her gaze on the bench clerk — by any measure an exceptionally attractive and athletic young Hispanic woman. The clerk was wearing an inappropriately short skirt for a courtroom. She smiled at the judge and enjoyed an appreciative smile in return, causing her to blush. Judge Kerry nodded her head, a non-verbal cue for the clerk to fulfill her duties.

The pretty bench clerk slowly read from a printed document she held, careful to convey the details with the utmost accuracy. She had a delightfully melodic, Hispanic accent. From a purely technical perspective, her English was flawless.

"Under Title 9 of the Carmel-by-the-Sea Municipal Code, the following charges have been filed: Per Section 9.24 — disorderly conduct under section of the municipal code 647 (h).

"That's loitering, Your Honour," clarified the bench clerk. "Per Section 9.24 Criminal Trespass, Section 602 (a) — cutting down, destroying, or injuring wood or timber standing or growing upon the lands of the city of Carmel; and (b) — carrying away any kind of wood or timber lying on those lands."

The judge, looking intently at the young female clerk, raised one eyebrow and asked, "Is it alleged that the defendant stole timber or finished lumber?"

"I'm not sure, Your Honor. I think they were trees. Living ones. The District Attorney can perhaps clarify for you."

The judge nodded her acknowledgement, eyes locked on the clerk. The intensity of the attention she was paying the young lady had not gone unnoticed. Some in the courtroom began to be discomfited; not Robert Das, the defendant. He was somewhat aroused. The judge raised her palm to signal the clerk to take pause.

"I love your blouse, by the way. It's simply gorgeous! Where did you buy it?" Her comment came off as passively flirtatious.

The clerk smiled, tilted her head a little, and brushed her long brown hair away from her eyes. "Thank you, Your Honor. I'm flattered. It's from Banana Republic."

The judge returned the smile and nodded her head in acknowledgement. The attractive clerk continued reading the charges against the defendant.

"Under Section 602 (d) — digging, taking, or carrying away from any lot situated within the limits of any incorporated city, without the license of the owner or legal occupant, any earth, soil, or stone."

Judge Kerry looked over her reading glasses and interrupted the bench clerk again. "Clarify for me, please. What exactly did he… er, was he *alleged* to have stolen?"

"He carried away rocks, Your Honor."

"Rocks?"

"Yes, Your Honor. Rocks. Nothing on the charge file indicates their size or mineral composition." The clerk continued once more. "Under Section 602 (f) — maliciously tearing down, damaging, mutilating, or destroying any sign, signboard, or notice placed upon, or affixed to, any property belonging to the state, or to any city, county, city and county, town, or village, or upon any property of any person, by the state or by an automobile association, which sign, signboard, or notice is intended to indicate or designate a road or a highway, or is intended to direct travelers from one point to another. Under Section 602 (i) — willfully opening, tearing down, or otherwise destroying any fence on the enclosed land of another…"

The judge interrupted again.

"He stole a fence?"

"He is alleged to have stolen fence boards from a property, Your Honor."

"Oh. City property or private?"

"Private, Your Honor."

"Got it. By the way, do you think that these judicial robes make me look fat?"

"No, actually; black is very slimming on you. You're rocking that robe, Your Honor. A double string of pearls might be a nice way to accessorize it, though."

"You're sweet. Thank you. You look very nice too. That skirt is… wow. But please, carry on."

The discourse between the two, and the entire morning, was out of the ordinary. Nonetheless, the clerk continued to read out the litany of charges.

"Section 602 (n) — driving a vehicle, as defined in Section 670 of the Vehicle Code, upon real property belonging to, or lawfully occupied by, another and known not to be open to the public; Section 602 (o) — refusing or failing to leave land, real property, or structures belonging to or lawfully occupied by another and not open to the public, upon request to leave by a peace officer"

"That's squatting, Your Honor," Robert said, to provide clarity, and to hasten the process.

"You're not invited to speak at this point, Mr. Das," the judge chided.

"Section 602 (q) — refusing or failing to leave a public building of a public agency during those hours of the day or night when the building is closed to the public."

Robert rocked on his heels as he listened to the list of charges filed against him. He struggled to keep his eyes open. I want to sleep, he thought. I need to sleep.

Judge Kerry looked bored — or horny. Maybe both. Robert couldn't be certain. She had a far-off, dreamy look in her eyes, a slight part in her lips, and seemed clearly disinterested in the proceedings. The judge did not make eye contact with Robert. Her Honor continued to direct her comments and questions to the bench clerk — chin resting in her hands and her elbows on the bench. While the judge ogled the clerk, the clerk, in turn, gazed at Robert sympathetically and, he perceived, rather seductively. He noticed and alternated his attention between the judge and the clerk. Once the charges had all been read and recorded by the court stenographer, the judge advised Robert of his constitutional rights to a jury or court trial, the right to a court-appointed attorney, and the presumption of innocence.

Robert rolled his eyes and waited for her to finish. "I choose to represent myself, Your Honor."

"These are serious charges, Mr. Das. I would recommend that you retain trained counsel, or at least a public defender, to represent you. Your demeanor here in my court suggests that you don't take these charges very seriously." She paused, waiting for a response, and cleared her throat. "Very well then. How do you plead to the charges, Mr. Das?"

"No contest, Your Honor." Robert eyed the bench clerk and proffered a confident wink.

The judge looked over, for the first time, to inspect the defendant. "Do you consider red golf slacks appropriate attire for my court?" she asked. Her furrowed brow and facial expression conveyed irritation, followed by confusion. A moment later, the look on her face suggested recognition.

"Have we met before, Mr. Das? I mean, have you been before my bench in the past? You look awfully familiar."

"Yes, Your Honor. Funny, I realized it just now myself. I graduated from Stanford Law with you. You don't remember me, do you? I helped you through second semester. You were thinking of dropping out. Struggling with Civil Procedure, if I recall."

"Rob? Rob Das?" the judge exclaimed excitedly before tempering her enthusiasm.

He offered a half-smile and shrugged — the best he could do, given the gravity of the situation. The judge struggled for words. She turned and surveyed the prosecution, the bench clerk, and the bailiff with wide eyes and a raised brow. She was uncertain if it had been entirely appropriate for her to acknowledge knowing the defendant on a personal level, even if it had been more than a decade since she'd seen him.

"How could you do all this, Rob? You're a lawyer! What the hell happened?"

Robert took advantage of the momentary distraction in the courtroom. Vaulting over the low wall defining the defendant's box, Robert sprinted for the back of the court. Dropping his shoulder, he launched himself like a ram into the heavy courtroom door. Between his mass and momentum, the door readily surrendered and swung open hard, the bronze door handles denting the wood paneling behind. The sultry bench clerk called out, "Run, Rob!" drawing a mixed look of confusion, anger, and hurt from the judge. The guard in the lobby could barely get out a word, let alone apprehend him, before Robert pushed through the front glass doors of the courthouse. He jumped all four front steps and sprinted across the parking lot, heading west.

The Monterey County Superior Courthouse sits like a castle on a stubby, natural mesa, bounded by twenty-foot-high earthen sides. The busy Pacific Coast Highway, running along the west side of the courthouse, acts like a moat, keeping people in or out, depending on your perspective. Robert stumbled and rolled down its steep embankment. He ran as quickly as a man bound in handcuffs can, along the treed slope that paralleled the highway. A host of court security officers set out in chase. Two pursued him on foot and another pair headed for a court vehicle.

If I can only make it to the woods, Robert thought. Frantic shouting rang in his ears, motivating his pace. *These bright red slacks*, he concluded, *are unlikely to help camouflage me right now. Why did I wear red golf slacks?* A low, steel guardrail separated him from traffic flying by at 70 miles per hour. He dismissed the idea of evading the guards by crossing the highway. Two court sheriffs, a woman and man, jumped into a Court Services–marked Chevy Suburban. The two remained parked, engine running and siren blaring, while they vigorously debated which route they should take.

"Take Aquahito to Farragut Road and cut him off there!"

"No. We should take Alan to Bergin Drive and then to Leahy Road. We need to get out ahead of him!"

"No. You're way off. Look at the map."

"He's getting away."

"We're going to get fired. It'll be your fault."

"No, it'll be *your* fault!"

Meanwhile, the voices chasing on foot grew more faint. Robert looked over his shoulder to gauge his lead on the pursuers. He had gained some ground. The posse had been right on his heels a moment ago. It was bewildering to see nobody chasing any longer. *Where did they go?* he wondered.

Robert continued running, shocked by how quickly he reached the forest and how dusky it had quite suddenly become. Once in the dim wood and certain he had fled his captors, he finally relaxed. This was his safe zone. The shouting and sound of sirens faded. All was silent. Only the faint chirp of crickets outside and the sound of his own labored breathing nudged the peaceful night.

After several aborted attempts, Robert opened his heavy eyes. Disoriented by the deep sleep and incredibly vivid and peculiar dream, he stared into the blackness of the small, makeshift cabin. It was dark: so much so he couldn't see his feet, let alone the walls. He swung his legs out over the cot on which he had been lying and sat up. Night sweat dampened his clothing and the thin sheet covering him. Like smelling salts, the rich, organic odors of the shack tickled his nose. These were familiar smells — a combination of natural, earthy musk and his own body odor. Robert inhaled and held it, wiped his face and neck with the bed sheet, and rubbed his eyes before releasing his breath with an audible sigh. His current reality was more extraordinary than the dream. But the solitude he enjoyed provided opportunity for introspection and healing. There was no thought of trading the dream for his current existence. Real life can never be bartered for a fantasy.

The dream faded quickly, as all do. His nocturnal erection, however, remained unabated. It had been almost two years since Robert had enjoyed sex with a woman. He was hardly at fault for retaining a vision of the pretty Hispanic bench clerk in the short skirt as the rest of the fantasy evaporated into the cool night air. She was exquisite. He couldn't get her out of his mind — and didn't want to.

"Jules," he whispered, before lying back down and drifting back to sleep.

chapter 3

Sunrise on the Monterey Peninsula can be anticlimactic. After being spoiled by the spectacular sunsets, one rising early might be disappointed by the subtlety of the morning. The contrast is dramatic. The theatre of stars eventually fades and is replaced by a wash of dull light that makes every turn, every view, into a very convincing watercolor painting by an artist trying to conserve her expensive paints. It's downright boring — at first. On the crescent beach at Carmel-by-the-Sea, or Carmel, as most often called, first light is always subject to postponement. The coastal range, with Mount Toro and Jacks Peak, sequesters the dawn each morning. The Del Monte Forest provides backup and curtains the rising sun, until it feels it's time to throw them open — requiring the entire Carmel Valley to squint.

Dawn competes for dominance with the cool morning fog that often overwhelms the coast and inland for several miles. Once the conflict gets settled, the dim light of morning eventually transforms grey, vague shapes and shadows into recognizable landmarks. You can begin to discern subtle colors and the gentle movement of trees. Light arrives at the western edge of the peninsula, where land meets the Pacific, last. Standing by the water's edge, one begins to appreciate that the sound heard in the darkness has a vast sea behind it. At different points along the coast, that ocean reluctantly surrenders to a sloping beach; ends in a draw after an indecisive battle against jagged rocks; or is defeated and sent into retreat by cliffs reinforced by a battalion of granite. The warfare between ocean and land repeats itself in perpetuity and the dispute between light and dark gets settled — every twenty-four hours.

Once dawn arrives, you'd enjoy a first glimpse of what holds back the light: the mountains that loom over the peninsula to the east and south. If there weren't already too many peaks, rocks, domes, and mountains named *Sentinel*, one viewing the range might be tempted to adopt the name. The ridge affords the coast protection from marauding invaders rolling in from across the Pacific, rear guard to the rocks and cliffs that contain the sea below. The coast along this stretch of the California shoreline is melodramatic, an exaggeration of how one might paint a bold and rugged coastline in one's imagination: coastal rocks, foamy surf, fine sand beaches, gnarled trees, quivering forests, looming mountains. Yet the beauty of the area is authentic. There is no shortage of spectacularly beautiful places in this world, but the Monterey Peninsula, like a favored and spoiled child, enjoys an unfair share of gifts.

With the benefit of first light, you start to appreciate the fauna of the area, too. Standing by the coast, you can pick out the low-flying silhouette of top-heavy pelicans and an overstatement of unruly, raucous birds, including western gulls, crows, jays, and blackbirds. On the beach, a disorderly assortment of shorebirds emerges to begin grooming random stretches of sand for the human replacement crew, scheduled to arrive a few hours later. In the surf, on a good day, you might see California sea lions, harbor seals, sea otters, and an occasional orca or grey whale performing without reward or applause. The one thing that seems to draw all the birds and beasts together is the expanse of beach at Carmel.

The beach is, in a word, magical. Roughly a mile in length, it mimics a scythe's gentle curve. Adorned by white sand and pounded by turquoise blue surf, it does a pretty good imitation of a bleached Caribbean shoreline. At night, it hosts turtles, crabs, and shorebirds, who all clock out at dawn and turn it over to the day shift: dogs. Their human companions are welcome join them, but Carmel Beach City Park is a dog's paradise. The canines often equal the residents and visitors that shuffle in the deep sand, trying their best to keep up. Local ordinances here allow dogs off leash, and daily the beach becomes a playground for breeds of all sizes and shapes. Dogs don't express the spectrum of facial expression we do. If, however, you've seen a dog running on a beach, greeting other dogs and leaping carefree into the ocean surge, you have seen pure, unadulterated joy.

No matter the species that gather, the beach is at its best on the shoulders of the day — dawn and dusk. The low light softens the bright white sand and the surf melds into the beach. As the day shift departs, the night shift wings in to clean up the mess, and balance is restored again.

Turning your back to the glowing sky on the western horizon, your attention might be drawn to the mountains to the east. One pinnacle stands head and shoulders above the rest and demands to get equal consideration as the beach. Jacks Peak is the highest point on the Monterey Peninsula: the guardian that monitors Carmel. Jacks Peak County Park offers the best day-hiking in the area and incorporates about one third of the mountain, including its summit. There are a hundred scenic walks in and around Carmel but people tackle Jacks, when the weather cooperates, for the vista it affords, high over the peninsula. One thousand feet in altitude, it provides for the best view of the small cities of Carmel-by-the-Sea, Pacific Grove, Monterey, Seaside, and Sand City to the north and west; the Carmel Valley to the south and east; and, to the southwest, a knob of rock, Point Lobos, punctuates the sea and defines the southern rim of Carmel Bay. Acclaimed local artist Francis McComas called Lobos "the greatest meeting of land and water in the world." He was spot on. Its beauty is more evident when you're closer, at sea level. But even from Jacks, it's damned impressive.

On a clear day, if you look northwest from the peak, you can catch a glimpse of sporadic bursts of unnaturally green and sharply defined fairways on the nineteen golf courses that dominate the peninsula. The courses and intermittent forest coverage are, in turn, punctuated and divided by a sharp black line. Highway 1, the Cabrillo Highway, passes through on its way south to equally awe-inspiring scenery along the coast, at Big Sur.

If driving, you'd likely take Jacks Peak Road to its summit. It's a steep, narrow, and winding strip of pavement and the only guardrails are the trees at its precipitous edges. It's tempting to slow at every break in the trees — not for fear of driving off the shoulder, which would be unfortunate, but to enjoy the astonishing views below. Jacks Peak stands proud and takes the full brunt of winds from the Pacific. The road and trails are closed to motor and foot traffic during storms, for reasons that become entirely obvious if you've been on its pinnacle. Storm or not, it's almost always cool and windy at the peak, just enough to make a strenuous hike more comfortable. Leaving your car behind, your walk through the trails takes a more purposeful course. If you allow yourself, you can enjoy a truly religious interaction with the flora of the park. The forests of the Monterey Peninsula feature some of the rarest endangered species of trees in the state, and, you will pass through one of only three remaining native stands of Monterey pine. The resilient pines stand on guard beside vigilant groves of live oaks, nut-bearing pinyon pines, redwoods stunted by high winds, and, as you leave the peak and descend toward to the peninsula proper, the rare *cupressus macrocarpa*, or Monterey cypress, is finally introduced to the hiker. This species of cypress is native to the Central Coast of California and is now confined to two small, relict populations. Those reside at

Cypress Point, near Pebble Beach, and at Point Lobos, south of Carmel-by-the-Sea. There, these refugees are protected within the bosom of the state park.

If you arrived at Jacks on foot, once ready to descend you'd want to head due west down a well-worn dirt trail. Your trip down will be easier. Gravity will do most of the work for you. The trail ends in the front yard of a ranch-style home at the foot of the peak. From there, you can pick up an easier path on Loma Alta Road. After a thirty-minute walk past more homes and a horse farm, after dodging cars crossing the Cabrillo Highway, you'd find yourself in the Carmel Woods, a section of the greater Del Monte Forest. The Del Monte Forest incorporates the better part of the Monterey Peninsula — ten square miles in all, aligned between Monterey, Pacific Grove, and Carmel. It includes many of the famous and immaculately manicured public and private golf courses in the area: Pebble Beach, Spyglass, Poppy Hills and Cypress Point.

It's taking considerable license to continue to call the Del Monte a forest. Residential development and golf courses have almost completely encroached on the cypress and pine forests that once dominated the landscape in this corner of California. Developers and homeowners, particularly those with the net worth to build houses valued upwards of twenty million dollars, are partial to naming their streets "Forest," "Woods," "Evergreen," "Grove," or "Glade." I suspect it reinforces the natural element and environment that residents want to believe they live in, even if builders bulldozed an acre of old growth to build a new home and then spent a quarter of a million dollars on filling the yard with plants and trees that aren't exactly native to the area. Perhaps it's unfair to be so critical. At the very least, Pine Meadows Way, near the Carmel Woods, is lined by, well, pine trees.

The homes in Carmel are, with few exceptions, exceedingly attractive. Residents spare no expense in ensuring their exterior design and landscaping conforms to the expectations of their neighbors and the community. Most of the peninsula is a high-rent neighborhood in which only the wealthy can afford to live, and it shows. There are no apologies for wealth among its residents; nor, arguably, should there be. Whether through inheritance, good luck, or years of hard work, those that make Carmel and area their home delight in the good fortune of being able to afford to live in one of the most stunning neighborhoods in the world.

Urban encroachment is an insidious force that rarely spares picturesque areas of the world. Natural beauty attracts people that want to live near, to enjoy it, regardless of the impact. Carmel is no exception. After the last fifty years of active development, only a small segment of the east end of the Del Monte remains forested. It's a managed forest, and not that densely treed. Light and shadow interplay along its forest floor and the breeze is barely slowed by the foliage. The well-manicured and well-managed residences of the Carmel Woods mirror the orderly wood that surrounds them.

Carmel Woods, as it exists today, is completely hemmed in and held captive by Ronda Road to the west, Sunridge Road to the north, and 17-Mile Drive on the eastern and southern perimeter. The infamous 17-Mile Drive has been attracting tourists since its opening in 1881. I use the term *infamous* because the community of 17-Mile Drive is the only residential neighborhood, of which I'm aware, that demands a ten-dollar toll from visitors. Small guard booths, manned during the day, collect a fee and offer a full-color tourist map in exchange from permanent gated points at one of five entry sites, including those at Carmel, Pacific Grove, and the Cabrillo Highway. To be honest, once you've experienced the drive on a clear and sunny day, you're unlikely to begrudge the fee or the traffic. More likely, you'll compare the value received to any museum or art gallery for which you've shelled out twenty dollars and enjoyed equally. The peninsula evokes tremendous emotion. Each turn of the head creates a new composition that inspires pause and appreciation for its form, movement, and color. You'll be convinced that each wind-worn and purposefully bent Cypress that you pass along the western edge of the peninsula drive has been carefully crafted by an artist as a sculptural installation, to be picked up and moved to the next museum in its world tour after a three-month showing.

If flying over the area, you'd note that the collection of residential neighborhoods, woods, and golf courses, equally divide the prized and highly priced nub of land resting almost exactly halfway between the northern and southern borders of California. The manicured golf courses seem to all touch one another like a game of connect-the-dots — that is, when ground fog clears enough to view them all.

Carmel Woods itself is fewer than two miles in length, north to south, and less than one mile at its widest point. This, the largest tract of forest on the peninsula proper, is divided by Ronda and Sunridge Roads where they intersect. The Carmel Woods is now completely encircled by well-kept and expensive rancher, Spanish, Tudor, and a smattering of smart, contemporary-style homes. Those residences enjoy a daily mix of sun and shade and attract an annual mix of high maintenance costs and astronomic property taxes.

The southern segment of the Carmel Woods features a sharply sloped traversable ravine that runs north-south and encompasses roughly a square mile of forest hemmed in by 17-Mile Drive, and Ronda, Sunridge, and Spruance roads. If you strolled through the gulley, crossed at either Ronda or Sunridge, and hiked due north, you'd soon run out of forest coverage and wind up dodging dimpled missiles on the driving range or adjacent tee boxes, at the ninth hole at Poppy Hills Golf Course.

Continuing north through the woods for almost a mile and crossing Congress Road, you would find yourself standing on the eighth hole of the Dunes course at the very private, very posh Monterey Peninsula Country Club. You can walk through the intermittent forest coverage and cross few roads to access every course on the peninsula without even having to pass through someone's backyard. All forms of wildlife that share the area with residents appreciate its trees. Most residents of the area are otherwise uninterested in the woods.

Outside of the wilds of Carmel Valley, to the east and south, the compact grove of pine and cypress that define the Carmel Woods still represents the quietest and most private enclave on the Monterey Peninsula. There's a well-used dirt trail that traverses the woods and runs roughly parallel to the ravine from Sunridge down to Del Ciervo Road. Individuals inclined to take a hike through this part of the woods seldom stray off the path onto the rough edges of the gulley. You can walk through trails on the undulating, high segments in the woods shared by black-tail deer, pheasants, a few bobcats, on rare occasions a black bear, riders on horseback, and the occasional off-leash dog. It's not a particularly demanding trek if you remain on the trail. From 17-Mile Drive, on the south fringe of the woods, there's a slight grade when headed north. Upon retracing your path, you'd enjoy a downhill lift, thanks to gravity, that makes the hike seem downright easy.

It's not the density of the tree coverage that dissuades hikers from leaving the trail — it's the tangle of fallen trees and stumps that makes progress challenging. The gulley is even more uninviting. Frequently, you can't glimpse the bottom of it. It's more densely treed and in shadow for much of the day. When the mist rolls in, the ravine — the lowest point in the woods — retains its foggy veil even after the sun burns the haze off the remainder of the peninsula. On an otherwise sunny morning, it's astonishing to arrive at the edge of the ravine to see it filled to the brim with white fog, adding to its air of mystery. The gulch, and the entire Carmel Woods, were a great place for myths and stories to be born — fueled by the vivid imagination of bored teenagers who explore the woods on long summer nights prompted by beers and a judicious helping of peer pressure.

It was assumed for some time that stories of a wild man living in the ravine were nothing but the product of the overactive imagination of kids tromping the woods. Variations of the tale, as it evolved, ran from the inhabitation of the woods by a young Sasquatch; a dramatic account centered on a runaway, who camped out and stole food from local garbage cans to survive; and a theatrical mythology surrounding an unshaven, unintelligible, and unpredictable hermit whose home had been foreclosed by a local bank. He apparently refused to leave his home and, under threat of forcible eviction, decided to camp out in the woods. Missing pets, building materials, garden gnomes, and cars, as well as a few local divorces, were all variously attributed to a stranger who had taken up residence in the woods. The folklore made for interesting coffee shop gossip and late-night, alcohol-soaked cocktail party stories. But none of the stories were taken completely seriously. Even amongst those who did see an occasional person disappear into the gulley, no one got a good clear look at the individual, or was convinced that he was, in fact, a homeless man who made the woods his abode. Some residents expressed concern about *anyone* skulking about or loitering in the woods, legitimately or otherwise. Many considered the forest to represent a security risk despite the beauty and privacy the woods afforded. For some, any activity in the woods put them on the defensive — they were concerned that someone might be casing homes to burgle them when the owners departed.

In any event, it became obvious to some locals that, over the span of two years, *someone* was going in and out of the gulley quite regularly. What proved uncertain was whether that some-one was a resident, a visiting tourist, an enthusiastic naturalist, or a legitimately homeless person. To most, the latter theory seemed the least plausible.

To be sure, there is unambiguous evidence of a homeless population in the neighboring city of Monterey. Around the waterfront and tourist areas and on the streets leading into the city, there is a regular procession of persons seeking handouts, their entire lives contained in a shopping cart purloined from a local grocery store. But just miles away, few residents of neighboring Carmel had much, if any, exposure to homelessness, and none were aware of any displaced population taking up residence in Carmel itself. It is, after all, one of the wealthiest small cities in North America. You don't walk down Ocean Avenue and see down-on-their-luck individuals panhandling like you might in San Francisco or Los Angeles. It just doesn't happen. Carmel is beautiful, clean, well-kept, well-coiffed, well-buttoned, and well-policed. The city caters to residents and tourists who enjoy significant net worth and are ready to spend it.

The majority of residents were unaware of any rumors of someone living in the woods. If they were, their primary concern related to the security of their homes. Given the significant wealth and assets accumulated within the residences of the neighborhood, the area had become the target of burglars and at least one violent home invasion in recent years. Not long before, smash-and-grab robbers successfully burgled the Coach leather goods store. If any jewelry stores had been robbed, I'm unaware. I suspect it's easier for thieves to fence a hundred stolen purses than a single fifty-thousand-dollar necklace. No matter the rumors, residences surrounding the woods were well-secured, well-alarmed, well-armed, video-monitored, and locked down, making their owners unperturbed by any stories of the so-called Hermit that may or may not have made the woods his home.

There were a greater number of believers among the golfers that frequented the courses lying within the Del Monte. Many of the local courses enjoy forest borders. An unseen voice had made its presence known, in a most subtle and unthreatening way, over the previous year or so. Like the deer that also call the local woods home, the Hermit might peek his head out early in the morning or at dusk and hightail it when seen or approached. Nobody knew the identity or motive of the elusive stranger or whether he was truly a hermit, in the traditional sense, or merely an eccentric local resident hanging around the woods. The hermit story seemed to command greater curiosity and audience back in the clubhouse over nineteenth-hole cocktails. It became a source of status to declare that you had seen the Hermit. It elicited howls of laughter if bar patrons heard that he called you out, from the safety of the woods, after witnessing you kick your ball from the rough to a better position on the fairway. If nothing else, the Hermit had kept golfers honest. That proved to be sufficient reason to raise one's beer glass or order another round. Or two.

As for the woods, one must only take a walk through them to appreciate their serenity and relative seclusion, among a sea of handsome mansions and heavily trafficked roads. If one were looking for a quiet, contemplative site to ponder life for a couple of hours, this would be an idyllic spot. For someone with longer-term plans, it was an ideal, tranquil place to remain purposefully hidden. If one were homeless, voluntarily or otherwise, there could be far worse places in which you might find yourself. The Monterey Peninsula, while on occasion damp and chilly, allows for year-round outdoor living — at least for the hardy and unpampered. It's an idyllic location for someone who wishes to access the infrastructure and resources of nearby Carmel. It is also the perfect place for someone who might want to interact with society on his or her own terms.

chapter 4

As happens so frequently in early spring, morning fog softened the subtle division of greens that delineate the woods, rough, and fairways at Poppy Hills Golf Club. It would be hours before it burned off fully. Poppy Hills is a lovely, 164-acre, eighteen-hole, seven-thousand-yard, public course that sits north of Ronda Road and south of the Forest Lake reservoir, on the east side of the Carmel Woods. The front nine lies south of Lopez and golfers must traverse the road to get to the back nine. You'd be advised to pay attention if you cross here, though. Regrettably, but through nobody's fault, a clump of trees obscures a bend in the road, right at this spot. I have no confirmation if a golfer has ever been struck and killed here, but I can imagine there have been some close calls. Many a distracted tourist enjoying the 17-Mile Drive and trying to catch a glimpse of each golf course on the loop has failed to see pedestrians, warning signs notwithstanding. Regular golfers who pass here have adopted a policy of running, not walking, across this stretch of road. If within earshot, you can hear their golf shoe cleats clicking on the tarmac like tiny, shodden, horse hooves.

The east side of the course, demarcated by the western edge of the longest unbroken tract of the Carmel Woods, is not quite a mile and a half at its longest. That chunk of forest, like Poppy Hills itself, enjoys an abundance of wildlife — likely more than any other of the local courses. Predominantly deer. Depending on your perspective, this might be a blessing or a curse. I doubt the deer consider human opinion in any event. While it might be a subjective appraisal, Poppy Hills is quite possibly also the quietest course in the area. The forest buffer insulates it from the many roads, heavy traffic, and residential neighborhoods that overwhelm the peninsula.

The clubhouse clock clicked ten minutes past eight when the ambitious first foursome of the morning made the turn at the ninth hole. The golfers hustled across Lopez without harm and approached the tee box on the tenth hole — a 527-yard (from the pro tee) beast of a hole. If the distance isn't intimidating enough, the hole will thwart your par attempt with a large pond that overpowers the fairway and guards the green jealously. On this misty morning, the silence of the course provoked a kind of quiet reverence for nature that one might otherwise save for Sunday church service. Three handsome does and a buck grazing in the rough bolted for forest cover upon hearing the distinctive *tink* of the first drive.

Each golfer skillfully placed his ball on the fairway, and together they proceeded down the green for the follow-up. The golf carts left glistening paths on the morning dew. The foursome spoke in hushed tones as they eased out of their electric carriages and strode toward one golfer's ball. It lay on the right-hand side of the fairway, ten feet from the edge of the still-shadowed woods. The golfers ignored a rustle in the trees behind them: they knew the area was teeming with deer and a variety of other creatures. The wild animals that abound in the area were used to golfers, though they still kept a safe distance.

"All right, then. Who's up for a cold beer now?" said one of the foursome.

"Good God man, it's only eight in the morning. I'll pass, thanks," replied another.

"I'll have one," said a third golfer. "If it's cold."

"Thanks. It *was* sweet. I'm in the zone today," said the fourth.

"*What?*" questioned the other.

"I said thanks… for the compliment. I was happy with that drive too."

"I didn't say anything. It was a good drive, though."

"Quit fucking with me, Rod." He looked irritated and stopped what he had been doing.

"Look, you pured the drive. But I didn't say anything."

"I was sure you said, 'Nice drive.' That's all. I was thanking you. I'm not making a big deal about it. Whatever. You're away."

"Did you *need* a compliment? Seriously, it was a great drive."

The first golfer, farthest away from the green, was away. For those unfamiliar with the game, the golfer farthest from the hole, or cup, after a stroke, enjoys the right to hit his or her shot first. It's golf etiquette. It's among a hundred formal or generally accepted rules that define the game and make it so damn frustrating to learn.

"Okay guys, help me out here. What's your call on this — drive the pond or lay up?" asked the first golfer.

"Lay up. You've still got about 170 yards to the pond," advised the second golfer.

"No way. Drive it, you pussy. You won't birdie if you don't," said the fourth golfer.

"Yup," said the third. "Take that big-ass three wood and hit it off the deck. Better yet, I'll bet you twenty bucks you can't clear the pond with a one iron."

"Even God can't hit a one iron," offered the more cautious second golfer, trying to sound clever.

A loud, unmistakable, but unseen voice emanating from the woods to their right, rang out. The foursome heard it clearly and it startled them.

"Ancient joke, buddy. Lay up! Play the conservative shot."

The foursome spun to see who had called out. Straining to glimpse through the trees, bobbing their heads side to side like barn owls, the group spotted the back of a man walking deliberately away into the depth of the forest, his longish, unkempt hair peeking out from beneath the brim a bucket hat.

"Who — who the hell was that guy? A greens keeper or something?"

"He looks like Spackler. You know, from *Caddyshack*."

All of them laughed nervously, as one might walking through a cemetery, at night.

"Gentlemen, allow me to introduce you to the Hermit of Carmel. Well, at least that's what some golfers around here call him. I don't know if he's truly a hermit. Been hanging around here for a couple of years now. Seems to like golf. He's been spotted around a few courses in the area, I'm told. My buddy thinks he might have seen him over at Cypress. Anyway, the guy evidently collects balls and sort of watches people play. It would be a little creepy, except he sometimes throws bad drives back onto the fairway. Haven't met anyone who calls that a drop yet. Nobody knows much about him or where he lives, but he hangs around in the woods, apparently. Harmless, really, I suppose."

"That's bizarre. What about course management? Don't they send security after him?"

"Nah. Why bother? He's not hurting anyone. Security shoos him away now and then. I did hear that Cypress called the cops once. Someone reported that a driver they left at the tee box was gone when he went back, after putting out. They blamed the hermit, but who knows. Could just as easily have been the following foursome. It doesn't matter how rich they are; some golfers, if they find a club, will keep the damn thing."

"Well, he must have a home. Are there actually homeless people in Carmel? Shit. That blows my mind. *Never* seen anyone panhandling there."

"Well, if he's of the 'reclusive genius' variety of hermits, I suspect he knows the course pretty well. I'd take his advice in any event, Jack. Better lay up."

"Hmmm… okay. Three iron it is, then."

A shout from deeper in the woods caught the attention of the golfers once again.

"Prudent decision!" advised the Hermit, in a most thoughtful and judicious manner.

The golfers spun once more to try to catch a glimpse of the elusive golf coach through the low light and forest coverage. The Hermit had disappeared. His footsteps on dried foliage faded. All fell silent once more save for muffled dialogue as the foursome played their respective second shots off the fairway. One with extraordinary hearing might have heard a faint sound — a plop — as a golf ball landed in the pond. It didn't take auditory superpowers to hear the expletives that followed.

chapter 5

Juliana was born and raised, until age sixteen, in Hermosillo — a city of about 700,000 in the Mexican state of Sonora. It's the capital and economic center of Sonora, the largest city in the state, and qualifies as a model city. It has held onto its cultural and architectural past, while at the same time embracing the modern Mexico. Hermosillo was once known as Pictic. During the Mexican War of Independence, the State of Sonora and its capital, Pictic, stayed loyal to the Spanish Crown. A general from the area, Alejo García Conde, was tasked by the Spanish with quelling attempts at liberation and defeated insurgent leader José María González Hermosillo. But, as the saying goes, one man's insurgent is another man's freedom fighter. After the insurgency and eventual independence from Spain eleven years later, the insurgents were declared heroes and the town adopted and embraced the name of Hermosillo. It would become a much larger metropolis — the current population is straining its infrastructure. The city lies about three hours' drive from the Arizona border and about an hour and a half from Bahia de Kino to the west, at the shores of the breathtakingly beautiful Sea of Cortez.

Despite its relative proximity to the sea, Juliana only remembered traveling from her home to the coast a few times as a young girl. Her father, a chemical engineer, worked long hours and had little opportunity to enjoy time off, even for a weekend. Juliana's father eventually landed a job in California, and she and her family moved to the Los Angeles area. There, she discovered the wonders of teenage American boys and the beaches south of their new home in El Segundo, a stone's throw south of the ever-expanding runways of LAX. She did not lament the move from her extended family in Mexico, as did several of her siblings. Juliana embraced her host country, all of southern California, and the city to which they relocated. Her spotty English improved greatly after she entered grade eleven, and she made friends easily. It was among and with her new Californian friends that she gained the easier-to-say, one-syllable nickname Jules. She relived her infrequent trips to the coast as a young girl almost daily now. Her new home provided easy access to the coastal beach cities and towns, accessible by a simple right-hand turn when she was headed south. Jeans gave way to cut-offs, so she'd look like the other teenage girls, and she let her lovely brown hair grow long and hang free.

Jules flourished in the last two years of her academic career at El Segundo High School. With a 30 percent Latino enrolment, she didn't look the least out of place at ESHS. She felt at home the very first day she walked in the front door as a new student. It only occurred to her why the school had felt so familiar months later. Its exterior façade and interior halls and classrooms had appeared in many Hollywood television series and movies depicting school-aged characters and settings that she'd watched, dubbed, back in Mexico.

With extra babysitting cash, Jules bought branded tees and became an enthusiastic supporter of all ESHS Eagles sports teams. Despite her athletic capabilities and inclination, her parents demanded that her focus on academics supersede her commitment to varsity sports. So, she hit the books. Jules's sincere interest in animals and the natural world directed her to the sciences. She logged A's in chemistry and biology, clinching her scholarships across the state by the second semester of twelfth grade.

Like many teenagers in SoCal, Juliana became magnetically attracted to the beach for its natural beauty — the cold, relentless surf, the white sand, the fresh air that rolls in off the vast Pacific — and, for the social scene and interactions it promised. An intensely beautiful Latino girl with deep brown eyes, a wide smile, and a capacity for intelligent conversation did not have to work hard to attract the attention of boys congregating around the beaches. Manhattan Beach, Hermosa Beach, Redondo Beach — the succession of cities south of LA were all mostly identical. But they offered enough variety when one wanted to socialize with friends, tease boys, rollerblade along the waterfront, or argue about who sold the very best fish tacos.

Sixteen and anxious to start dating, Juliana kept an open mind and a discerning eye. Boys buzzed in from every angle, but her self-confidence, sharp wit, intelligence, and outspoken nature worked well to keep the flies away. She became quite adept at sizing boys up for compatibility and then batting them away with little energy spent. She knew what she wanted and ignored pressure to have a "steady" and to "lose it" — a priority for girls at age sixteen.

As it turned out, there were a lot of good-looking boys, and many were damn good at kissing, a skill that Jules valued. But most fell flat when they opened their mouths to speak. "Hey, pretty *conchita*. Wanna go back to my car and see my *pene?*"

"*Déjame solo*, idiot," she'd commonly respond. *How can such a beautiful specimen of a male fail so quickly when he speaks?* she'd often wonder to herself and say to her girlfriends.

Stupidity (an admittedly subjective measure) and smoking were two turn-offs that quickly terminated further engagement, no matter how many bottles of Corona and lime clouded her judgment. Then came Robert. Rob. *Robbie*, as it turned out, was not an acceptable name, even if used affectionately. Juliana met Rob, a boy with the soul and maturity of a much older man: a boy destined to be her future husband and best friend, at Manhattan Beach. Manhattan was on the other side of the foul oil refineries separating her home from the first accessible beach to the south. It would have made for a better cocktail party story to introduce the *"Rob and Jules meeting"* as a more romantic affair — eyes locking on that very first date or during a chance meeting on the beach at sunset. That's not the way it happened, though. People often meet because of an unintended and unexpected life collision. Sometimes that happens quite literally.

One day, while rollerblading along the recreational path bordering the beach, Juliana found herself forced to make a split-second decision — a defensive move — to avoid a collision with a grey-haired woman walking her pampered Shih Tzu. The path that day mirrored car traffic out on Highway 405. Legions of beach enthusiasts, representing all activities permitted on the path, choked the lanes. There were bumper-to-bumper, ass-to-ass walkers, runners, skaters, cyclists, and scooters. She even noted a couple of those contraptions that look like an elliptical exercise machine on wheels. Juliana skated like she drove a car: fast. And recklessly. The throngs of people frustrated her efforts to put the pedal to the metal, like a sports car in heavy traffic. Jules put her braking and steering to the test in a valiant effort to dodge an oncoming runner who strayed from the opposite lane of the path. Played in slow motion, it might have appeared like a well-choreographed dance — except people got hurt.

The flushed and perspiring runner, wearing nothing more than sneakers and a Speedo, had moved out of his assigned lane to avoid a scooter rider. A dog walker, reaction time slowed by her advancing age, overreacted to the runner — albeit in slow motion. She faltered to her left, into Jules's kinetic path. The elderly dog walker turned her head in time to watch Jules attempt an emergency stop, dragging her left skate sideways. Jules raised her hands, an instinctive and self-protective move, and prepared for the impending collision with the senior and her small dog. Alternatives flashed through her head. Jules envisioned a conceivable scenario in which she could guide all parties and herself to safety, her arms parting them like Moses, the Red Sea — ensuring a satisfactory ending to this unsuccessful attempt by three humans and one dog to occupy the same physical space at the same time.

Those familiar with Newton's First Law of Motion will know that an object in motion continues in motion, at the same speed, and in the same direction, unless acted upon by an unbalanced force. No unbalanced force interceded in this case, unless you acknowledge that all three — or four of them, if you include the dog — were decidedly unbalanced in the second before they collided. That said, Jules did successfully circumvent a full-on, full-force smackdown of the old lady. She adeptly moved the woman out of her way with a glancing stroke of her forearm. Unfortunately, Jules rolled into the leash attached to her vulnerable pet. Rolling at speed into the now knee-height leash, resulted in the total and immediate loss of Jules's balance.

The dog got sucked into the mess like a string of yarn might into a vacuum nozzle. The canine became airborne along with Jules as they launched, this time in the same direction. Jules and dog looked like one single biological entity attempting flight: the old lady dragged behind on the tether like those advertising banners airplanes tow on parallel passes of the beach. Collisions are almost always unexpected, and this incident proved to be no exception.

The sweaty runner, unaware of the morass he had created, avoided the human and animal shrapnel altogether. But the two women, young and old, and the Shih Tzu (of unknown age), were about to further complicate the situation with the involuntary addition of an unsuspecting young man. He was, perhaps for the better, completely unaware of the biological cluster bomb zeroing in on him.

Rob had parted with his friends some twenty minutes previous. In need of some privacy, or at least what solitude a crowded Sunday afternoon Manhattan Beach could offer, he was sitting peacefully. Focus, to the exclusion of everything around him, was a personality trait of the young Robert Das. That focus manifested itself often as either a blessing or a curse. Today, he completely zoned out the bustle of the beach to simply take in its beauty. This was Rob's church. He sat worshipping this Sunday afternoon, hunched over on his pew: the guardrail separating the recreational path and the beach.

Rob had been facing the ocean and lacked any view of the path behind him. He blocked out the noise of the people, bikes, and skateboards, and focused on the organic sounds of the ocean and the gulls. That made Rob's involuntary participation in the collision, well, unexpected. Without forewarning, three females — two human and one canine — hit him forcefully in the center of his back. They delivered sufficient force to launch him to a landing spot, five feet away, on the beach. The ladies, motion and mass compelling them, slowed only slightly as they plowed into Rob, glanced off the guardrail, and arched into an inglorious heap atop the unsuspecting young man. The wind knocked out of him, Rob couldn't even yell out in pain. An empty wheeze was all he could manage before the lights went out. His head and faced were buried in the sand, in a shallow crater formed by the force and weight of a meteorite comprised of one senior citizen, one young woman, one young man, and one diminutive but adorable dog. Rob's inability to inhale might have been a blessing in disguise. A reactive scream or attempt to breath, at this point, would have resulted in an immediate ingestion of sand, adding insult to the real injury he suffered.

Thankfully, nobody lost consciousness. All avoided head trauma, despite the violence of the collision. Sand, it turns out, can dissipate the force of a fall quite effectively. This is something that beach volleyball players learn the first time they launch themselves to dig a low ball. The old woman let out the first exclamation, a muffled grunt. As the last over the railing, she wound up on top of the heap. Her immediate concern, of course, was for her dog. It had had the misfortune of becoming sandwiched between herself and Juliana. Jules's face, it turned out, had come to rest awkwardly in the middle of Rob's buttocks, likely saving her from facial abrasion on the gritty sand. The old lady, at first, could not get up. She gradually and clumsily rolled off the heap formed by Jules, the little dog, and Rob, to determine the fate of her beloved pet — whom everyone within earshot soon learned, had a name. It became obvious because the woman kept repeatedly saying it: "Daisy… Daisy… Daisy!!" with increasing volume and heightened level of concern, as the dog remained motionless and unresponsive.

As it turns out, dogs can have the wind knocked out of them too. The pup was unable to move for a few seconds as she gathered in enough air to react and talk. Daisy finally talked. My goodness, did she talk. She yipped. She yelped. She cried. She whelped. She howled. She whimpered. The old lady rose to her knees on the hot beach, her dress gathered around her, dusted with white sand. Her left arm, possibly injured, hung limp beside her. The woman gathered Daisy with her right arm and pulled the pup against her body, in what might have been her best effort to start one-armed doggy CPR. Or perhaps she wanted to protect her dog, not knowing if the messy collision had yet concluded.

Freed from the weight and burden of the woman and dog atop her, Juliana now too slowly arose, first to her knees. She looked down at the stranger beneath her. Or at least looked down at the exquisite ass she had become unexpectedly and intimately familiar with. As far as she could tell, the victim, lying face down and not moving, was a young man in board shorts and a T-shirt. He was barefoot, but it was quite possible that his shoes had been knocked free in the accident. Head rising, breathing once again, but still looking down, Rob propped himself up with one elbow, spat out a mouthful of sand, and raised the other hand to his face. He carefully rubbed the mask of grit out of his eyes, his nose, and off his face. Rob groaned as he rolled over onto his back and looked up at whatever, or whoever, had tackled him from behind. Kneeling over him and saying something at first unintelligible, appeared a dark form of what might have been a girl. She, if it was a she, was backlit by the sun, her features obscured. He squinted and attempted to rise. His senses once again operational, he could now discern the voice of a young woman asking him, repeatedly, if he was hurt. Or at least that the interpretation of her delightfully musical Spanish, a language you can't help but pick up and gain limited proficiency in if you're raised in Southern California.

"Lo siento mucho. Estas bien? No pude detenerme a tiempo. Puedes escucharme? Estás herido?" Like many people who speak more than one language, Juliana often reverted to her mother tongue when excited or scared. And she spoke rapidly. She didn't realize she wasn't speaking English either. Juliana turned to check on the elderly woman and repeated the same questions. *"Lo siento mucho. Estas bien? Estás herido?"*

The old woman didn't understand Spanish and looked at her blankly. With the discipline and focus of a first responder, Jules divided her attention and concern equally between the two people and dog. She apologized again, in Spanish, and tried to help both the woman and Rob to their feet, genuinely concerned for their wellbeing. A small crowd gathered. Several people who witnessed the collision approached to offer help, focusing their attention on the most elderly of the human tangle. Somebody asked if he should call 911, but it became evident that care wasn't necessary. The victims of the collision were bruised a little, shocked a lot, but eventually able to get up and walk, or at least limp away. The runner, who caused the entire morass, had long since fled the scene.

It was there in the hot sand, on his knees, that Rob first saw Juliana. She knelt in front of him, looking directly into his eyes. He returned the inspection, still blinking the sand and tears out of his eyes. One arriving on the scene, and having not seen the accident, might have misinterpreted the scene. You could have been convinced you were witnessing an emotional young man proposing marriage to his girlfriend. That would have been romantic. It wasn't. But as it turned out, it did make for great cocktail-party or family-gathering fodder in the future, when people asked how Rob and Jules met. Their response, always the same, and stated in unison: "*Una colision.*"

Perhaps it was the blow. Maybe it was the summer heat. Possibly it was the sun, behind her, creating a halo over her head. All Rob knew at that moment was that Juliana was the most beautiful girl he had ever seen. He remained on his knees for what seemed an unreasonable amount of time, not saying anything altogether intelligible, though quite capable of speaking clearly. Rob might have been feigning injury and seeking sympathy, to improve his chances with this breathtaking young girl. She appeared to him to be about his age. Jules offered her hand and helped Rob to his feet. Several others attended the woman and her poor dog, the one victim of the crash who might have experienced the worst. The dog responded well to the attention. Her tailed commenced wagging forthwith. Kind and gentle words, loving strokes, and offers of dog treats followed. A kindly couple helped the senior, brushing the sand off her and offering to walk her and her dog home. She graciously accepted.

At this point, the assembled crowd began to largely ignore Jules and Rob. The two appeared shaken but were clearly in decent shape. If they cared, it didn't show. Something other than a violent collision had transpired. The two were in their own world, oblivious to the accident in which they had both played a central role. Jules and Rob stared at each other for another minute of awkward silence before one gave in and spoke.

"Hola. Estoy bien gracias. Mi nombre es Rob, por cierto. Quién eres tú? Cómo estás?" asked Rob.

"I'm all right, thanks," replied Juliana. "I speak English, by the way. I don't know what to say. I'm sorry if I hurt you. I couldn't stop. Honestly."

"It's okay. Your knee is bleeding, though," Rob noted, pointing at her leg. "I've got a first-aid kit in my Jeep. Can I help you? Do you need a ride to a clinic, or your home, or anything? Do you live close by? I'm Rob Das. Did I tell you that already? What's your name, anyway? You're beautiful. Did I just say that out loud? God, I'm an idiot. I'm sorry for being so forward. What's your name again?"

"I didn't tell you my name." Juliana smiled broadly.

And so it began. The thoughtful young man of few and carefully chosen words was struck with verbal dysentery, for which there was no known medical cure.

chapter 6

The year Rob and Juliana met, she was a senior in high school. He was enjoying a post high-school gap year before heading to the University of California for his eventual undergrad. In his typical self-deprecating style, Rob more candidly referred to it as his "nap year." He acknowledged that he didn't get much done beyond surfing, eating burgers, trying to keep his Jeep running, chasing girls, and, well, napping. As it turned out, it was even more satisfying to nap on the beach than at home. To his amazement, Rob's girl-chasing days ended abruptly the day he met Juliana. By October, his daily pilgrimage to the beach had turned into daily drives from his parents' place in east Manhattan Beach to Jules's home to hang out, listen to music, make out, and talk about their plans for life. Rob's summer guise soon faded. His hair darkened to its natural dark brown. Later he would say Jules saved him both from becoming a beach bum and likely from skin cancer. Her family liked Robert and he had a standing invitation to weekend family dinners. Jules's sisters bestowed a nickname on him: Robo, pronounced with first "o" short, second "o" long. *Roberto*, her parents called him. Behind the mop of hair, flip-flops, and his infernal smoke-belching Jeep, they could see an intelligent, responsible, and ambitious young man. Hanging out and making out evolved into deep and thoughtful conversations as both matured from teenagers to adults, it seemed, over one season.

The summer romance blossomed into something with staying power. Robert and Juliana became inseparable. The early days of any romance are the most intense, as anyone who has ever fallen in love can attest. It's a time of mutual discovery and optimism. For Jules and Rob, that included a physical, intellectual, emotional, and spiritual discovery that shaped their relationship forever.

Both had strong language skills, but Rob was undeniably the quiet one. When he had something to say, he said it, for certain. Juliana was incontestably more talkative, particularly when amongst her family — people she loved and trusted. When hanging with her sisters, Jules could maintain a running dialogue, without break, for an hour. No exaggeration. Rob saw it firsthand. Spoken in rapid-fire Spanish, those exchanges were impossible to keep up with. As a couple, however, Rob and Jules found their level — a frequency, pace, and depth of conversation that fell somewhere between their comfort zones and communication needs.

Juliana learned early in their relationship that Robert, while social, felt most comfortable with and required time for solitude. He sought that outdoors. Many find deep spirituality within nature. It evokes an almost religious response and zeal in some. Robert's churches included any desolate section of beach in Northern California, the rugged canyons surrounding Los Angeles, and the Mojave Desert: resplendent in its Joshua trees and Monadnock outcroppings. The late Albert Einstein is best known as a theoretical physicist. He deserves greater credit for his deep philosophical take on the natural world, which went beyond egg-head science. The one quote Rob retained and recited, if only in his own head, went something like: *"Look deep into nature, and then you will understand everything better."*

Juliana learned early in the relationship that Rob was a deep and thoughtful young man. When he needed to work out a problem, get away from the urban jungle and tangle of highways of LA, to *understand everything better*, Rob would disappear for days in the many and disparate natural environments that make California so unique and cherished by naturalists — its deserts, mountains, forests, woodlands, and rugged coastal headlands. He made frequent pilgrimages, with Jules now in the jump seat, to Joshua Tree National Park, Yosemite, Death Valley, and north, up the famous California State Route 1. It's often referred to as the Pacific Coast Highway (PCH for short) or "Highway 1." Rob headed north on the #1 many dozen times and memorized each tight turn in the famously bendy stretch of highway. Throughout his twenties, he'd camp on several stretches of beach near Big Sur, or at Point Lobos Sate Reserve, on the southern end of the Monterey Peninsula.

His Jeep Wrangler, with soft top and steel push bars, was Robert's escape pod: frequently adorned with a mountain bike, a surfboard, a kayak, or all three. Robert, Juliana figured out, was so much deeper than a tanned, handsome southern California surfer dude that the flip-flops, toothy smile, and Jeep might have implied. He wasn't particularly political but was deeply principled and his values guided his actions and behavior. Rob would never have considered himself an activist; he felt no compulsion to impose his values on other people or change the rules to match his worldview. He was prepared to play within the established structure of government and the law, respectful of its place and function in society — to ensure civility and order. It was no surprise when, after finishing his undergrad at UC, he followed Jules to Stanford, where Rob completed a Juris Doctor (JD) degree. His parents were understandably proud.

Rob learned that Jules was kind and deeply empathetic. He witnessed that in their very first accidental meeting. She helped anyone and embraced every cause when she perceived oppression or identified an underdog. Jules definitely leaned left. Rob leaned right. They respected each other enough to disagree on political issues and still find room for love for one another.

Jules, like Rob, treasured the outdoors — the ocean, deserts, and mountains of California, and, across the border, the Baja Peninsula of Mexico. She was a complete science geek and proud of it. It was rare for the two of them to watch sitcoms on TV. She would insist, politely of course, that they watch PBS's *NOVA* and *Nature* — anything educational and related to science and natural history. Rob was more than willing to comply. Any time they didn't spend as a couple, was spent together with relatives. As for most raised in a Latin American culture, Jules prioritized her family, and, fortunately for Rob, he was now part of that tribe. He offered no complaint.

Among her passions, Jules was an unapologetic defender of Mexico and its pre-Columbian history. She considered herself a Mexican nationalist — lowercase, and not to be misconstrued as supporting the agenda of the Nationalist Front of Mexico — the activist organization and movement that, among other things, seeks return of territories in the Southwestern US, to Mexico. Born and raised, she continued to advocate for Mexico, its tremendous history and potential for the future. The violence and continuing deterioration of the security in her home country, catalyzed by the drug trade, disturbed her deeply. If anyone within earshot engaged in debate about or critique of Mexico, Jules was all over it like a Saltillo blanket. She would never back down and always claimed the last word.

Her commitment to academics paid off too. Jules earned a well-deserved scholarship to Stanford. She followed in her proud father's footsteps by achieving a degree and a career in chemical engineering. With employment offers in hand two months before even graduating, both Jules and Rob felt secure. Both of them exuded the kind of confidence that one only ever seems to enjoy in one's mid-twenties. At that age, everyone has a certain sense of invincibility and feels convinced they are going to change the world.

Two weeks after the grad ceremony, while still living in their own respective apartments, Rob and Jules met for dinner at their favorite restaurant in Palo Alto. While it certainly could have been more romantic, Rob, with utmost sincerity and genuine adoration, blurted it out: "Marry me?" Jules replied, "Of course," as though it was a forgone conclusion. "What took you so long to ask?"

Neither had ever imagined an alternative outcome from the day they met. The couple slipped the wedding into their rapidly filling professional calendars and the rest was history, as they say. To family members and close friends, Jules and Rob's honeymoon plans were rather boring and uninspiring, given their financial means and adventurous natures. The couple could have gone anywhere. The newlyweds might have travelled to Venice to repeat their vows and love for one another from the Bridge of Sighs overlooking the Grand Canal. A thatched-roof suite on the beach in French Polynesia might have provided a dreamy setting, too. Jules and Rob could have walked hand in hand down the banks of the Seine under the shadow of the Eiffel Tower on their way to find their own clean and well-lighted place. Instead, Jules and Rob decided to go to their favorite place in California, Point Lobos Nature Reserve, for some hiking, camping, and sea kayaking.

"Where do you want to go for our honeymoon, babe?"

"Lobos?"

"Yup. Let's pack."

It was as simple a process as the decision to wed.

At Lobos, they connected with nature on their own terms and pace. Rob and Jules had been to the park nine or ten times and never tired of the place. They remained in awe of its rugged beauty, the diversity of the ecosystem, and the wonderfully luxurious distraction of nearby Carmel.

chapter 7

Jules and Rob felt liberated at Lobos and loved its atmosphere — the briny air, ghostly, stunted and twisted trees, and the magical play of light. And its scent is an elixir. It's a combination — a permanent potpourri — of ocean, seaweed, pine, and wildflowers that always seemed to be in bloom. As much as they appreciated the elements, if Rob and Jules needed a break from nature, and longed for a soft bed, an expensive glass of wine, and a great dinner, Carmel was only a ten-minute drive away. That's exactly where they went after three days and nights tenting at Lobos.

Upon arrival in town, the lovers pulled up to the curb at the Cypress Inn. They desperately hoped to get a room, despite lack of a reservation. Rob wanted to leave the car out front, at least until he knew if there was or was not, any vacancy. But an enthusiastic parking valet greeted them and smiled broadly — pausing long enough to convey the non-verbal tip invitation, before climbing into their car and driving away. Rob and Jules looked the part of the newly married couple, hands and arms all over each other as they entered the hotel lobby. The two swayed nervously as they stood at the front desk and giggled like kids before inquiring about a room. The troubled look and furrowed brow on the reception clerk suggested a negative response.

"We need a little luxury. But we'll take anything you've got," Rob said. "A broom closet if necessary." Jules pulled Rob close to her. It might have been a consciously affectionate move, or, unconsciously, an attempt to demonstrate how small a space they could occupy, in the hotel, if necessary.

"Hmmm, let me see if I can find anything. We're really full tonight," said the young reception clerk, apologetically, as she alternated her gaze between keyboard and computer screen. "The broom closet has already been booked, I'm afraid." She tried her best to keep a straight face. The slightest uplift of the corners of her mouth gave her away.

From outside the glass entry doors, the valet easily read the young couple's body language. The newlyweds scored a suite — an expensive one at that. Rob and Jules literally jumped for joy. With the room confirmed, the valet put the car keys away for safekeeping, while fingering the ten-dollar tip Rob had deftly pressed into his hand.

The Cypress is a pretty Mediterranean-style hotel, in the center of town. I know it's officially a city, but it feels like a town. The hotel was founded in 1929 and originally named *Hotel La Ribera*, then *Cypress West* when it changed hands in the sixties. In the eighties, businessman Dennis LeVett and notable local resident, actress, and animal rights activist Doris Day bought the hotel. It's been maintained to the highest standards since. Jules and Rob always loved its ambience and the fact that it's a dog-friendly hotel. By that, I mean it's typically filled with dogs, in most rooms and common spaces — the restaurant, lounge, lobby, and courtyards. Even though the married couple didn't have a pet, they loved to see dogs slouched low in oversized wingback chairs, around the roaring fire, in the living room. Canines frequently occupy all the parlor chairs, leaving their compliant and doting human companions to stand or sit on the floor. A few times every week, a pianist and a singer provide live entertainment, as if the dogs weren't enough. The occasional disagreement between dogs at the Cypress can rival that of two intoxicated bar patrons in its clamor and commotion. Personally,

I'd take barking dogs over arrogant and disagreeable drunks any day. Except at 6 in the morning.

On their first night at Cypress, Jules and Rob didn't leave their room, despite their dinner reservation. While one might reasonably anticipate newlyweds to consummate their vows on the first night of a honeymoon, in which they enjoyed some privacy and comfort. Jules and Rob made the mistake, or not, of indulging in the complimentary sherry discovered in their suite. The provision of cream sherry was and remains a hallmark of the hotel. The innkeepers thoughtfully endow each guest room with a generously sized crystal decanter filled with the nectar, temptingly placed on the dresser. It's the first thing one might notice upon unlocking the room. Rob opened the decanter and sniffed its contents. Neither had ever tasted sherry. Jules did the honors. She poured them each a full glass, to try it. Etiquette demands one drink sherry in small, fluted glass, half the size of a white wine glass. The hotel, however, had provided only highball glasses, and the couple didn't know any better. The cream sherry was, well, creamy. The first glass went down smoothly and disappeared quickly.

"Pour me another, babe, please", said Rob. He reached for the table lamp to compensate for the failing light in the room. The incandescent light lent the room a toasty hue, not dissimilar to the tone of the sherry.

"Coming up. Or is it bottoms up?" Jules' faculties had already become compromised. But she did as asked. Two glasses. Full. Again. They downed it. And then drained another. It was rich. Like... cream. "This is inedible," Jules confirmed, then corrected herself. "I mean, incredible." Rob looked and her and chuckled. "You're getting tipsy."

Sherry might be the most perfect, most versatile drink ever invented. It can be enjoyed for breakfast, brunch, lunch, dinner (before or after), on a picnic, in bed, over fruit, in a soup, with or without food, and, if passion takes you there, over bare skin and licked off slowly. In this case, most of it was consumed orally and with unintended haste. It was decadent. And potent. Ever the chemist, Jules pondered its complex chemical composition, surface tension and lastly, alcoholic content. About that time, she began to wonder if *all* the rooms at the hotel were novel in their ability to spin on a vertical axis. Jules sat, to stabilize the room a little, and put her feet up on the bed. Looking glass-eyed at Rob, she attempted a scrunched-up kissing face. "You are so hanshum," she slurred. "I'm gonna make you ver-wey… happy t'night."

She adorably brushed her hair away from her face and sucked in a deep breath. Then her head fell — quite suddenly and heavily — to her chest. Jules was out. A gentle snore escaped her partly opened mouth. Rob stared at her for a time, while he enjoyed a fourth glass of sherry. He appreciated how beautiful she was, even when drunk — her brown hair flowing over her shoulders, across her clavicle and draped across her perky breasts. He chuckled and thought to himself, smugly, that she couldn't handle her liquor like he. The evening hadn't panned out as he'd intended, but Rob was hardly fazed. He knew that as a couple they could count on many years of delicious, sherry-induced sex in the future. For now, Jules earned a tender kiss on the forehead.

Inclined to take a shower before bed, Rob began to undress. Lifting one leg off the ground, he attempted to remove his pants. Disoriented by the effect of consuming four full glasses of sherry inside forty minutes, he stumbled, regained his balance momentarily, and fell hard on the Persian rug. His hands remained clutched on the pants and didn't break his fall — at all. And the rug offered no cushioning whatsoever. The pain was mercifully brief though. First, he cried out; then he laughed. Rob was drunk, and nothing hurts all that much when you're drunk. It's God's way of protecting idiots. He continued to undress from the relative safety of his grounded position. Successfully disrobed, Rob stood with some difficulty, balancing first with one foot, then one hand, the second foot, and then the remaining hand. He did a pretty good imitation of a newborn calf struggling to its feet. Rob teetered into the bathroom, one hand on the wall for support. The feeling of cold ceramic on his bare feet was the last conscious memory Rob had of that evening.

When the sun rose the next morning, Rob remained asleep, lying lengthwise in the five-foot-long bathtub — his feet and head propped up on either end. He was snoring loudly. A dog in the adjacent suite growled in response. Towels and the shower curtain were heaped about the room. A dozen broken and bent shower curtain rings lay strewn across the tiled floor. Water was still running in the sink but, thankfully, not in the tub. Jules at some point in the evening had succumbed to gravity's pull and slunk from her sitting position to a heap on the floor that was not immediately recognizable as human. Rob didn't remember doing so but must have been aware enough to remove his watch and place it on the bathroom vanity, before collapsing in the bathtub. The watch, at least, was unharmed. The sherry was harmed — terminally. The sherry was depleted.

Jules and Rob remained at the Cypress for three enchanting nights. They swore off the sherry thereafter. Neither were inclined to endure a hang-over for three consecutive mornings. Early each morning, after a bite and strong black coffee, they held hands and walked together along the streets that formed an almost perfect perpendicular grid pattern in the town center. Many of the cottages and homes forming the residential part of town are ranchers and bungalows, delightfully unique and embracing a variety of architectural styles, from classic Tudor to shingle style. Some do a great impression of a grown-up treehouse, or something that might have been rendered in a children's storybook, complete with a thatched roof. Ocean Avenue, a block north of the Cypress Inn, lays east-west and features a steep incline from the center of town down to the beach.

In Carmel, as in Lobos, Jules and Rob capped each evening of their romantic honeymoon with a ritual sit, on a log, sand, or rock, resting their heads against one another, to watch the breathtaking sunsets over the Pacific. The show was rarely disappointing, and they had a ticket to each performance. The French poet Gérard de Nerval said, "The first man who compared a woman to a rose was a poet, the second, an imbecile." You'll understand why I'm resistant to offer a cliché related to the best things in life being free — or something like that.

chapter 8

Back home, Jules unpacked their collection of gear and clothes, hoping to get their lives tidied up. It was time to return to a normal routine. The smell of Lobos clung to each article of clothing she removed from the suitcase. It was a good and comforting smell — the antithesis of the odor of Los Angeles. Jules breathed it in, smiling as each whiff triggered another pleasant and deeply ingrained memory of their latest and most memorable trip. She laid everything out methodically on the bed in a grid that unintentionally mimicked the street pattern of Carmel.

She called out to Rob. "Babe, did you get all the suitcases out of the car yet? I'm missing a bag."

"Yup. The car is empty now. Damn, which one was it? Anything valuable gone? Is the camera there? Do you have your knapsack? Remember you took it off at that lookout, on the last hike."

"Nope, I've got the knapsack. Missing the small night bag with makeup and girl stuff. That's all, I think. No big deal. Hon, I'm exhausted. But a good tired. Outdoors tired."

Rob needed to personally survey the situation and confirm what might be missing. He sauntered into the bedroom wearing boxer shorts and a T-shirt. Sporting a couple of days' growth on his face, he looked entirely content, as newly married men often do.

"What was your favorite part of the honeymoon, babe?" Rob gargled, a toothbrush poking out the corner of his mouth.

"You."

"No. Seriously. What part?"

"The hike at Point Lobos. The South Shore trail was the best. It's always inspiring. The rocks. The ocean. I wish I could paint. But next time we go to Carmel, I want to go scuba diving. Can we? I'll take the certification course."

"Definitely, *amante*. Or a little golf perhaps?"

"Rob, I'm so sorry you didn't get to play golf on the peninsula. You sacrificed for me. Thank you. Why don't you do a guys' weekend up there sometime soon?"

"Don't worry. I enjoyed every minute of the trip. I'll get up there for golf soon. Hey look, I've still got some of that clamshell powder on my shoes." He lifted the shoes up to show her the soles. "It's from that path at Lobos. Remember? It's from all the shellfish harvested by native fishers for hundreds of years. Cool, huh? History on my feet!"

"Let's see," she said, regarding the shell dust, chemist that she was. "Calcium carbonate. That is cool. Love that about you. You're interested in everything in the world."

"Love that you love me."

They shared a long look into one another's eyes. Juliana smiled and cupped Robert's face in her hands and kissed him. She pressed her cheek up next to his and whispered, in her best seductive voice, "This can go one of two ways right now, mister."

"I'm tired, but I think I've got a little left in me. Let me help you finish unpacking this stuff first. Then I'm going to shower and we'll consider your two options."

He started toward the bed and open suitcase.

"Wait, what's the second option?"

Jules smiled, dropped her nightgown to the floor, sat on the bed, and smiled mischievously. "*El desembalaje puede esperar hasta otro momento.*"

Robert wasn't certain he translated it correctly, but the non-verbal communication was clear. He ran to the bathroom and cranked the shower handle over. "I need no more than three minutes!" he shouted. He hurriedly undressed, slipped into the stall, and made his best effort to rapidly wash all the important bits. "I've got to get up early to get into work too, honey. Time to play catch up on my files," he yelled over the sound of the water.

He jumped back out of the shower in two minutes and fifty seconds and blot-dried with a towel. Still dripping, he skipped back to the dimly lit bedroom wearing nothing but an erection. "Hey babe, do you want to try…"

Robert's voice trailed off as he returned to the room and saw Jules, still naked, curled in a fetal position, eyes closed. She was in a deep sleep already. He sighed, a little disappointed at the lost opportunity. Exhausted himself, he was also secretly grateful. This time, the sea air was to blame — not the sherry. His erection had already called it a night — awaiting its next cue, in the morning. Rob pulled the duvet up to Jules's shoulders, leaned over to kiss her cheek, and listened to her slow, peaceful breathing. He set the alarm and slid gently into his side of the bed so not to wake her.

Rob unclasped his watch, took it off his wrist, and stared at it for a minute. It was Jules's wedding gift to him: a Rolex with a black dial and large, white, luminous dots forming the hour markers. It had become Rob's very favorite possession, and he didn't consider himself to be into material things. In the dim light of the bedroom, the hour markers glowed brilliantly. Rather than squinting at the alarm clock on Jules's side of the bed, he had become accustomed to wearing his watch to bed. By simply lifting his wrist and viewing the glowing hands and hour markers, he could tell the time. You could have read a book in the dark from its luminescence. Rob flipped the watch over and ran his thumb over the inscription on the caseback. He could feel each letter of the inscription as if it were in braille. Slipping it back on his wrist, he snapped the stainless flip lock clasp closed.

Jules had agonized over what she would give Rob for months before the wedding. It had to be something with permanence. Ideally, it would be something he would be able to look at frequently to remind him of her. She contemplated a painting featuring Carmel or Point Lobos. But art is so subjective, and she was never sure he'd like her choice. Jules also pondered buying Rob a new set of golf clubs. As he hit his mid-twenties, Rob's recreational interests had become a little less risky. Kayaking, scuba diving, and rock climbing eventually ceded their dominance to golf. He hadn't played it at all during his teenage years. The game revealed itself to Rob as his legal career developed. Peers and clients invited him to play, at first, in tournaments. To be social and to develop lasting professional relationships, he took up the game, albeit reluctantly. Slowly, Rob's focused and passionate (Jules would have described it as Obsessive-Compulsive Disorder) character kicked in and he became obsessed with golf, as many do. Rob had, however, bought himself a new set of sticks, after receipt of a previous year's bonus, so she discarded the idea.

One weekend, while out shopping with one of her sisters, Jules passed a jewelry shop. A Rolex-branded clock hung on the outside wall of the building. Passing the store, she stopped, backtracked, and leaned in to look at several rows of glimmering timepieces in the front window. They were all stunning. One watch in particular, caught her eye. The tent card in front of it labeled it as an "Explorer II." *That's Rob*, she might have thought. *An Explorer*. She made the decision, and bought it that day, despite her sister's protest.

"That's *loco*, Juliana. That cost like a third of my annual take-home pay," she argued.

"Who cares? Amortize it over thirty years, and that's only five bucks a week. Skip one premium coffee a week, you've got yourself a great watch — a tool, a keepsake, a memory, and the only piece of jewelry Rob is likely to wear — for life. Other than the wedding ring, that is." She smiled at the thought and continued to defend her case. "I don't think that's such a bad deal. I should get it engraved. Oh, what should it say?"

Jules's sister abandoned the debate and offered a suggestion. "What about, 'Our love is timeless'? Get it? Timeless."

"I get it, but that's lame. How about '*Mi amor, mi vida, mi mejor amigo*'?"

"*Cursi. Compra el maldito reloj!*"

"Watch me," said Jules, completely aware of her atrocious pun. She smiled, summoned some courage, and presented her credit card: eliciting a nod of approval from the saleswoman assisting her. Even the rich green box it came in was exquisite. It was Rob's favorite color.

Rob, on the other hand, experienced no angst, agony, or uncertainty when considering a wedding gift for Jules. He had the idea for the gift before he even asked Jules for her hand. Raised Catholic, Jules always said she wanted a traditional Mexican wedding. One tradition common in Hispanic wedding ceremonies is the use of *El Lazo de Matrimonio*, El Lazo for short — in English, "the loop." The Loop, or lasso, is a traditional rope, beaded or bejeweled, placed over the heads and upon the shoulders of the marrying couple as they share their vows. The loop is a statement of union and perpetual love. Rob sought a local artisan jeweler to make a custom Lazo from genuine pearls and sterling silver, with two loops and a crucifix, to embellish the ceremony. After the wedding was concluded, one loop could be removed, providing for a more conventional rosary, albeit a little on the longish side. It was the artisan who suggested that, given its length, the lasso could be doubled up to serve as a pearl necklace for more formal occasions. Always the practical and resourceful man, Rob thought a piece of jewelry that served three purposes was great value. He placed a deposit of a thousand dollars and returned a month later to pick up what he hoped Jules would cherish forever. The Lazo was a work of art — flawless. Even the handcrafted wooden box in which it was presented was lovely.

"*Arroje esto alrededor de la pequeña señora y nunca la deje ir,*" said the Hispanic artist, as he presented it to Robert.

Rob nodded in agreement. "*Gracias.*"

Rob and Jules had intended to share their respective gifts with one another the night before wedding. When Jules mentioned going out to purchase a Lazo, Rob felt the necessity to advance the mutual gifting timeline. After a debate about who should open theirs first, they both welled up with tears upon unboxing their respective tokens of love — both of which, quite romantically, reflected a theme of permanence. I expect it was mere coincidence that both gifts turned out to be something one could wear, and forever.

chapter 9

Life is fundamentally unpredictable. For better and sometimes for worse, its unpredictability is the only predictable part. Most of us, I suspect, understand that at an elementary level, but feign shock when the unexpected catches up with us in due course. Robert did not expect Jules to enter his life when and how she did. It was completely unanticipated, even if for better. Neither predicted that they'd rarely leave each other's side for a more than a day over their ten-year marriage. Jules was guarded when it came to men and relationships. She had no idea that the concept of a soulmate was more than a simple cliché served up liberally in romance novels and chick flicks. Rob did not anticipate Jules's miscarriage sixteen weeks into pregnancy. They were both astonished and emotionally incapacitated when Rob's father and Jules's mother both succumbed to cancers, six months after initial diagnosis and within three months of each other.

But they also didn't presume that Rob would achieve partner status at his law firm after only five years of toiling as a civil litigator. He was pleasantly surprised when his clients were victorious with consistency that did not go unnoticed by Rob's partners. Jules, too, was successful in her career. Her ascendency to middle management at Exxon-Mobil (Long Beach) was a source of great pride for everyone, especially her extended family, who would have otherwise predicted an athletic career. Life is unpredictable.

Jules and Rob became each other's greatest champions: their own mutual admiration society. Consummate foodies, in one of the world's best cities to be so, they celebrated even the smallest achievements with dinner out. In fact, the last time Rob saw Jules, they had discussed dinner plans and agreed to meet at a new Thai restaurant. They wanted to give it their personal review, and to congratulate each just for making it through another busy work week. It was merely an excuse to go out. They planned to each go directly from work and meet at six-ish. It was pouring rain — a rarity in the summer, in Los Angeles. Rob arrived at the place early, as usual. Jules was uncharacteristically late. Rob did not anticipate the call on his cell phone from Jules's closest and dearest sister, Maria.

"Hey, Marie. What's up?" he asked anxiously. For reasons, uncertain to him at that moment, he feared her answer. She was unresponsive for an uncomfortably long time, though Rob could still hear her halting respiration, as if she were panting from exercise.

"Maria?… Maria?"

Then Maria started sobbing. The news she reported was unexpected. All Rob remembered was Maria's labored breathing and the distinct and unforgettable words *accident* and *UCLA Medical Center*. Maria hung up.

Anyone who has experienced any circumstance in which they are compelled to rush to a hospital, not knowing what they will find there, will acknowledge how difficult it is to drive a car in that state. Between the adrenaline-induced shaking, and the tears obscuring your view, it's damn near impossible. It's always advisable to catch a ride from a friend or take a cab instead. Rob didn't. He drove, as fast as the LA traffic would allow on a Friday at 6 p.m. His hand mimicked the car's wipers, rubbing the tears from his eyes in tempo with the blades slapping rain from the windshield. Maria had sounded grave and it scared the hell out of him. The aphorism, "There are no atheists in foxholes," proved true. Rob was not the least bit religious, but he prayed for the first time as he exited the highway and sped along surface streets to UCLA. It was a hell of a long thirty minutes, but he made it. He parked haphazardly in a no parking zone near the entrance to the Emergency patient entrance, and almost ran straight into the automatic doors before they had chance to open.

Regrettably, the scene at the ER had been played out hundreds, perhaps thousands of times: entangling so many devastated families. Even the most hardened medical professionals and administrative staff must be impacted by it. Family members from both Rob and Jules's side, came streaming in from every door and hallway of UCLA-MC, converging on the ER, hoping to get news and her health status. In the movies, people pace anxiously and look down the hall, awaiting a kindly physician to come in and deliver a status report. By the time Rob arrived, there was no pacing, no physicians, no status report — just a lot of family members crying loudly and consoling one another. He didn't even have to ask about her condition. It was obvious. Jules was gone. He stood frozen for a moment and looked at each person at the room, documenting the picture as one might a crime scene. Then the involuntary shaking started. His knees failed him first and he crumpled to the tiled floor. The tears flowed in torrents and continued unabated for an hour, as he remained on the floor, knees tucked up into his chest and arms wrapped around them, head drooped low. Family members were divided over whether to give him space or wrap their arms around him.

When Rob asked if he could see Jules, as loved ones often do, the hospital administrator looked at Rob with sympathetic eyes and shook her head.

"Honestly, Mr. Das, I don't think that you would want to see her right now. You should confer with the extended family and make a service and burial decision. If you choose to have a service and an open casket, I expect that the funeral home will ensure that your late wife will look much more like you remembered her. I know that's difficult to hear. I am truly sorry for your loss."

And then she left. Robert began to weep again the moment she used the term "late wife." It wasn't as though he hadn't understood the gravity of the situation. The use of the two words, together, formed an incomprehensible summary of Jules's relationship to Rob. He shook at the thought that he'd have to use those words again and again.

Rob later learned from the police that a young adult driving her parents' SUV well above the speed limit, and unaccustomed to the added danger associated with rain-slicked roads, was texting while driving and, distracted, missed a bend in the road. By all accounts, she crossed the center line before looking up from her phone. Realizing her error, she overcorrected to the right, hydroplaned, and put the car into a spin. She crossed the center line a second time and ran head-on into Jules's convertible VW Beetle. The young driver survived with few injuries. Jules was declared dead on arrival at ULCA but was reportedly unresponsive and without a pulse, when the EMS arrived on scene. The police were still at the accident scene wrapping up their investigation while everyone else was completely unraveling at the hospital.

Rob went home past midnight, after hospital administration were done with him, as next of kin. Back home, he remained awake all night. He tried drinking straight vodka to dull the pain. Sickened by it, he ran to the bathroom, dropped to his knees and vomited. On the bathroom floor, he assumed a seated, fetal position: arms locked around his bent knees, and unconsciously began rocking back and forth. Rocking, research has proven, releases endorphins. Babies like to be rocked because the endorphin release is soothing. Even animals, particularly those imprisoned in zoos and circuses, rock repeatedly, to soothe their stress. Robert rocked himself until dawn.

The rain finally stopped as first light peeked through the drapes shortly after 5:30 a.m. Rob moved from the bathroom to the living room couch, and, as he lay in a catatonic and sleepless state, the irony struck him at once, like a punch in the stomach. He had both met and lost Juliana in an unexpected collision.

chapter 10

It was an uncharacteristically, but appropriately dreary day in Los Angeles. Dressed in a black suit and pressed white French cuff shirt, Robert sat on the edge of the bed which he had shared every night with Juliana. He was on the right side — her side — bent deeply, face buried in his hands: his body heaving as he sobbed uncontrollably. On the bed beside him lay a framed picture of him and Juliana from their wedding day. The photographer had captured them in a jubilant moment, like they were sharing a private joke. Beside the frame, in a small heap of silver and translucent pearls, lay one half of the Lazo rosary he had gifted Jules just before their wedding. The other half, including the crucifix, remained with Jules upon burial. Her sisters protested that it should remain with the family, but Robert, as her husband, enjoyed the final decision. Rivulets of tears streamed down Robert's cleanly shaven face and dampened the black tie constricting his neck. Grief etched and shadowed his face in the poorly lit bedroom. He looked twenty years older. Rob ran his suit sleeve across his face, capturing the tears and blotting the mucus running from his nose. Maria walked into the bedroom on tiptoes, afraid to disturb him. He heard her anyway.

"Roberto? Rob. I'm sorry to bother you. It's okay, you know, if you want to stay in here. Maybe we should have held the wake at our home instead. Is there anything I can do or get for you? Do you have more coffee somewhere? I can make up another pot for the guests."

"No. Let me compose myself. I can do this. Really. I will be out in a few minutes to thank everyone for coming. Umm, there should be more coffee beans above the stove, in the cupboard to the right. There's a grinder in the pantry. Jules likes her coffee fresh. He unconsciously spoke of her as if still alive.

"I found the grinder already. I'll look after it, Rob. I've got it covered."

It sounded like a party in the living room, making Robert feel even more uncomfortable. There were close to a hundred guests occupying every main-floor room of Robert and Juliana's modest home. Most of them congregated around the living room and adjacent kitchen. It was Rob's first exposure to some of the Mexican traditions for a wake. The candles and flowers seemed appropriate, as did the ton of food. All three scents battled for olfactory dominance. Mexicans, he learned, observe death as part of life. The sound of celebratory laughter, alongside the sound of sobbing, threw Rob a little off guard; as did the group of older men engaged in a raucous game of cards and dominos on the dining table. Rob thought it callous at the time. The upbeat ranchera music disturbed him too. He was *not* a Vincente Fernandez fan (the Frank Sinatra of ranchera), or of the entire musical genre, for that matter — something he hadn't been able to bring himself to tell Jules when she was alive. She and her family listened to it constantly. It drove him absolutely loco. The things men do for love.

"*Cómo va la comida Maria?*" Rob was doing his best to help but was barely keeping it together.

"*Mucho.* Take as much time as you need, Rob."

Maria feigned composure too. But her tears and running nose gave her away. She was hurting as much as anyone else. Siblings are frequently close, but Jules and Maria were emotionally conjoined. They behaved like fraternal twins. As hard struck as she was by Jules death, Maria was grateful that their mother did not have to experience the anguish of burying a child. It most surely would have sent her to an early grave. *Ella habría muerto de pena.*

"Does the music have to be so fucking loud?" Robert asked rhetorically. Maria had already left the room, inadvertently leaving the door ajar. The music was excruciating. He followed her out to the living room. "Can you please turn the music down a little?"

Days later, after he struggled to settle himself, Robert attended to the depressing but necessary legal details associated with Jules's death. The funeral and burial were over, but he had to look after payment for services; write and submit the obituary for the papers; obtain a death certificate; correspond with life insurance carriers and lawyers; write thank-you letters to the team at UCLA Medical Center, who were so helpful, and to those who attended the funeral or sent condolences; and throw out the flowers that had served their purpose and were past their prime. He hadn't yet even considered going back to Jules's burial plot to check on the installation of the headstone. Nobody had told him how long that would take, and he had neglected to ask. That was next on the list. *Ironic,* Rob thought, *that the pomp and responsibilities, cost and complication of death frequently exceed that of birth, graduation from college, and marriage combined* — the significant events in our lives that invite celebration and positive, hopeful prospects.

As the days passed, Robert contemplated a return to work. He knew, in his head and heart, that he wasn't emotionally equipped to do so. Rob could hardly muster the strength to get out of bed in the morning. But he didn't want to let his partners down or become a burden on the practice. His career, his personal health, his relationship with family were all deteriorating. His grief remained resilient. Robert was ill equipped to manage any of it, let alone achieve some definitive resolution.

A tour of Robert's home — their home — two weeks after his wife's death, offered evidence that things were not going well. He was rumpled and unshaven, and the house was a disaster. Dirty dishes piled up in the sink. Laundry lay heaped high in the bedroom. Garbage decomposed in the garage. Concerned for his wellbeing, José, one of Roberts' partners from the law firm, arrived at the house one afternoon, unannounced. He knocked on the door gently, then loudly. There was no answer. He was relieved to find the front door unlocked but apprehensive about what he might find. José stepped lightly inside the small foyer and called out. "Robert! Are you home? It's José. Hey man, where are you?" The sights and smell of disorder were palpable.

"I'm in the garage," Robert shouted back.

José was relieved to hear Robert's voice. After a couple of false starts, José found the garage. He smiled and spread his arms, offering a hug, as he greeted Robert.

"How are you, man? You all right?"

They engaged in a brief man-hug, complete with two back pats and a soul handshake to finish it off.

"Been better. Thanks for asking. And I appreciate you coming to the funeral. What brings you here today?"

"Worried about you, of course. C'mon, man. We all miss you. I, er… we are all wondering what your timeline looks like — you know, to return to the practice. Your clients are all asking about you too. A lot of them conveyed their condolences and mailed personal notes. Who mails notes these days? It's nice, to be honest. Real nice. I only ever get email. Anyway, we've re-assigned some of your files to other partners, but, you know…"

Robert preempted José's sermon. He knew the direction it was going. "I'm not returning, José. I can't work. I can't even think. I have to leave."

"Where are you going?" asked José.

"No, I meant resign. Quit. Leave the firm."

"Whoa, Robert… Rob. I understand that you've had a traumatic month, and are… You should grieve Jules's death. It's understandable man. If you need more time, just say so. We have got your back, *amigo*. You don't need to quit the firm. Take another few weeks and think about it. Okay?"

"Sure. Thanks, José. I appreciate you checking on me. I'm good." Robert lied. Poorly. "I'll be in touch soon."

"Please do keep in touch, man. I mean it. If you need anything… anything at all, call me. Hey, you want to get drunk some night? Cathy never lets me go out anymore. Let's do it. We can stay here if you want. That's okay, man. I'll bring some wicked strong tequila and bag full of limes over. You need some company, man. I need some company! You down for that?"

Robert looked at him, forced a slight smile, as if tempted for a moment, and shook his head. José looked crushed. Mostly because that meant he couldn't go out drinking. He *was* genuinely worried about his partner. Rob looked withdrawn and sullen. Beaten.

José made one last attempt at cracking Rob's apparent resolve.

"Hey man, don't hide away in here, like a hermit or something. You've got to get back out there. It would be healthy to socialize. Going back to work would distract you from your grief. Trust me on this, man. When I lost my *padre*, I went back to work the next day. People thought it was cold, but it was the best thing for me, to process my loss."

Rob was unresponsive and maintained his stare at the floor. He didn't want José to pick up on his facial expression. The comment, though innocent enough, enraged him. *Your father died at age eighty-nine. He wasn't taken in the prime of life by some fucking teenager texting acronyms and emoticons!* he thought.

"I'll be in touch soon," Robert stated to assuage José's obvious and sincere concern. "Seriously, I'll survive this. I think the best thing for me, right now, is to simplify my life, and take time to figure things out."

"Don't try to do this on your own, man," said José, shaking his head gently.

Robert offered an unconvincing head nod. "Roger that."

José extended Rob one more hug and a closed-lip, sympathetic smile and sidled back to his car. He backed down the driveway, watching the doorway all the while, hoping that Robert might possibly beckon him back at the last moment, asking for something: asking for anything. Rob waved. But it was *good-bye*, not *come back*. Rob's business partner drove down the street, turned the corner, and disappeared.

Returning to the garage, Rob glanced at the golf bag leaning against the wall beside his car. It had been well over a month since he'd last played, and the clubs had collected a fine layer of grey Los Angeles dust. He brushed a swipe of dust off with his hands and, in turn, wiped his hands clean on his pants. Lifting a driver out of the bag calmly, he pulled the head cover off and studied the club from every angle. It was a TaylorMade M2, made from carbon fiber. It had been an uncharacteristically expensive purchase for Robert, but he'd rationalized it at the time. He gripped the club tightly, his left hand on the top of the shaft and right hand below, slightly overlapping his left thumb, right thumb outstretched as he was accustomed to. He placed the club head on the garage floor, assumed an appropriate stance for a drive off an imaginary tee, and looked up and forward, squinting, as if trying to see an imaginary green and its pin several hundred yards away. His position was good, squatting at the waist, elbows bent and close together. He addressed the invisible ball and commenced a gentle backswing in slow motion, as if trying to find the perfect speed and momentum for the drive. Turning his hips and shoulders away from his unseen target, Robert completed a gentle turn and held the club at the top of his backswing. He remained frozen for close to a minute.

With a rage that surprised even him, Robert swung the club with all his might into the adjacent drywall. The club missed the two-by-fours and plunged deeply between the studs, leaving a dark, gaping hole in the garage wall. He pulled out the club like a swordsman and struck the wall again and again and again. Robert's screams — intense, guttural and primal — drowned out the sound made by the impact and penetration of each thrust at the drywall enemy. On the fifth stroke, the surprisingly tough club found an intransigent wall stud, and the shaft and head of the club finally surrendered. Rather than bending, it splintered into a jagged mess, rendering the entire club useless. The garage wall, now pockmarked with deep holes, suffered a similar fate.

Panting from the exertion and uncontrolled release of emotion, Robert dropped the remains of the club and stared blankly at the cratered wall. He took a deep breath and held it. Anguish and grief were family relations who had invited pain to join them in his home. Pain evidently had an angry cousin. None were welcome. He wished the family reunion to be over.

chapter I I

To everyone's pleasant surprise, Robert returned to his practice in Los Angeles a week later. After greeting and hugging him, his workmates offered appropriate pleasantries, free-flowing tears, and sympathy. It was awkward, but Rob donned a fake smile to make everyone else feel less uncomfortable. Extracting himself from the reunion, he walked lethargically into his office. His partner José, followed him.

"If you don't mind, José, I'd like some privacy."

"Oh, hey, no problem, man. *Está todo bien.*"

The office, on a corner and befitting his partner status, was well decorated, if a little busy. It was adorned on every available horizontal surface — shelves, credenza, and desk — with a veritable gallery of framed photos, and one expressive pen and ink drawing of Jules. Some photos included Rob and Jules together, at formal affairs and in casual settings, including one of them wearing backpacks and hiking boots. Though the office was mainly crowded with personal mementos, a few professional awards and several degree certificates did somehow negotiate limited real estate on the walls. Rob surveyed the room. It looked unfamiliar. He regarded it as if for the first or the last time. It soon became clear that the latter was his verdict.

Robert made the very difficult decision to leave his practice. His partners, of course, tried again to convince him to remain. They offered a six-month paid leave to grieve and recuperate.

They offered counselling. They offered Rob a paid trip to Mexico to spend time with Juliana's family, if he needed it. They offered an operational role, managing the office, so he didn't have to engage lawyers, the court or clients, to ease him back. He had thanked them for their kindness and generosity with complete sincerity, but reflexively batted away every option they served up.

Robert returned to his car to fetch the boxes left over from packing his home. He proceeded to bundle up the contents of the office that he wanted to retain — pictures and personal belongings — sealing them with packing tape. He stopped, briefly, to look at the JD diploma on the wall. Not expecting he'd need it again, he left it where it hung.

Adele, Rob's administrative assistant of nine years, had been quietly watching him, hoping he would speak a little with her. Leaning against the frame of the door to his office, she cupped hand to her mouth and did her best to stifle a cry. Overcome with sorrow for Rob's loss and by the departure of her boss and favorite practice partner, she shook her head, wiped her tears away, and turned, leaving the office. Rob finally directed his attention to where she had been standing, alerted by the sound of her sobbing. She had already disappeared around the corner. Her heartfelt outreach had gone unanswered. Rob too did his best to control his emotions as he scooped up the pictures and drawing of Jules and piled them into the assembled boxes. It took two lazy-loads to the wagon to extract them. With each trip through the office, he did his best to avoid eye contact, certain that by doing so, he could control the dam of tears building in his eyes.

Though the house was once the center of their lives, Robert could no longer bear to live in the home he and Jules had made.

The rancher they'd bought in Santa Monica had great curb appeal, even if a little dated. Rough as it was inside, they'd made an offer the very day they toured it, with an agent. And while it was modest, Jules and Rob had both come to love the nest they created together. It reflected the lives they'd lived and included mementos and objet d'art from their travels — many of which revealed their passion for the outdoors. Without Jules, it felt like nothing more than a house. Rob made the decision to sell with little hesitation, and no regrets. He listed the house with a friend — a real estate agent who knew the neighborhood well and had an exemplary track record of quick home sales. It was time to leave.

After necessary drywall repairs in the garage, and some minor staging, the house was listed. It sold in only four days — an average length of time in the red-hot Santa Monica market and for their neighborhood. A young couple, first-time buyers, made a full-price offer less than an hour after viewing it. The couple did their best to maintain a good poker face during the initial showing. With twenty years of experience, the real estate agent saw through the bluff immediately. After thanking her, the couple made it no farther than their car. After sharing their giddy enthusiasm for the house, they marched right back up to the front stoop. The agent was engaged with the next potential buyers, and was presenting the newly renovated kitchen, when she was interrupted by the sound of the doorbell. Opening the door, the realtor was not surprised to see the couple to whom she had just said goodbye. They stood on the steps, barely able to control their youthful enthusiasm. Voices cracking under the stress and exhilaration of the situation, the couple announced their decision to make a full-price offer. The fact that the home was offered with a quick closing date and, at the buyer's option, fully furnished, appealed to the eager couple. They were first-time buyers with limited furniture that wasn't college-dorm quality.

Jules and Rob had been in that economic camp once themselves. The home equity he and Jules accumulated, as the frothy market drove their homes' value to unprecedented levels, provided Rob with sufficient resources on which to live comfortably. He didn't need or want the furniture and felt satisfied to pay it forward by including it with the house. The offer to purchase was drawn up and promptly countersigned by Rob, a few hours later.

A day before the legal closing, Robert hired cleaners to tidy the place. While they were doing their thing, he finished packing the last of his belongings. He'd given most of Jules's extensive collection of clothing, shoes, purses, and jewelry to her sisters. José received what remained of Robert's golf clubs. Everything else, he donated to charity. After the house was readied, he loaded the rear hatch of his station wagon. He jammed in several duffel bags filled with clothing, three pairs of shoes and toiletries, a knapsack, a camp cot and stove, three plastic bins filled with assorted camping gear, and limited memorabilia from his marriage. Everything he chose to keep fit in his car. Rob felt liberated to free himself of all the stuff he and Juliana had accumulated over their ten years of marriage.

While he and Jules had had a very open relationship with few secrets, he'd never dared to share a deep-seated resentment he harbored. Rob always felt heavily encumbered, and even suffocated, by all the material things they had acquired and sequestered in their home. He felt that he could shed most of what they had purchased, except for the art, photos, some favorite books, and, of course, the wedding present that never left his left wrist. He knew, however, that Jules enjoyed their lifestyle: the house, the furniture, the Nuova Simonelli espresso machine, monthly pedicures, annual vacations, and all the things that a professional couple with no kids and a double income could afford. Every weekend represented another forty-eight-hour shopping opportunity for Jules. Wanting to avoid potential confrontation through open dialogue, Rob said nothing. Every new load of designer clothes that made its way back home provided an opportunity for him to purse his lips and hone his passive-aggressive skills. And Jules, to his frustration, had dragged their credit score to the shaky side of 700.

The car loaded to the roof with all the possessions he valued or needed, Rob backed his Volvo Cross Country out of the garage, lowered the door, and slipped the remote control into the mailbox, as requested by his real estate agent. The wagon sat idling as he took one last look at the place, through the sun glare on the windshield. It was hot as hell and the lawn had been neglected. It had turned a golden tan — like a fall wheat crop. *As nice as it was, I won't miss maintaining the house,* he thought. He was thrilled to be now also unencumbered by a mortgage. Between the proceeds for the sale of the house, and the half-million-dollar payout from Jules's life insurance policy, Rob was financially comfortable and could afford to get away, and stay away, for a while.

With a sheet of sweat rolling down his forehead, Robert cranked the air conditioning to ice cold and the fan to high. He turned to the rear-view mirror, tilted it sideways, and regarded the unfamiliar man looking back. It was the first time he had observed his own image in weeks. He wore a blank, sorrowful look on his face. Rob was unshaven and his loss of appetite had resulted in a deficit of at least ten pounds now visible even to himself. Without further delay, he put the Volvo in drive, wound his way through the neighborhood, grabbed the first entrance ramp to Highway 405, and made his way to Highway 5. He turned on the radio and promptly shut it off again. The sound of tires on asphalt was about the only music he could bear to hear.

At Los Banos, almost six hours north of LA, Robert steered off the highway and swung west, on Highway 152, and then the 101, to Salinas. Salinas is the largest city in Monterey County and it's centered in one of California's most fertile agricultural zones, anchored by flower and vegetable farms, with some decent vineyards thrown in for good measure. It also happens to be the hometown of John Steinbeck, one of Rob's favorite writers, whom he discovered in high school when assigned *East of Eden,* for English class. Salinas lies in the middle of a gaping lowland that defines the start of the north-west to south-east canted Salinas Valley. Its climate is schizophrenic. Only eight miles from the Pacific, it welcomes the influence of the cool ocean zephyrs, while simultaneously battling the heat and dry that governs the central valley. In the summer, residents hope the former dominates.

Robert checked into the first motel in Salinas that had a vacancy sign, too drained to drive farther. After a shower to wash the day off, a pang of hunger screamed for attention. He hadn't eaten a thing all day. Robert wandered across the street to a diner and wolfed a burger without tasting it. He walked back to his room, collapsed on the bed, and fell asleep, beating the sun to the horizon. An alarm blaring in the empty room adjacent to his woke him at seven the next morning. *There's a special place in hell,* he thought, *for people who set their bedside clock radios in hotel rooms and depart before the alarm goes off.* He shook off his irritation and the night's sleep, gathered his thoughts, and attempted to define a plan — at least for the day. The morning sun had already starting seeping into the room, from behind the thick curtains.

Distracted, and in his haste to get the hell out of LA, Rob realized that he hadn't communicated much with his own family. He loved them and didn't want them to worry about his extended camping plan and get-my-shit-together scheme. After searching the motel room dresser and desk drawers, he was pleasantly surprised to learn that some motels still provided stationery, envelopes, and a pen. With a coffee in hand, Robert pulled the writing kit out and wrote a few short notes to those for whom he cared. The notes represented his best attempt to offer an explanation and outline his rather vague plan: they in-cluded a plea for them not to not worry and a solemn promise he'd return when he sorted out his grief. A stop at the front desk and quick query of the front desk manager pointed him in the direction of the closest post office. He threw the knapsack in the back seat of the car, promptly found the post office, posted the letters, and jumped back in the wagon. He sat in the car and stared at nothing, contemplating his journey.

A characteristically logical and methodical man, Rob was perplexed by his rush to make progress to an undefined des-tination. He had trouble processing the complex mood of the moment. Emotions bounced around in his head like bingo balls. He acknowledged that he had all five squares filled and could have called it. It wasn't a jackpot he wanted to claim, though. *Grief. Sadness. Guilt. Loneliness. Relief.* The fifth caught him off guard. *Where the hell did that come from? How can I feel relief?* His emotions turned on one another and he began to have feelings about his feelings. Deconstructing each, like a trained lawyer might, led him to the conclusion that his relief came from the deepest part of his psyche. He felt comforted by the newfound detachment from so many material things, which had previously weighed him down like a ship's anchor might a dinghy. Satisfied at having ruled out any deeply felt sense of encumbrance by the marriage itself, Rob felt better. He regained his focus, started the car, and wheeled out of the parking lot: foot heavy on the gas pedal, free to go as far as he pleased.

chapter *12*

Robert's first stop traced a familiar path back to the place that he and Jules had loved so much. Driving a short distance due west, he arrived at the Carmel Highlands and entrance to Point Lobos State Natural Reserve. He rolled the car into the hard-packed dirt parking lot at Whaler's Cove, among the first cars to arrive that morning. He threw on a jacket before stepping out of the car. It was predictably cool, made more so by the offshore breeze. Like opening the fridge door, you can predictably escape even the most sweltering days, inland, by leaning into the coast and the headlands formed at the Carmel Highlands. Locking the car, he shouldered his daypack, snatched a bottle of water, and headed off for a brisk hike — the kind he had enjoyed with Jules so many times in this familiar place. Rob hoofed it to and scrambled up Skull Head Rock, the highest promontory on the reserve. Panting heavily from an exercise tackled many times before, and quite easily, he realized he had lost his base of fitness. After a well-earned rest at the peak, he surveyed the dangerously steep edge of the cliff.

The ocean below provided its spectacular performance for free. He sat there for close to forty minutes, recovering from the exertion and taking it in. Breathing deeply, he sucked the cool, damp ocean air into his lungs. The coastal oxygen here has mysterious and unique properties that somehow can either bestow energy or fatigue you. Today, Robert experienced the latter. It was an entirely new and different level of tired. Robert looked down at the churning froth that obscured the base of the cliff and shuffled ever closer to its precipice. His eyes welled with tears as thoughts of Jules and their shared life played on a continuous reel in his head. He missed her more than ever. Inhaling deeply, he contemplated his present and the future. Neither seemed the least bit appealing to him.

He closed his eyes, hoping to contain his negative thoughts and squeeze the tears out. Jumping head first off Skull Rock — aptly named given his current state of mind — seemed a reasonable default resolution. It would at least be quick, he thought, contrasting the pain he'd experienced over the previous two months. If the fall onto the serrated rocks didn't kill him immediately, the pounding ocean would surely crush him against the rocks. If that didn't work, the roiling ocean along this stretch of the Pacific coast would drown him within a few more seconds. The cove one hundred yards away at Monastery Beach was nicknamed "Mortuary Beach" by locals for the number of divers it had claimed due to its notoriously powerful undertow. And these were people who entered the water voluntarily — for recreation — with scuba equipment, dive buddies, and back-up safety gear. He opened his eyes and wiped tears away with his palms. Jules would be furious at him, in Spanish, for even contemplating suicide. Whenever she broke into high-speed and passionate Spanish (a not infrequent occurrence), he always knew he was in deep shit.

"Nunca pienses en hacer algo tan estúpido de nuevo!"

While rejecting the notion of self-harm, Robert did throw his cell phone off the cliff — a symbolic release from his previous life, and a ritualistic sacrifice to the Gods of Simplicity. He watched it spiral down and just clear the jagged base, creating a diminutive splash in the frothy surf below. It became obvious that had he chosen to jump, he wouldn't have cleared the rocks.

A mental picture of the outcome and ensuing mess made him wince. He looked away. The horror of the thought was surpassed only by the sudden realization that he had forgotten to terminate his cell data plan.

The sound of angry Spanish still ringing in his head, Robert struggled around Lobos for another two hours, unenthusiastically absorbing the sights, sounds, and smells that he'd shared with Jules during better times. On an emotional level, he couldn't figure out if he was taking her along on one last visit, saying goodbye, or both. He wanted to believe he heard her offer comforting and loving support. He still, however, had no plan. He felt nothing but sorrow and emptiness. He had slumped into a deep depression and should really have been under the care of a physician, supported by weekly appointments with a psychologist. But Robert was damn stubborn, and though he recognized his sorrowful state, he sought no one's help or offers of support. He wanted to escape from everything and deal with his grief on his terms, as misplaced and poorly chosen as those terms might turn out to be.

Leaving Lobos, Robert drove a few miles north, into Carmel, to buy some groceries. He had contemplated continuing his drive northward along the coast to camp out when and wherever he landed. Vancouver Island was high on his list of possible destinations, the non-plan he had concocted. Even coastal Alaska had been given limited consideration. On the outskirts of town, at the Carmel Rancho Shopping Center, he withdrew cash from an ATM and bought some food: two sandwiches, some energy bars, a few drinks, and two large jugs of water. The car demanded equal attention. A low gas indicator light demanded a break. Fueled and provisioned, the car pointed north on Hwy 1. It didn't get far. Lured by roadway signs for 17-Mile Drive, Robert exited the highway and headed into the heart of the Monterey Peninsula. He and Jules had traversed the 17-Mile Drive loop many times. Along this route, a familiar sign on Lopez Road caught his attention. The sign summoned him to Poppy Hills Golf Course, a course he had played years before. Feeling a tad nostalgic, he swung into the car lot, parking well away from other vehicles.

Robert got out and leaned against the hood of the car. He gazed toward the clubhouse, scanned the driving range, and squinted to view the fairway at number one — all within his sightline. Hands pushed deep in his pockets, Robert sauntered toward the driving range. He engaged a pre-game warm up on this very spot by hitting a bucket of balls. Believing he owed himself this pleasure again, Robert bought a bucket and rented a well-abused driver — a one wood. The reference is dying out, given that no drivers or golf clubs of any persuasion are made from wood anymore. Successive generations of golfers have taken to renaming those clubs *metals* or *metal woods*. Even those terms are falling from favor. The latest drivers are more likely made from a composite. The game, like every other sport, continues to be redefined by technological change — much to the lament of traditionalists. Robert wasn't one. He embraced *any* advance that might improve his game. At this moment, though, his clothes and hiking shoes were completely inappropriate for the chore. His stride to the tee, however, suggested that this was a man who knew what he was doing, regardless of the uniform — like an off-duty police officer in sweatpants who, while out buying milk, stumbles upon a crime in progress, and neutralizes an armed robber.

Substandard club in one hand and wire basket full of balls in another, he found himself a bare patch of artificial grass on the tee line. While his game proved a little rusty, the action of swinging the club again sparked an enthusiasm in Robert precisely when he needed it. He appreciated the smell of the freshly cut grass and the satisfying sound the clubface makes when you hit a ball square on the sweet spot. It's a very distinct sound that can be felt as much as heard. It resonates in your chest. Without so much as a glance, you can tell when the other golfers on the tee line have connected well, too. The sound is unmistakable. A single, perfectly executed drive, out to 250 yards, can make up for twenty flubbed, duffed, hooked, sliced, shanked, and pulled drives that end up in the woods. Every amateur golfer knows and embraces this theology. For many, it's the only thing that keeps them coming back to this game again and again. You remember the great holes or entire courses that you've played out successfully and conveniently forget the bad ones. Psychologists call it *motivated forgetting*. Psychology aside, I suspect this rationalization, by golfers, falls into the same category of things from which God saves idiots. Without it, I suspect there would be exponentially fewer golf enthusiasts in the world.

Robert's few first cuts at the ball were not pretty. He hoped to hell that nobody was watching. His game was rusty. Robert topped the first two drives and trimmed the grass. Overcompensating on the next swing, he inadvertently got under the ball, resulting in a terrible moon shot that landed thirty yards ahead of him. It was embarrassing for an experienced golfer. After a trio of hooks deep into the woods, he finally dialed in the once familiar drive. *Keep your left arm straight. Slow down your back swing. Don't let the contact distract you and make you lift your head.* Robert mentally coached himself through a refresher course and got back in the zone. He found his signature draw again and, as the bucket of balls drained, increased his distance. Several sailed out past the 250-yard marker.

By the time Robert had finished driving the bucket, his arms ached. He had transferred his internal anger and pain through the club, down its shaft, and into every single ball teed. He struck each with increasing ferocity and an accompanying, exaggerated grunt. Other golfers began to take notice and react with some concern. A few drives rolled out to the 300-yard marker and the woods beyond. He still had the power, if not the consistency. Robert walked back to the car, leaned against the fender, massaged his arms, and watched — silently critiquing the other golfers at the range. Some were good. Some were terrible. He tried not to be too judgmental. They were all adherents to a shared religion. Or *cult*, depending on your perspective.

Robert eased into his parked car to grab a drink of water and eat some of the food picked up earlier. After devouring a sandwich, he closed his eyes, weary from the hike at Lobos and his personal war with the golf balls. Sleep snuck up on him swiftly.

A loud and very close knocking sound eventually awakened him. Robert roused with a start, grunted, and, half awake, looked for the source of the thumping. A rotund man dressed in a security uniform pounded on his car window, without response, before he finally woke. Robert fumbled for the electric window button. A clearly irritated security guard glared at him for a half a minute, sniffing the air — presumably wondering if this sleeping guy, in the now dark parking lot of Poppy Hills, was passed out drunk. It had happened many times before. Golfers who visit Porter's, the club lounge at Poppy (more generally referred to at all golf courses as the *Nineteenth Hole*), had been known to imbibe more than a few drinks, complementing that which they might have consumed rounding the previous eighteen. It was the guard's job to make certain that they all left the premises when the course closed, soberly if possible. The course was well past its posted closing time. Robert's car was conspicuous as the only vehicle remaining in the lot. He tried to explain. The painfully bright flashlight directed at his face was not helping anything. Its intensity forced him to close his eyes while he spoke.

"Sorry, pal. I fell asleep. I had a long day. Can you turn that thing off, please? You're blinding me!"

"You have to leave right now. The club closed an hour ago. Have you been drinking, sir? California has a zero-tolerance policy, you know. I'd encourage you to call a cab."

"I haven't been drinking. I told you that I fell asleep. I hit a bucket of balls and nodded off."

"Uh-huh. You sure you don't mean a bucket of beers?"

The guard, a wannabe cop, shone his flashlight around Robert's car as though searching for contraband. He did a complete walk around the wagon and peered into every window, front, back, and sides.

"What the hell are you doing?" Robert asked, irritated.

"What's all the gear for?" asked the guard, suspicious of Robert's presence and intent.

"I'm going camping."

"Sure you are. You understand that this is not a campground. Right?"

"Well aware."

The guard jotted something down in a small notebook he carried in his breast pocket and tucked it away. He used the pencil end to pick wax from one ear.

"You have a safe drive home now," he said in a cynical tone, slapping the roof of the wagon twice.

Robert gave him a bleary-eyed look, punched the automatic window button, to punctuate the conversation, started the car, and wheeled out of the parking lot. He hung a random right out of the lot onto Lopez Road, unsure where he was going next or where he'd spend the night. About sixty yards down the road, he clobbered the brakes. He'd spotted, with the aid of the moonlight, a packed dirt trail as wide as the car on the right side of the road. It appeared to lead into the woods that bordered Poppy Hills. The trail, he felt certain, portended something more significant. He imagined it to be the kind of place young people (or older, married types tempting the boundaries of fidelity) went to park and make out. Robert turned in slowly and flipped on the high beams. There were no lovers or cheaters in sight — only trees and long shadows cast by the headlights. He drove in tentatively, far enough to ensure the vehicle would be obscured from sight. The sound of tangled branches scratching the sides of his car had the same effect as fingernails on a chalkboard. It sent chills up Robert's spine, making him grimace. The paint on the Volvo was surely scratched horribly. He came to a stop, shut off the car, killed the headlights, reclined his seat as far back as it would go, and attempted to resume his much-deserved sleep. It was delightfully fresh and quiet in the woods, save for the crickets. Robert was certain he heard a distant owl hooting, in angry Spanish, as he drifted off to sleep again.

chapter 13

The light was still dim in the morning when Robert first stirred. He could barely move. His body ached from the hike, from driving the bucket of balls, and from the uncomfortable and sleepless night in the front seat of the car. The wagon's windows had fogged over from his warm breath converging with the cool night air. He wiped the side window with his shirtsleeve to peer out. Easing his worn body out of the car, he groaned, attempting to stand upright and straighten his atrophied legs. They were stiff as tree trunks and felt as heavy. He tried stomping them awake. The exertion forced him to draw fast, short breaths. A pungent smell of pine and cypress teased his nostrils as stood and inhaled deeply. Dawn light punctuated the tree coverage and turned the woods a lovely dappled orange. If he had been half asleep, he was now fully awake from the cacophony of sounds — crows rudely ordering breakfast and woodpeckers self-sufficiently preparing their own. Robert turned a slow circle to regard the wooded environment into which he had stumbled, or rolled, the previous night. The forest surrounding him seemed industrious in an entirely natural way. The morning shift had already begun. Robert might have been considered inappropriately late for work. He'd ask the boss for leniency — his first day and all....

Nature called, quite literally, and he started into the woods a few yards to release a much-needed morning drain. A burst of activity startled him. That's the way it is with a forest. Regarding it externally, it appears peacefully vacant. Sneak a peek behind the curtain, and it's full of life. A deer bounded at the sound of Robert's footfall. Squirrels strategically repositioned themselves on the opposite side of the trees and skittered up the trunk, their claws nipping at the bark. A ruffed grouse took to low-altitude flight to put some distance between herself and the urinating biped. The grouse scared Robert more, I'm certain, than he scared the fleet bird.

It was an event. The woods — a theatre. It proved to be a surreal but seminal moment. Robert developed that characteristic, unnerving, focused look on his face: the kind that allowed him to block out everything else, sights and sounds, and turn his attention to the problem at hand. He knew he had a problem. He knew the source. He understood how it was manifesting itself and impacting his mental health. That's where Robert's rationality ended. An injured man rarely makes sound decisions, particularly when it comes to self-diagnosis and self-prescribed treatment. At this moment, however, Robert was certain that he had identified an appropriate medication. Rather than engaging those who loved and cared for him — those who wanted to help shoulder his burden of grief — Robert convinced himself that solitude would hasten his convalescence. At the moment, this place and this time seemed as good as any to start.

Robert was surprised how deep into the woods he had inadvertently walked, lost in thought. He found his way back soon enough. Back at the car, he hefted the tailgate and yanked out duffel bags, backpacks, plastic bins, food, and the water he had bought. The backpack slung over his shoulder was reserved for the most precious possessions — the few mementos of Jules he'd brought. He laid the gear all out in neat rows just inside the forest edge, beside the dirt trail. Rob did a quick visual inventory and catalogued it mentally. He commenced moving all the gear, load by load, deeper into the woods and out of sight from anyone who might meander up the trail. The car remained where it had been parked. Robert never gave it consideration after that. His attention turned to establishing a temporary base in the woods. It was unclear where, geographically, he had chosen to drop his gear. The closest intersection he recalled lay at Ronda and Sunridge roads. This *felt* like a private and secure site. Robert has no idea when or if he might be seen, but he decided, right then and there, he'd make the Carmel Woods his home.

Three days later, a Volvo wagon was spotted being towed out of the woods. A local homeowner, whose daily routine included a healthy walk in the woods, had spied it for two consecutive days before calling the police. You couldn't blame her. It most definitely looked out of place. When he parked it, Robert hadn't considered what he'd do with the car. Clearly, it hadn't been hidden that successfully. The police were on scene and traced the vehicle to its rightful owner. The registration in the glove box made it altogether uncomplicated for the responding officer.

"I'm not going to make detective over this discovery," the slightly disappointed cop told his partner. "How come I can't solve some real crimes?"

"Maybe a missing person case. Those are cool."

"Could be a murder and auto theft."

"How about carjacking."

"True. You see any blood or anything?"

"Unfortunately, no. Car's pretty clean actually. Bunch of boxes in the back. Maybe a home robbery. Check the glove compartment for the registration."

There was no evidence of any crime at the scene. Finding a car in the woods, six hours away from its registered owner's address, perhaps convinced the police officer that kids or gang members had stolen the vehicle: likely for a joy ride. Had the car been snatched by professionals, he might have reasoned, this late model Volvo would have been either on a container ship headed to Asia, to be reborn with a new VIN, or chopped in Los Angeles. The officer wrote a few details in a notepad and requested a tow to the impound yard in Salinas, where it would eventually sit and collect dust — for quite some time. The police report of the recovered vehicle never triggered further investigation. There was no corresponding report of a stolen Volvo wagon filed in Los Angeles. It was eventually declared an unclaimed vehicle and destined for public auction. Half of Robert's life, or what little of it endured, remained entombed in the vehicle, waiting for its day of rediscovery.

chapter 14

It took Robert a few days to complete a cursory ground reconnaissance of the surrounding woods, map them to his memory, and seek out a more suitable, long-term location to set up camp. Like any experienced wilderness camper, he sought a dry, flat place (it's not fun to wake up in the middle of the night having rolled up against the tent wall); a place with a balance of light and shade from the sun (same for being awakened by the light at seven in the morning, rolled up against the tent wall); a break from the wind (tent blown down, in the blazing sun, rolled against the tent wall); and, of course, in his case, an assurance of absolute privacy. He simply wanted to be comfortable for his short stay. Robert wasn't planning on extended residence. He never thought of himself as a survivalist, a prepper, or a hermit of all things. Recluse… maybe. Eccentric? He'd own that. The term made him sound more interesting than he imagined himself to genuinely be.

Robert had sufficient financial means, of course, but was just not inclined to get another house, stay in a hotel, or buy a house, trailer home, condo, houseboat, or any of the other more socially acceptable forms of temporary or long-term habitation. They all seemed so… permanent. And social. Except the houseboat. The houseboat might be an option. Robert resolved to survive on his own terms: to rediscover the nature that he had once embraced, and to live simply, all while negotiating his way through crushing grief. He carried that anguish with him constantly, like a fifty-pound rucksack that he could never un-shoulder. Above all, Robert hoped that he'd find peace in the Carmel Woods.

It's not entirely productive to judge Robert or to consider his response as overly dramatic or unproductive. People deal with grief in distinct and very personal ways. Another experiencing such a deep sense of loss might have taken his life, or worse yet, that of another. There can be power in grief, though. Like any other emotion, it has the potential to drive positive outcomes. For some, it stimulates self-reflection and personal growth. Channeled, it can be harnessed as an agent of change — a catalyst to greater self-confidence, self-reliance, and ability to better manage life's challenges. Grief aside, Robert's immediate task was to create a place to live, even if he might never call it a home.

On his third day of reconnaissance, Robert stumbled, quite literally, down the gulley running off Del Ciervo, near its intersection with a quiet section of 17-Mile Drive. The ravine here canted at a near thirty-degree slope, its descent this day slick from rain and runoff. He lost his footing on his second step and slid on his ass for eight feet. A half-rotted stump stopped his momentum. Struggling back to his feet and brushing the pine needles, dirt, and moss off his pants, he carried on more cautiously. At the bottom of the shallow valley, Robert conducted a quick visual survey. This is an adequate spot, he thought, a contender for sure. The gulley was far enough from any of the established paths that crisscrossed the woods. Any semi-permanent shelter he might build would be well below the view plane of anyone strolling past, even if they were close to the ravine. The canopy of pines and cypress, he assessed, would shade the site from the hot sun and the rain. There were no homes altogether near. The closest faced in the opposite direction from the woods, providing a sound and visual buffer. Every one of the residences that bordered this section of the woods featured a solid privacy fence as high as bylaws allowed, to their benefit and his. Robert even envisioned the potential for operating a small camp stove or some arrangement of fireplace, if committed to constructing a fixed cabin. After pacing off the length of the gulley — south to north — he became even more enamored with its potential. The northern end of the ravine, while near a residential cul-de-sac, ended at Costanilla Way. After one crosses this thinly trafficked section of road, the woods continue unabated until the southern edge of the green at Poppy Hills. The southern end of the ravine, in turn, leads to 17-Mile Drive. That road, in turn, leads south to the Carmel Gate, with its toll shack at Carmel Way — the main road leading into town and Carmel Beach.

Though he was certainly roughing it, all the resources Robert might need, beyond those that he brought with him or could access within the wood itself, were within a reasonable walk away. A marked and well-used trail ran parallel to the gulch. It remained more than a hundred feet away, even at its closest approach. The relative dimness of the ravine and the steepness of its slopes were likely to dissuade casual hikers from venturing in, he imagined, even if they chose to stray from the main trail. There was nothing to view in the ravine, really. It was shadowy and empty. And the path to approach it, from the trail, was arduous. The entire gulley also provided for a convenient, natural windbreak — something that might be useful when the furious ocean winds spilled into the interior of the Monterey Peninsula. Robert mapped out potential ingress and egress routes up to the ravine edge. There were three routes that provided clear passage, and several alternative paths for a clandestine exit, if required.

Satisfied that he had identified a nearly perfect campsite, Robert hustled back to his initial, makeshift camp. His tent and supplies remained safely tucked behind a large tree on the side facing away from the closest trail. He broke down the tent, bagged it, and collected all the gear he had accessed over the previous days. It was at that point that he caught a whiff of himself. He stank. His body odor, after four days without a bath or shower, had caught up with him. In his enthusiasm to establish a suitable campsite, he'd neglected to consider his personal hygiene. He also took note of the fact that he had also consumed most of his drinking water. Robert mentally logged an agenda for his next set of tasks: wash self, wash dirty clothes, find a source for water and fill jugs, get more food. It took three trips from his temporary camp to move his bags and bins to the ravine. It was draining. Now conscious of it, his body odor became more obvious. Better make that a priority. He removed his shirt and tossed it in a black plastic bag. Using the remaining water sloshing around the bottom of the jug, he soaked a clean towel and scrubbed his underarms. The towel got tossed in the black bag too. Robert dug deep into the duffel bag and pulled out a stick of deodorant, applied a swath, and felt more human at once.

While the ravine proved to be well sequestered, the plain above captured a variety of neighborhood and traffic sounds. Now and then, when the wind was blowing from the west and all else was quiet, he heard a faint noise. It came and went, swirling with the breeze. It navigated the tangle of tree coverage and proved as sweet a sound as that of children playing — at least to Robert. It was barely audible but unmistakable — the echoes of golfers — at Poppy Hills or Pebble Beach, he presumed. That sound was punctuated by the resonance of a driver connecting with a golf ball: its distinctive tink, mixed with an almost sub-audible tone of players yakking and, undoubtedly, bullshitting. Robert stopped for a minute to enjoy it vicariously. Four tinks, measured out in almost chronologically accurate sixty-second intervals, marked the play of four experienced golfers hitting their respective drives from a tee box. Robert was now tucked in amongst some of the greatest courses in the United States, if not the world. One might compare it to the excitement a tennis enthusiast would experience after moving into a flat across the street from the All England Lawn Tennis Club at Wimbledon in London.

His gear safely tucked away, Robert considered a more specific location at which to establish a permanent camp. Logic suggested that, when it rained, water would likely to pool at the bottom of the ravine. That would make for a swampy home. Robert spied a dry, level spot, halfway up the slope: thirty feet by thirty feet. It featured a balance of tree cover. One section was clear save for sporadic deadfall. A natural berm of earth at the end of the flat, closest to the forest plain above, provided excellent concealment. He dragged his gear the last hundred feet to this site: his camp. The sun drooped low and, as predicted, it became dark in the ravine well before the rest of the surrounding woods. Sitting on an overturned plastic bin, Robert allowed himself rest. He surveyed the site once more and smiled. I can make this work, he thought, as a squirrel watched him suspiciously.

The squirrel dashed off to score another pinecone and Robert found himself alone. An air of calm enveloped the gulley. He paused to listen to the lovely silence of it all. From his bad, he snatched two energy bars, gobbled them with ferocity, and chased them down with a bottle of orange Gatorade. He didn't care for energy drinks but knew them to be effective in replenishing electrolytes lost through perspiration. Too tired to erect the tent for the night, Robert pulled out the bivy sack he'd packed; took off his boots; and slid in: covering his head with the hood to keep out the cool and wetness of the morning dew.

Jules had always envied Robert's ability to fall asleep so quickly and was frequently infuriated by it — especially when she lay awake for hours while he slept peacefully. A vision of Jules sleeping filled his last waking thought, and generated a reflexive smile, as he nodded off.

chapter 15

In the early morning, Robert jerked awake, reacting involuntarily to the overwhelming noises surrounding him. Caught in a waking dream, he perceived himself surrounded by police. They approached from all sides to execute a warrant for his arrest. There were voices shouting out, demanding he come out peacefully. A rustling of trees gave away their position as they advanced, guns drawn and ready for a fight — deadly force authorized. Seconds later and fully awake, he realized he was hearing the calls of aggressive crows, alerted to his presence, welcoming him to their neighborhood or perhaps requesting his immediate departure. Recalling earlier experiences at wilderness campsites, Robert understood that he would hereafter have to align his personal sleep and wake schedule with that of nature — the cycles and activities of the forest creatures with whom he now shared a small slice of the Carmel Woods.

At no time over the first week did Robert think of himself as a hermit. He had never fantasized about living off the land, hunting and killing his own food and sustaining himself for an indefinite period. He had no intention of living that way. In the moment, he considered himself to be merely camping, albeit alone and in an unauthorized campground. Despite or because of his loss and ensuing grief, Robert had become an accidental minimalist.

His food had run out now, and he desperately needed a shower, some food, and more water. He begrudged the necessity of leaving his campsite for the first time but acknowledged that even minimalists needed to eat. Paranoid that his stash of gear might be discovered, he laid pine boughs over the inventory and started to hike out of the gulley. Some fifty feet away, he stopped and looked back to determine how visible the site might be to anyone wandering near. He moved left and right to check it from all angles. It proved to be well concealed. That gave him a small sense of accomplishment and comfort.

His initial stash of food and water exhausted, Robert now faced some hard choices. The car was gone. If only he had parked it somewhere legal or accessible but well hidden, it might have been handy for fetching food and water. From his previous trips to the area, he knew of a small boutique grocery and liquor store downtown — Nielsen Brothers Market — a good two miles' walk from camp. He had a second option, the larger Safeway out by the highway at the Crossroads Carmel Plaza. The full-sized grocery store might be three miles, as the crow flies. Neither location was exceedingly far. He would only be able to buy as much food as would fit into the knapsack. Water would be the biggest challenge. It's heavy to carry more than you'd drink and cook with in a day. The average person uses 80 to 100 gallons, per day, in western society. A gallon weighs a little more than eight pounds. Haul that every day and you'll get in shape fast. Or, you'd decide to consume a whole lot less water. Robert, famished, opted for the faster, easier road into town and to Nielsen's. He carried a water jug in each hand and the empty knapsack over his shoulder. It would be his first trip into Carmel's center.

Officially, Carmel is a city — it was incorporated in 1916. But it doesn't look or feel like a city at all. Its population of 3,800 shrinks or swells depending on who's home. Many of the houses that grace the city are second homes for those wealthy enough to be able to afford a $5 million weekend cottage. The temporary population, comprised of tourists who fill the hotels and B&B's during peak months, likely double the numbers on any given weekend. Carmel has become the tourism and cultural center of Monterey County — central California, even — and is resplendent in its fine restaurants and wine bars, art galleries, and boutique shops. It hosts an artist colony; feeds and sleeps the thousands who attend the annual Concours d'Elégance at Pebble Beach, the prestigious car show for the automotive aristocracy; and, of course, hosts the tens of thousands of golfers who come to enjoy some of the best courses in the world. Once dominated by those engaged in music, theatre, and literary and visual arts, Carmel has become, well, a commune for the wealthy. They might be patrons of the arts, but few are artists themselves — at least professionally.

I'm not bashing the locale or its residents. Carmel is among the most beautiful and charming small cities in the world. I love it. It's just not a place for anyone living on the margins of society. Not that the reader should feel sorry for Robert. He chose his path. One might understand, however, how he might have been perceived as he walked into town.

With dirty clothes, unkempt, unwashed hair, and a week's growth on his face, Robert felt he looked every bit the errant camper. But anyone else catching a glimpse might have just as easily interpreted him as a homeless man on the prowl for his next handout or meal. Walking the populated streets of the city center, it dawned on him how out of place he must have appeared. He felt critical eyes on him, causing him considerable discomfort as he trudged his way up the Ocean Avenue hill. A police car cruised by him and slowed, taking a long, hard look, before continuing its morning patrol. Robert pulled on his bucket hat and donned a pair of sunglasses to ease his insecurity — not that anyone would have recognized him anyway. Distracted by his thoughts and discomfort with the situation, Robert neglected to look to his right as started across Ocean

Avenue. A driver in a Bentley Flying Spur, cruising from the direction of the beach, slammed on the brakes to avoid hitting him. It was a big, black, luxurious beast of a car: the opulence of the Orient Express rolling on rubber tires. The well-dressed and coiffed couple inside, driver and front passenger, gave Robert matching looks of contempt, visible through the downturned windows. The woman in the passenger seat shook her head in apparent disapproval. The driver raised both hands in exasperation and mouthed two words. It might not have been intended so, but Robert heard it nonetheless.

"Fucking bum!"

Robert was taken aback. He stood in the middle of the street, blocking the car's progress, and glared. The comment was as unexpected as it was hurtful. He understood that the comment was directed at him. Yet, he never thought of himself as a "bum," whatever "bum" meant. *Does that mean unemployed? A beggar? Homeless?* He hadn't thought of himself as homeless. And he hadn't asked for anything at all. Identifying as homeless would be an insult to those people who truly are homeless, genuinely without a place to live, and *not* by their own choosing. Robert had a place to live. He lived in the woods — exactly where he wanted to. Rob also had the means to buy a house in which to live if he chose. His shock at being on the receiving end of rude and thoughtless comment turned to hurt, then advanced quickly to anger. He was a passionate man.

Robert stopped and dropped his water jugs and knapsack like a hockey player preparing for a fight. Robert turned and walked intently the few yards it took to confront the Bentley and its occupants, rage driving his pace and stride. With clenched fists, he imagined the admonishment he'd deliver if the driver were unwise enough to remain. Approaching the sedan, he got a better look at the couple inside. The occupants appeared to be in their mid to late seventies, and any thoughts of a fight left his mind. Robert was unprepared to punch out a seventy-year-old man, even if he was an insensitive prick. Robert made his point with an open-handed slap of his two hands, palms down, on the expansive hood of the massive and expensive car. The hood, and voluminous engine bay underneath, reacted like a giant steel drum. It was loud. It startled even Robert, but he had made his point. The driver intended to make his. With Robert still standing in front, knees literally pressed against the bumper, the driver stared him in the eyes. With Bolero music ironically playing from his car stereo, the elderly driver revved the engine. The twin-turbocharged V8 roared like an angry bull teased and picked by a *banderillero*.

"Ah, you think you are *toro bravo* do you?" Robert yelled, thinking he would torment the aggressive driver. "You are but *cabestros*."

Robert had travelled to Mexico City with Jules several times and had once attended a bullfight at the Plaza de Toros — the world's largest bullring. If the driver knew Spanish, and was up on his bullfighting lexicon, he might have appreciated the intelligent insult. It was likely lost on him that he had just been called a castrated bull. Robert's actions likely only reinforced the driver's perception that he was dealing with an unstable, homeless vagrant who ought to be run out of Carmel. Flushed by rage, the driver glared at Robert, huffed through his flared nostrils and repositioned himself in the car seat. I'm sure it was unintentional, but the angry driver looked very much like a raging bull. He revved the engine once more — preparing to charge. Robert did not flinch. He watched as the driver's right hand moved slowly from the two o'clock position on the steering wheel down to the gearshift lever. Robert heard the gentle, metallic *cluck* as the transmission slipped into gear — DRIVE, he feared. The brave matador did not back down or avert his stare for a second.

"Prepárate para el viejo Estocada!" The *estocada*, Robert had learned in the bullring, was the final, killing thrust of the sword by the matador into the bull. The commotion caught the attention of several passers-by. On both sides of the street, walkers on Ocean Ave. stopped. One pulled out their phone to start recording the confrontation on video. An altercation between a car and a person might get interesting fast — and go viral faster. "He's going to run that man down." Robert overheard an unknown woman say.

The sedan lurched forward, taking Robert not by surprise — but onto its hood. As the car accelerated, he launched onto the windshield. Robert instinctively reached for anything he could. He got one hand on a windshield wiper arm. It would not hold him and bent under the strain. In an instant, he was catapulted onto the front edge of the roof. Rolling off the side, he caught one leg on the car mirror and landed on his ass — slightly bruised and mad as hell. There was no *"Olé!"* moment. The Bentley driver sped away, fearing danger in the form of an unpredictable, wild, angry and, apparently, Mexican hobo. It might have been the best outcome, frankly, for both parties. Robert picked himself up. He scanned for cuts and contusions but remained standing in the middle of the street, watching as the luxurious sedan reached the intersection and wheeled around the corner, ignoring the stop sign. The Bentley driver didn't strike him as a man who thought traffic laws and signs applied to him. Robert also noted that the car sported vanity plates: *MOREMNY.*

Robert cursed. *"Jodido imbécil!"* He brushed himself off. His pants were abraded and dirty. His hands were raw and rasped from the fall. No one, among those watching, offered to help him. He heard a few gasps, and a "Did you see that". One witness, outraged by what she saw, and sympathetic to the man on the ground, finally did come to his aid. "Are you alright sir?" She reached out and touched his shoulder. "Can I get you any help? I saw the whole thing. That man could have killed you. You people deserve to be here as much as anyone else. The police. Do you want me to call them?"

"No police, please," said Robert. "I'm alright." He nodded his head for reinforcement. "What do you mean by *you people*?"

"Do you need anything dear? Could you use some money, or some food? Here." She started to reach into her purse, one presumed, for money.

"Money? No! What do you think…" He caught himself and decided it would be imprudent to say more. He just shook his head, no. Still simmering, and a little bewildered, Robert left the scene and continued, at a quick pace, toward his destination. He wished to just pick up some grub and return to the woods, without delay. Everyone he passed on the street now, he imagined, was eyeing him — judging him. Was it coincidental that that woman just pulled her child closer to her as I approached? Arriving at the store, Robert placed the two water jugs outside and sheepishly walked in. He felt self-conscious at once, especially after noting the other patrons. They all looked like the couple in the Bentley. They wore expensive, branded clothes. Tom Ford sunglasses rested atop tops of their coiffed and styled hair. Dior and Hermes purses dangled from their arms. There must be some unspoken but learned etiquette, Robert observed, that dictates the manner with which wealthy women are instructed to properly hold their handbags. Place the strap in the crook of the elbow, forearms bent precisely five degrees above the horizontal plain and locked into position; keep the arm still as you walk; and lock or limit head movement similarly. He shook his head but avoided eye contact, as he made his way among the unfamiliar aisles and patrons.

Robert quickly located and bagged a small and carry-friendly selection of onions, carrots, tomatoes, cucumbers, garlic, and potatoes (all vegetables that keep well without refrigeration);

two French loaves; a wedge of dried parmesan cheese and small block of aged cheddar; tins of black beans and chick peas and a bag each of dried lentils, rice, and kidney beans; flour (he later wondered why); and lastly, a dozen eggs (which, for anyone who cares to know, can keep for two weeks if they are farm fresh and have never been refrigerated). His last-minute impulse buy, a treat, came in the form of thick-sliced smoked turkey. He'd have to eat that the same day.

The cashier gave him a dry look and quipped: "Will that be cash, sir?"

Robert fumed silently. Is he implying that I don't and couldn't have a debit or credit card? Am I just being paranoid? He pursed his lips and paid the otherwise congenial clerk, in cash, and departed without a word. Outside the store, he stuffed the food into his knapsack. It overflowed before he had completed the transfer. What remained, he slid into his pockets. Empty water jugs in hand, he headed down the hill on Ocean Avenue and stopped off at the public facilities that serve beach-goers. There was a small, low shower, for rinsing sandy feet, outside the building that housed the toilets. Robert assumed the water was potable — it was the only public source of water he had yet discovered. He filled both the two-gallon jugs. Making every effort to keep his head down, he glanced to each side, checking his peripheral, for reaction. Rob hefted the jugs and knapsack full of food, collectively weighing forty pounds, and headed back to the ravine via 17-Mile Drive.

Back at his tent, finally, Robert dropped the load and fell into a heap on the leaves and pine needles that carpeted his site. The outing had been both exhausting and humiliating. He was sore all over. And the driver, he thought — still smoldering. Obviously, the Bentley driver had been expressing his disdain with the presence of someone whose social standing did not meet his criteria of who should be able to enjoy Carmel, its beauty, and its infrastructure. The polarity between have and have-not's provoked thought Robert had only contemplated in a limited way. He had previously only considered it from the other side of the equation, as a successful, well-educated professional who had lived in an upscale neighbourhood, in a very nice house. His anger at being mistaken for a "bum" — whatever that meant — and the confrontation, forced Robert to reflect on the definition of "bum," and homelessness, and how it informed his self-image. He wondered if he might deny his unwitting social standing or acknowledge and embrace it. If nothing else, he felt greater empathy for those who were homeless, regardless of circumstance.

Perhaps he was being over reacting to a single, provocative event, but Robert felt as though he had to re-think his strategy for living — for surviving — in Carmel. *Should I accept social reaction and ignore it, or take a stealthier approach?* He also contemplated the risk of forcible eviction from his forest home, or even arrest, if he were outed as an illegal squatter in the woods. What Robert did know is that he had no desire for attention, and no motivation for fueling a mythology of a mysterious hermit living in the woods.

chapter 16

His immediate need and source for water, shelter, and food now addressed, Robert turned his attention to upgrading his temporary accommodations. The tent was not going to cut it for long. Now that fall was closing in, it got uncomfortably cold at night and when the fog rolled in. And, to add insult, he couldn't stand in the tent. That proved a source of incredible frustration on long, rainy days. If it got dark early, but he wasn't ready to retire, he'd lie and look at the roof of the tent. Anyone who has been sequestered in a tent over a rainy day can attest to the sheer insanity it can invoke. As challenging as it might prove to be, Robert became determined to build a permanent shelter — his cabin in the woods. The priority would be concealment, followed closely by a secondary goal: comfort. He envisioned a small, cozy, dry place in which to establish a new life: a very Thoreau-esque experiment — without the pond or the bean field. Or the emotional comfort of visitors.

Robert fired up his portable Primus camp stove and boiled water in the combination steel mug/French press that he cherished — an essential tool for a refined hermit. It made damned good coffee, and he enjoyed this small luxury. Sipping intermittently, and appreciating the warmth it distributed, he thought about his housing problem. "How will I construct a cabin here, and how the hell do I do it without detection? Robert whispered aloud. He had started to talk to himself, a trait that many people who find themselves alone for a long time, often adopt. He caught himself speaking this time, felt terribly self-conscious about it, and defaulted to simply *imagining* a few options.

The first and most basic potential solution, he imagined, was a lean-to type arrangement. He might place large branches against a fixed tree and cover the grid of limbs with fresh pine boughs. The benefits of this design would include: 1) a high degree of concealment; 2) ease of construction using existing, living flora and storm fall littered around the gulley; 3) ease of dismantlement and dispersal if detected; 4) potential for establishment of multiple shelters throughout the woods for security; 5) no tools or fasteners would be required, in theory. The downside of that design, Robert pondered, was that: 1) it may or may not offer much warmth or dryness; 2) it may or may not enjoy much longevity; 3) when the pines boughs inevitably lost their needles, the integrity would be compromised and allow in rain; 4) he couldn't consider any form of combustion inside the shelter, like a fire for cooking or warmth. Scratch that idea.

Robert then considered building a foundation of rocks and cutting the floor out of his tent, fastening the sides of the tent, along with the fiberglass reinforcing tent poles, to create a watertight roof. Most importantly, that design would provide standing headroom. Thinking through that option further, he decided against it. Though the headroom would be nice, the same prerequisites, for insulation and ability to maintain a fire, could not be satisfied. The coffee, black as always, proved delightfully strong this morning. Fuelled by caffeine-induced confidence, he turned his attention back to the concept of a permanent, fixed cabin. He reasoned that if he could build it from natural materials, it would remain well camouflaged and concealed. A structure of about eight by ten feet would hold the essentials for living, including his cot, a small table for eating that might double as a work bench, a wash station, a shelf or box for secure food storage, and the other accoutrements of his newly adopted lifestyle. Constructing some form of solid roof would ensure a dry home, and, by insulating the cabin with moss, leaves, and pine needles, as settlers once did, he could enjoy warmth on otherwise cold, damp days and nights. If designed well, and if he could find some steel pipe, Robert might even enjoy the extravagance of a fireplace. *No*, he reasoned, *a steady volume of smoke would give up my presence.* On the other hand, wood fires were limited to periods of complete darkness. The whiff of smoke might just be attributed to homes on the perimeter of the woods. That concept remained in contention.

As he sat among the deadfall and branches, contemplating how he could clear it all, Robert's spirits were lifted by thoughts of his favourite scientist, Albert Einstein. Einstein was quoted, if Robert remembered correctly, as stating: *"Out of clutter, find simplicity. From discord, find harmony. In the middle of difficulty lies opportunity."*

It seemed an appropriate reference for his current predicament. A nod to Einstein and vision of a cabin established in his head, Robert began to execute the construction to the best of his amateur hermit abilities.

Step 1: *Clear a twelve-by-twelve-foot section of the level area on which to site the cabin.* Fallen trees represented the biggest impediment to the clearing process. They were smack dab where he wanted to locate the cabin. And they were big. He searched the immediate vicinity, seeking a long straight branch with enough girth and strength to use as a pry bar. He would coax logs away from his building site, using Archimedes's principles of leverage. That initiative alone took him two full days of backbreaking work. Robert celebrated the clearing of his home site by eating the remaining chocolate he had packed. He felt like a colonial settler now, though he regretted not buying a larger camp saw to manage some of the more substantial wood. The one he did bring offered potential for pruning branches — to a maximum of three inches in diameter.

Step 2: *Create a cabin foundation*. Robert laid out a grid of rocks found about the site or dug out of the dirt. He hefted them one by one into place, over two arduous days. Flat rocks were hardest to move (they don't roll well) but best for his intended foundation.

Step 3: *Construct a sturdy floor*. He continued his quiet reconnaissance of the forest for makeshift floor joists. He sought consistently sized, straight and sturdy branches that could be dragged back. These would form the basis of the cabin floor joists.

It was on one of these forays that he came close, for the first time, to walkers using the trail. He lay low and listened to the voices of a man and woman, perhaps husband and wife, as their voices became louder and then, faded away. On weekends, he reasoned there would always be an increase of foot traffic. Sporadically, over the course of the next three days, Robert found and wrestled an assortment of small trees and limbs back to his camp. He'd drag them for fifty feet and stop to listen for interlopers. In the end, he collected almost twenty limbs — all would play a role in the construction phase.

Across the rock foundation, he lay the straightest branches in parallel and bound them with rope. These formed the rough equivalent of joists, on which he could lay some form of flat, finished floor. At that point, Robert wished he had hauled additional tools and materials. As it were, he had only planned to hit the road for some extended camping. He remained unprepared for this level of commitment to permanency. The local hardware store could undoubtedly fulfill his needs. This setup made good use of what he had.

After completing the floor base, Robert stepped back a few feet, to regard his rough creation. He scrunched his nose. It looked like something a castaway on a deserted island might have erected. He tried to temper his discouragement. The thing that perturbed him most was the floor support structure. When he walked on the stick floor, it gave. He bounced. And it was uneven. His ankles rolled when he walked on it. He tested the strength of the floor by jumping up and down. On his third leap, he discovered why, exactly, building codes were created and enforced. Even in his more svelte form, Robert produced sufficient mass to push the branches past their breaking point. With a terrific crack, heard throughout the woods, the branches, lashed together, gave way. Robert plunged through the sticks and wound up standing thigh-deep in the middle of the cabin foundation. It was emasculating to acknowledge the inadequacy of his design and construction technique. He was also stuck, wedged snugly in between the limbs. I mean literally stuck. Robert could not move his legs. He tried, of course, to raise one, hoping to step out. He tried squatting and using his arms and hands to jack his lower body out. Neither effort proved successful. Robert remembered the multi-tool he kept in his pocket. He drew it and unfolded the knife. The only option remaining was to cut the adjoining joists. He leaned to each side and cut through the lashings that held the other branches together. In time, he freed a section of the makeshift sub-floor. He bullied the logs out of the way until he could once again move his legs and scramble back up and out. It was embarrassing. He was grateful nobody had witnessed and videotaped the whole affair. *I'd be trending on social media right now.*

Scanning the mess he'd created, he re-evaluated his plan. *This won't do. I need some plywood or a bunch of flat boards to make a sub-floor.* Three weeks later, after a seemingly unconnected series of complaints to City Hall, someone in municipal government concluded that *every* road and directional sign on 17-Mile Drive, from Carmel Way to the northern tollgate at Highway 1, had mysteriously gone missing. It was the most scandalous event in recent Carmel history. The sign thefts made headlines in the *Carmel Pine Cone*: the local newspaper. Furious real estate agents assumed teenagers had absconded with their *FOR SALE* signs and dutifully replaced them every two or three days, for two weeks, before calling both the local police and City Hall. Though sometimes practical for drivers, road-side signs are, all in all, ugly: a visual blight. Having served their original purpose, they now fulfilled a more *socially respectable* role as a much-needed parquet floor — composed of steel, wood, and corrugated plastic — in Robert's cabin. What remained of the signage, eventually assumed duty as a dining tabletop. He still needed to consider alternative options, and more substantial building materials, for the walls, and the all-important roof. As a temporary measure, Rob pitched his tent on top of the platform composed of his stone foundation, tree joists, and floor made from assorted road signs. It was solid, dry, and level, if nothing else, and made a good base on which to rest his tent and cot. He leapt up and down. The jump-test was successful. Progress proved rewarding.

Weeks passed as Robert continued work on the cabin. His fear of being sighted by locals settled, in the absence of human activity. There were almost daily human incursions in the woods, but people dutifully kept to the trails. While Robert was acutely aware of them, he became acclimatized to their presence. He could hear them, if not see them, from his location low in the ravine. To be sure, Robert *was* spotted, a couple of times, as he tromped through the woods, on his way to town. Each day, he began to wander farther from his cabin — gaining confidence that his domicile in the woods, which he assumed was not actually legal, would not be discovered. He started to use the well-worn trails, like everyone else. Those were infinitely more comfortable and convenient than slogging over fallen trees and deep bush, as primary ingress and egress paths through the forest. Robert's original tactic, when people came close, was to lie low, literally, on the forest floor. If tree coverage allowed, he'd sneak behind and remain still, until the threat passed. It occurred to him that that might invite suspicion, if seen doing so. He decided to alter the protocol. Thereafter, if spied, he would simply wave and continue onward. To his surprise, the strategy worked. When he was seen from a distance, few paid him mind. Nobody cared — a marked difference from his experience to date in the town center.

chapter 17

It was late October. In the shade of the forest, the temperature became less comfortable. The cold and damp motivated Robert to complete the cabin as quickly as possible. His forest and community explorations uncovered multiple sources for materials that might be appropriated and used as walls and a roof. Robert was a principled man and a former lawyer. That personal quality and the profession don't always go hand-in-hand. Still, he struggled with the concept of theft on an ethical level. He felt dreadfully guilty stealing the road and real estate signs, but he needed to complete his home or risk hypothermia. All options were on the table or, the forest floor, as it were. His alternatives for accumulating the necessary building supplies did include legitimately purchasing them at a building centre. He had no clue how he might transport the materials to a location near his camp. Nor could he figure how to wrestle lumber, plywood, and siding up the hill to the plain and down the gulley to his camp. Access to his Volvo might have come in handy right then. Robert's commitment from withdrawal from his previous, materialistic life, proved to be firm. Even renting a car seemed hypocritical at this point. He was all-in.

The homes that bordered the woods near his camp represented potential worth considering. Most backed onto the woods, offering him easy access to yards, storage sheds, garages, and a convenient path to and from the forest. Some of the residents had already taken to storing (or disposing of) unwanted junk in their backyards, placing them on the far side of their property fences. Local by-laws prohibited that, of course, but people did it anyway. Some homeowners stored cords of firewood, lawn furniture, broken birdbaths, and outgrown kiddie pools in what they'd casually refer to as *out back*. Robert even spotted a toilet, presumably the remnants of a renovation, behind someone's yard. The refuse was, in places, unattractive, though out-of-sight to anyone other than those passing in the woods.

Robert decided, where possible, to take the ethical high road. He'd scavenge for supplies as a first option. He began scouting the surrounding neighbourhoods, late at night or early in the morning, on garbage day, to seek out anything that might help his cabin-in-progress. Consumers in Western society, he already knew, disposed of half of everything they bought. He'd use that to his advantage. And so, our erstwhile hermit added *picking* to his regular routine. Robert was rarely alone during his nocturnal wanderings. He shared the still and lamp-lit streets with raccoons scrounging a meal and, more than once, a black bear — ass-deep in an organic recycling bin it had knocked over. When not dodging bears, Robert combed the residential streets in a noble quest for scrap wood, where he found himself rummaging through the discarded remains of gross consumerism. It was tempting to pick up every piece of renovation waste onto which he stumbled, during his walkabout. Construction leftovers were plentiful in a neighbourhood known for its fine and well-maintained homes. Nary had a week had gone by when at least one fine home wasn't undergoing renovation. The telltale discards from demolition disclosed which home was subject to restoration, and what they were tackling: kitchen, bathroom, den, or dining room.

Robert's greatest score materialized when he stumbled upon contractors replacing a backyard fence, on the forest side of Sunset Lane, bordering the woods. The pounding hammers, groaning pry bars and grunting manual labourers could be heard clearly in his gulley. The contractors spent the first day on the job dismantling the fence for removal. They stacked the remains at the curb of the homeowners who'd contracted them, for pick up and disposal the next day. Nightfall was Robert's cue to investigate. Like a two-legged raccoon, he scampered out as soon as it got dark, the streets quiet. The work crew scratched their collective heads when, upon returning the next morning, discovered the bulk of the demolished fence missing — carted off by an efficient, industrious and unseen junkman.

"Did you order the waste-removal truck to pick up the old fence last night?" the supervisor questioned his foreman.

"Nope. Not me. I assumed you did. The homeowners, maybe?"

"That's strange," said the supervisor. "Somebody must have taken it!"

"I don't care," quipped the foreman. "Makes my job easier."

The homeowners were, quite surprisingly, furious. They were angry as hell. They had intended to throw out the wood and pay a removal and disposal fee to do so yet considered its mysterious disappearance as property theft. Absurdly, the owners even reported the incident to the police. It was the first among a series of incidents that aroused suspicions in the neighbourhood and increased vigilance among Carmel residents. The events motivated a few new volunteers for the local Neighbourhood Watch chapter.

Robert, on the other hand, was elated. He considered the find to be significant — his El Dorado. He carted off three to four boards at a time under his arms. By daybreak, he had relocated them all to his building site and laid each out beside the cabin foundation — more than sixty boards in all. Each board measured one inch thick, eight inches wide and eight feet long. They were faded and cracked, from many years of exposure, but made from unpainted western cedar. Western cedar lasts for fifteen to twenty years, even if left untreated. They were perfect, if a little tired looking. He hardly slept that night: excited and anxious to build cabin walls and a roof, which had been delayed for too long. As he lay sleepless in his tent, he wondered how he would fasten it all without exposing his presence. He couldn't avoid detection if he hammered away. Robert remembered watching a documentary on traditional Japanese carpentry techniques for building furniture, and even homes, without the use of nails or screws. Buddhist temples built using these methods were still standing, a thousand years later. He also thought about a stitch-and-glue method for building small boats from plywood. Perhaps he could successfully build without nails and screws at all. He drifted off to sleep once again, pondering and planning, and celebrating his resourcefulness and developing hermit craftsmanship. Robert was certain that he heard that Spanish owl again — this time offering a more soothing and encouraging tone.

chapter 18

Robert spent the next two weeks laboriously attempting to complete the cabin, including its walls, from the planks, boards, chunks of plywood, and castaways he had accumulated. As he acquired them, the building materials were stacked in neat piles, organized by size. Branches or boughs were overlaid to temporarily conceal them. Robert dreaded the thought of having to go into Carmel again to buy the supplies he required to finish the cabin. It was bad enough that he had to make weekly forays into town for groceries. He looked a mess and knew it. By now, his clothes were terribly dirty, his hair, twice the length that he had previously kept it, and he had a pretty darn good start on a hermit beard. Among those items he intended to buy were a bucket and toilet plunger. He intended to use it for something other than you might have assumed. He'd use them to hand wash his clothes. It was a technique Rob had learned in camping trips, and it worked well. Fill the bucket with water and a little laundry soap, add dirty clothes, plunge away for about five minutes, empty the bucket, rinse clothes in fresh water, and hang the clothes over a line drawn between trees. *Voila*: clean clothes. It had yet to occur to Robert that it would prove hard to dry his clothes in the depth and low light of the forest ravine.

Rob recited and repeated his hardware list as he reluctantly started out for Knapp Hardware at Mission and Eighth. His knapsack adorned his shoulder, as usual. For this trip, Robert also brought an empty duffel bag rolled up and stuffed inside the pack. *This*, Robert thought to himself, *is the last time I go out in public, during the day.* He pulled a bucket hat down low over his head, partly to hide his oily and scraggly hair and, to hide his face and identity.

Robert appreciated disorder. Disorder, to him, seemed somehow more natural — more organic. Knapp's would fit anyone's definition of disorder, at least outwardly. If ever there was a hardware store made for a hermit, this was it. The store reminded him of an old oak tree: one that remained stubbornly rooted in a former farm field, refusing to surrender to urban encroachment and residential development. Hardware that might have been labelled, priced, and organized neatly on shelves, looked much like leaves around its base — arbitrarily cast by the wind. Knapp is an anachronism among retail stores. Unlike the big box stores that dominate the retail trade, including the enormous Home Depot in Seaside, Knapp Hardware is a small and intimate store: the kind your grandfather used to drag you to as a boy.

Other than food, Knapp has everything you could possibly need. The place is celebrated (or cursed, depending on your perspective) for its narrow aisles stocked ceiling-high with shelves and racks. A ladder is required to access some of the stock. The family-owned store and its employees, all of whom have worked there, on average, for twenty years, know exactly where everything is: even if what you need is buried under a decade of boxes and other goods, in some remote corner of the stockroom. They offer tools that you can't find at large chain stores, including, as it turned out, a manual hand drill. That was the first item on Robert's list. Yes, for all of those under the age of say, thirty-five, drills did not always come with a lithium battery pack. Carpenters still use hand drills, large and small, when they need precise control, or if they happen to like making furniture completely by hand. Or, if they're Mennonites or Hutterites and eschew power tools.

The sound of the brass cowbell hanging on the front door reinforced the old-school ambience of the hardware store. It clanged when Robert entered the store. He received a friendly nod of acknowledgement by a clerk and offered a furtive grin in return.

"Can I help you, sir?" asked an older gentleman wearing an apron appropriate for a very traditional hardware store. The man might have been the owner or one of the thirty-year veterans.

"Thank you, but I expect I can find what I'm looking for," Robert replied.

"Just yell if I can help you find what you need. Some stock, we just can't find space for," he said, somewhat apologetically. "On second thought, let me know if there is anything you *can't* find." He paused for a moment and held up his index finger as if to make a point. "In all chaos, there is a cosmos — in all disorder, a secret order."

"Excuse me?"

"Carl Jung," said the gentleman, whose appearance belied deeper intellectual interests.

"Oh, I get it," said Robert. "Clever."

"He was on the cover of The Beatles' *Sargent Pepper's Lonely Hearts Club Band*. Bet you didn't know that. Did you?"

"I did not," Robert responded, respectfully. He returned his focus to assembling supplies. Getting no response, the man attempted to bait Robert into conversation once more. "And what's your public persona?" Robert did not bite and continued his task.

Robert studied the store layout from his position at the front, grabbed a shopping cart, and set off purposefully, throwing items he needed as he discovered them among the secret order. It was tempting to buy more than he needed. He might have built a two-thousand-square-foot home with what was available in the shop. Robert repeated his mantra again. *Keep it simple. Keep it light. Keep it small. Only buy what is necessary!*

He picked up a dozen galvanized tie plates, a large box of deck screws, a set of drill bits, a set of driver bits to fit a drill, a set of four good-quality chisels of varying widths, an axe to supplement the small hatchet he already had, a bucket and toilet plunger, laundry soap, heavy-duty garbage bags, a large plastic bin (to serve for dried food storage), three rolls of duct tape, a can opener, a bag of tea candles, three one-pound propane containers, a large nylon tarp, four eye bolts and fifty feet of heavy gauge wire, three large galvanized gate hinges, galvanized turnbuckles, galvanized carriage bolts, nuts and washers, and a painted steel latch that might be used to secure a backyard fence.

"We can deliver all this if it's more convenient, sir," offered the gentlemen, who had by now introduced himself as the owner of the store.

"I can manage it by myself, thanks," Robert deflected.

While he could have used the backside of his axe, Robert also picked out a hammer.

"Do you have a hand drill — a large one?" Robert asked hopefully.

A little surprised by the request, the owner replied, "Well, we don't get much call for those anymore, but I believe that I have a couple out back. I'll be back in a few minutes."

Robert waited, impatiently. It's not that he was fundamentally an impatient man. The opposite was true. He just felt exposed and uncomfortable in a public setting, now, and in the physical state he acknowledged himself to be. He acted like one might expect of a robber casing a shop, head and eyes darting and scanning as if he were keeping an eye peeled for the law, all the while planning a hasty exit out the back door. Robert caught an accidental glimpse of himself in the reflection of glass door of the shop.

I really do look like a bum, he silently acknowledged.

The owner came back beaming and proudly holding up what Robert was seeking as if it were some ancient treasure, lost to time.

"They're also called a hand brace. Haven't sold one in ages, but we've got a few left. I think they still sell them at speciality woodworking stores, too," he offered. "Whatever do you want one of these for? If nothing else, you'll have this for life. You'll go through three electric drills before this one even starts to show wear."

The shop owner rang in and totalled Robert's supplies at the checkout counter.

"Vacation project?" the owner looked up and asked, to make small talk. It seemed reasonable that the shopper might have been working on a project during some time off. A veteran of many a project himself, the storeowner embraced the credo of not shaving while on vacation. The owner's curiosity was further piqued when Robert placed each item into his knapsack and, once that was filled, into the heavy nylon duffel bag.

"Oh, sorry, but there's one more thing I need. Can you cut me about one hundred feet of quarter-inch braided line from one of those reels?"

"Certainly. Three-strand or solid braid?"

"Whichever is strongest, please. Black if you have it."

"That would be solid braid. What do you need it for?" the shop owner asked, innocently enough, and to be helpful. "Not going to hang yourself, I hope." He laughed a half-laugh. He half meant it.

"Hadn't planned on it, but we'll see how the week goes. Solid braid is fine, thanks."

The bill came to $289.78. Robert counted out $300 in fifty-dollar bills. He coiled the rope, added it to the duffel, and snugged the bag, bloated with supplies, closed. Then he hoisted the knapsack and duffel bag — one over each shoulder.

The owner opened the door for him and asked, "Can I help you to your car, sir?"

"That won't be necessary." Robert squinted as he transitioned from the low light.

The owner-manager stood on the sidewalk, scratched his head as Robert adjusted his load. "You must live close by if you're going to haul all that on your back. Not one of them survivalists are you?" he wondered aloud. He watched Robert's awkward gait as he struggled down Eighth Avenue, readjusting and wrestling the weight every ten paces or so — his future on his back. Robert didn't answer his question. "Man and his symbols indeed," the manager said, to nobody in particular. The comment must have made sense to him. He shook his head and went back into the store, no doubt pleased he had at least sold a hand drill — old inventory for sure — for the first time in twenty years.

Three blocks away, and entirely focused on his burden, Robert was startled by an loud honk behind him. He swung around to see the red and white lights of a police car, stopped ten feet behind him. An officer wearing sunglasses motioned something to Robert, which he interpreted as 'get out of the way.' Robert dutifully moved off the gutter of the street to ensure he was fully on the sidewalk. He turned and continued his progress. The cop honked his horn again, this time, an extended blast. Robert stopped and turned again. The officer from the City of Carmel Police Department put his squad in park, exited the car, and walked determinedly toward Robert. The cop stopped no more than two feet from Robert's face, close enough for him to feel his hot breath and suffer his less-than-minty breath.

"Good morning, sir. Where are you headed today?"

"Why do you ask? Have I broken a law?"

"Whoa, partner. Let's not get defensive. I was just asking where you were going. I haven't seen you around here before. Do you live here in Carmel?"

"I'm just travelling through but thank you for your interest. Good day and keep up the good work, officer." Robert turned and took one step in the opposite direction. He hoped that the interaction was over. It was not.

"I'd like to see some identification," the cop said in a rather insistent and authoritative voice. He couldn't have been more than thirty years old. He carried a Glock though and that spoke louder than words. Robert reluctantly reached into his knapsack and produced a California driver's license. He knew it was expired. "Remain here, please, sir. I'll be right back."

Carmel's finest went back to his car, slipped inside, and began tapping at the laptop extending from the dash of his vehicle. Robert could see his lips moving but was a little rusty on his lip-reading skills. After what seemed an eternity, the officer returned to the sidewalk, where Robert had remained firmly planted, as directed.

"Your driver's license is expired, sir. Do you have anything else? Any other form of identification, like a passport?"

"No, I don't carry a passport unless I'm travelling to another country," said Robert. "We are still in the United States, aren't we? Why have you detained me?"

"I haven't detained you. I have lawfully requested your identification, and, unfortunately, it is not valid. Therefore, I have no means to adequately identify you. The law allows me to request identification, and requires you to always carry adequate ID."

"This is harassment. Plain and simple."

"Look, I'm not harassing you. I'm guessing you have wandered down here from Monterey. I'd be willing to give you a ride back and save you the burden of carrying your stuff all the way back to the shelter tonight. Are you staying at Shelter Outreach?"

Robert had to make up his mind, and quickly. He figured he had three options: 1) Drop the bags and run. He was certain that despite the age difference, Robert was in better shape and could outrun the cop, if the officer opted for a foot chase. If he could make it to the woods, he would be home free; 2) accept the offer of a ride to the shelter in Monterey, and end up fifteen miles away from his camp, with fifty pounds to haul back, on foot; or 3) argue his way out of this, as he'd been trained to do in law school. Option two might have been the most prudent decision, but passionate personalities do not frequently follow the rational path. Robert was a passionate man. He opted for number three and did his best to sound like a lawyer.

"I strenuously object to your Terry stop, officer." He looked at the name plate on his uniform for the first time and continued. "Officer Torres. You have no reasonable suspicion that I have been involved in any illegal activity. I demand that I be allowed to continue on my way!"

"You have just created a suspicion. Please empty your bags on the sidewalk, sir."

"I do not consent to a search."

"Open the bag now!" demanded the cop. He looked pissed and did that thing that some cops do to increase the level of intimidation: he placed his hand atop his service weapon.

Robert reluctantly opened his bags. He pulled out the receipt from the goods he had purchased at Knapp's and handed it to the cop. The officer removed his sunglasses and squinted at the receipt. It included the date and time of the purchase: exactly twenty-one minutes before. The officer opened the bag, pulled out a few items, compared them to the receipt, and looked frustrated by what he saw. Then he spied the Rolex on Robert's wrist. The cop looked like a hungry dog that had just been served a dish of steak. Raw steak.

"I expect the owner of that Rolex would appreciate its return."

"It's my watch!" Robert shouted, a little too loudly and way too passionately.

"I'm going to ask you to turn around and place your hands behind you, sir," said the cop, as he strong-armed Robert over to the hood of his car and kicked his legs apart.

This is going to be a long day, thought Robert.

"You are making a mistake, and it's going to reflect poorly on your department, officer."

Handcuffed and now in the back of the squad car, Robert's hopes of lawyering his way out of detention had failed miserably. The station was only a block away. It seemed ridiculous to drive one block in the back of the police car. They could have walked.

"The lights and siren are a bit much, don't you think," Robert said, from the back seat.

After being led inside and instructed to wait in a secure reception area, Robert was at least asked if he wished a glass of water. He graciously accepted. Torres forcibly removed his watch and asked an administrative staff member to check on the serial number against a state-wide stolen-property database. The sergeant on duty had been called in off the streets and arrived back at the station shortly later. They didn't make that many street arrests in Carmel. The sergeant met and spoke with the officer and Robert together to investigate the circumstances of the situation calmly. The young officer explained to his superior that he had a "hunch" that Robert was possibly in possession of stolen property — the watch, specifically. Homeless people, he reasoned with his sergeant, didn't wear $10,000 Rolex watches. Or watches at all, for that matter.

Robert went full lawyer on him this time. "Gentlemen, I am a lawyer, called to the bar in the State of California. Feel free to verify that on your databases. That said, I'd like to speak with another lawyer before we go much further. You have broken a great number of legal statutes governing police conduct, and the Fourth Amendment of the US Constitution. Reasonable suspicion must constitute significantly more than an individual police officer's *gut* feeling or hunch. To justify a Terry stop, or stop-and-frisk, a police officer must be able to point to specific, objective facts that made his or her suspicion reasonable. You have failed the test of reasonable cause for search and seizure and detention — not to mention grossly violated my civil rights."

The civilian administrator interjected. "The serial number does not show up on the stolen-property database, sir — state or federal."

"That's because it's not stolen!" Robert shouted.

The sergeant interceded. "Whoa now, everybody. Let's take this down a notch. No one has accused anyone of anything." Robert didn't know if they were purposefully playing "good cop/bad cop," but it worked. The sergeant was somewhat politer than the officer who had detained him. Robert softened his approach and tone, hoping that reason and rationality would win the day.

"The watch belongs to me. My late wife gave it to me as a wedding gift — years ago. It's mine. Please don't take it from me."

The administrator piped in with some new information, gleaned from her computer.

"Sir," she said to the sergeant, "I see that Mr. Das' car has been logged in the stolen-vehicle database."

The sergeant looked over her shoulder, squinting at the computer screen. The senior officer looked back at Robert, still squinting — an expression that seemed curious rather than suspicious.

"Do you own a 2011 Volvo XC-70?" quizzed the sergeant.

"Yes, I do," replied Robert.

"It was stolen?"

"Sure."

It seemed to be the most appropriately vague response to the question. Further explanation or detail might have made the made the exercise infinitely more complex and complicated. Robert preferred to avoid that, given the current circumstance.

"Did you know that your car has been recovered?"

"No, I didn't. That's why I was walking with fifty pounds on my back and not driving, comfortably, with the gear in the trunk. But thank you for letting me know. I appreciate it."

The sergeant looked at Robert with a puzzled expression.

"According to our records, your car was reported as stolen and recovered more than two months ago! It's in the Salinas compound yard. I'm confused. Why didn't you claim your vehicle after it was recovered, Mr. Das?"

"I haven't needed it," replied Robert, truthfully.

All three employees of the Carmel Police Department looked at one another, perplexed.

"Officer Torres, please return Mr. Das' watch and release him immediately. Please accept our apologies, sir. We've had a rash of thefts in the city — especially road signs, for some reason. It's bizarre, to tell the truth. Anyway, we want to ensure Carmel remains safe for you and everyone else. Can we give you a lift with your duffel? It looks very heavy."

"No, thank you," Robert stated emphatically. "Fuck you," he added under breath.

Robert fumed as he walked out, his afternoon completely shot. After the door to the station closed, the sergeant motioned for the young officer to come closer.

"Keep an eye out for him around town. Something just doesn't add up with this guy."

"Gladly, sir. I think he's trouble."

Back on the sidewalk in front of the station, Robert hefted his bags, then plodded back to the woods. Arriving back at his cabin home, he collapsed on the cot and enjoyed a much-deserved nap.

chapter 19

I won't bore the reader with too many additional details surrounding the design and execution of Robert's hand-crafted cabin. Suffice it to say that he was proud of the result. Completed without the use of any power tools, in relative silence and stealth, Robert had used the cedar fence and other scraps to make a weather-tight, makeshift home. The hand brace became his most valuable and frequently used tool. The brace did double duty — drilling holes and, with a driver head, driving deck screws to fasten the boards into the log sill plates he had laid as a foundation for his cabin. Other than the squeaking of screws turning into hard, dried wood, he had made very little noise and perceived that his construction project had, to date, gone completely undetected. To ensure the sides of the cabin were square and reinforced, he inserted eye screws into each corner of the interior walls, top and bottom, and strung the steel wire on a diagonal, tightening it with turnbuckles. He did that on the three sides, to allow for the door he planned to put in the front of the cabin, along with a small window.

Robert had faced the cabin to the south, hoping to maximize the light that would grace his cabin once he'd installed a window. The door was the easier of the two additions. He designed and built, from the remaining lengths of fence, a traditional barn-style door, with vertical boards braced by a Z-pattern. The door was hung with the galvanized fence-gate hardware, and Robert sacrificed a leather belt, to create a door handle. The fence-gate latch he installed last. It served to keep the door closed securely from either the inside or out. Robert crafted roof trusses and rafters on the ground, using a hodge-podge of the remaining fence boards and two-by-four remnants. Laid out in a roughly ninety-degree frame, he braced each triangular set of boards with the galvanized tie plates, hoping it was enough to keep them together until the whole thing became reinforced with a solid roof. Two sets of hands would have made the exercise a hell of a lot easier, he thought, as he hefted the makeshift truss to rest on the top of the cabin sides. He rather inconveniently ran out of scrap plywood with which to cover the roof. Over the following days, road signs around 17-Mile Drive began to disappear once again. Carmel city administration managers were not amused.

The cabin walls, made from faded cedar, blended in perfectly with the surrounding cedar, cypress, and pines. The roof, however, stuck out like a sore thumb. The directional road signs, with their reflective type and corresponding directional arrows, were not the least veiled. As a matter of fact, if you pointed a flashlight at the cabin in the dark, it lit up like a Christmas tree. You could read the words *Exit - Pacific Grove* from two hundred yards away. Robert cut down some branches from surrounding trees, strung them together with the braided rope, and draped them across both sides of the roof to help better conceal it. As the greenery died off every few weeks, he would replace the boughs to maintain a living roof of sorts.

Other than the window, the cabin was complete. It was, nonetheless, dark inside. Robert moved in with his supplies — clothing, cot, food, bins, tools, and discarded, re-purposed furniture. Finally, he had a relatively comfortable, dry, warm, and entirely livable place to call home. Frequently over the next several days, he'd stand outside and admire his creation — as much living art as a practical shelter. He had never thought of himself as a handyman, but he had learned as he built, or jury-rigged, the structure. And the cabin turned out to be well camouflaged. From over fifty feet away, and from most angles, the cabin was undetectable. The shade of the ravine contributed further to cloaking the unnatural and illegal structure. And the low-lying fog, which not-infrequently engulfed the ravine, contributed to its almost invisible presence. Though the mature trees surrounding the cabin added to the cover, Robert did fear the occasional Pacific cyclone that might sweep in from the west. The greatest risk to the cabin, he felt, came from falling trees, or detection by a hiker. Either might result in a very bad day: the former, catastrophic, were he inside and caught unawares.

The cabin was far from perfect. Light peeked through the cracks in the walls. Even moderate winds sailed straight through. As Robert walked across the floor, the structure creaked, groaned and swayed, like an arthritic old man climbing steep, off-camber stairs. The hut moved and undulated — an organic, living thing. It moved with him and spoke to him when stressed but the forces of the weather. It provided Robert with comfort and company as a conversational companion. But a fierce wind — even that filtered by the Carmel Woods — could challenge its structural integrity.

chapter 20

Inside the cabin it was reasonably muted, save for the sound of an occasional squirrel using the roof as a convenient bridge between trees. Outside, it was quiet but far from silent. Sound squeezed between the cypress and pine to entertain or irritate Robert, daily. An insult of unwelcome noises from — the aggravating sound of pneumatic guns nailing a new roof; the *beep-beep-beep* of trucks reversing; parentally-unsupervised teenagers with a free afternoon and a portable stereo; and, the occasional teenager-unsupervised adults with a free evening and cocktail party on the deck — all made the list of sounds that Robert wished he could have barred from his natural home. Sounds he welcomed included those produced by the high boughs that rose above the ravine and caught the passing winds; well-rested and talkative birds engaging one another at dawn; and the sounds of crickets seeking a mate — their chirps providing humans with an effective means to determine the temperature. Count the number of chirps in fifteen seconds and add thirty-seven. It works. Try it.

During his months of surviving in the woods, Robert had slowly but surely begun to stray from his ethical stance and initial commitment of fulfilling his needs through legitimate purchases or scavenging discards to survive. He felt guilty when he stole, but increasingly less so, especially when he was pilfering from the Pebble Beach Corporation — the business entity that owns and maintains 17-Mile Drive. Its five tollbooths, like guard towers at a maximum-security prison, control each entry point. Robert had begun to deeply resent the intrusion that the 17-Mile Drive, hosting hundreds of thousands of annual tourists in cars, vans, and campers, introduced to the otherwise pristine and rare forest that the Del Monte had once been. The winding road and the developments and expansive homes accessed from it had now completely hemmed in and encroached on this once great tract of forest. Robert thought of the Del Monte as a wild animal in a zoo, unable to truly live freely. It wasn't a purely metaphorical reference. The forest he had begun to know so intimately was indeed a living, breathing organism that reacted to the environment and stresses placed on it, man-made and otherwise: mostly the former. If the Del Monte were capable of rocking back and forth to soothe itself, it most surely would be doing so right now.

Robert had appropriated a window from the Pebble Beach Corporation, to provide some much-needed light in his cabin. The window frame came conveniently painted forest green. It fit in perfectly with his cabin's design theme and emphasis on blending in with the surrounding foliage. One of the corporation's employees, arriving early in the morning at the Carmel Gate tollbooth to begin her collection of ten dollars per vehicle, hadn't noticed anything unusual for at least five minutes. The cool morning breeze in the otherwise enclosed booth gave it away. She called head office repeatedly to inquire about when they might replace the window — assumed to have been purposefully removed during a previous shift. Surprisingly, nobody had record of a requisition for a broken window repair. Administration committed to send someone later to review the situation.

"Tell me again. Which booth had its window broken?" corporate administration quizzed the caller.

"No, you don't understand," she argued with the manager, "it's not broken. It's missing. Gone. Not there. Frame and all. There's nothing but a hole in the wall where the window used to be."

"You're right, I don't understand. Start from the beginning, please."

chapter *21*

The months of subsistence, punctuated by the significant phys-ical exertion required to make his situation less uncomfortable and tedious, took its toll on Robert. Modern consumers in de-veloped nations take for granted the labor and infrastructure that underpin and support our collective lives: housing, food, clothing, and energy production. Most of us have no visibil-ity into the manufacturing, wholesale and retail distribution framework that enable us to constantly consume. If removed from that pervasive infrastructure, we would appreciate how survival becomes a full-time job — and not an easy one. Past generations certainly knew it. The vast majority of us have lost those skills.

Robert cheated a little, of course. He borrowed, he stole, he recycled and reused the output of modern society's propensity to consume and discard. He used guile, creativity, resourcefulness, and, occasionally, duplicity, to get what he needed to maintain his lifestyle. Robert drew the line at dumpster diving for food, preferring to endure the discomfort of interacting with shoppers at the grocery store and hauling food back to the woods. He was neither proud nor ashamed of the events, both involuntary and voluntary, that had led to his current situation. Everyone, regardless of circumstances, wealth, geographic location, politi-cal environment, personal security, and resources, learns to adapt and survive. It's human nature. *Every* living organism seems to have an innate will to endure. A man with no sense of purpose and no reason to rise each morning, however, cannot survive, regardless of the environment in which he lives.

Robert developed a sense of purpose early on in his self-imposed exile. One might think that in the absence of a formal job, a man might be inclined to sleep late every day. He did not. Robert rose before the sun. The simple act of surviving had helped him develop a greater sense of purpose. Anyone who occasionally camps in the bush can attest to the fact that it becomes old after a week. Experienced outdoors people and frequent campers might shrug off a little hardship and lack of creature comforts for a second week. A commitment to living in the woods without electricity, running water, sewage, refrigeration, broadband access, and touch-of-the-finger temperature control takes a whole other level of personal sacrifice and discipline. Robert never did anything by half measures.

His lifestyle, Robert felt, did have some advantages. It was hard work, but the sense of accomplishment that comes with self-sufficiency can in itself, be quite rewarding. If nothing else, the demands of his life were sufficiently distracting that they diluted the impact of the grief that threatened to consume him. Robert did enjoy the quiet and his commune with nature. It reminded him of his youth, marked as it was by frequent camping trips throughout the wilds of California. The universe didn't reveal itself in the Carmel Woods, but then Robert had no expectation it would. He appreciated the solitude and freedom. His cabin in the woods allowed him to go when and as he pleased. Robert was Huck Finn, personified, and grown up — something many men have dreamed of, even if only briefly and unrealistically. He did occasionally wish for a Widow Douglas to save him, but his hermit life was tolerable, for a time.

After establishing his camp and cabin, Robert began to create a more regular routine. He eventually dispensed with his paranoia-induced morning reconnaissance to scout for human intrusion in *his* gulley. Robert became confident that the cabin and his presence were adequately concealed. That confidence allowed him to turn his attention to a routine and a purpose. He also made the conscious decision that to protect his home and self, and to avoid arousing suspicion among locals, he had to *look* less hermit-like. To Robert, that meant paying greater attention to his physical appearance, cleaning his clothes regularly, maintaining personal hygiene by washing more often, and shaving regularly.

The western end of Ocean Avenue dead-ends in a tight circle at the beach. Here, the city of Carmel has marked off a hundred parking spaces for visitors accessing the beach. It's the busiest corner of town from April to September, with frequent traffic jams as people shoehorn themselves into a parking spot as close to the beach as possible. Curiously, it's a most respectful form of traffic jam. I've never witnessed arguments or road rage over a spot yet. Despite the bottlenecks, something about the beach elicits a sense of peacefulness and calm in most people. Traffic for commuters headed to work tends to have an entirely different effect. Nearing the beach, a different attitude tends to overpower any bad mood you might have been experiencing, even minutes ago. You arrive and smell the beach before you even see it. It's a potent elixir. If you've brought your dog, she'll be pacing in the back seat right now, whimpering as she anticipates the joy she remembered from her last visit. The sound of kids laughing, waves crashing, dogs barking, and car locks beeping merges into an extended stanza of music overseen by an invisible maestro. *Música de playa. Alegro.* It becomes significantly quieter over the fall and winter months and the music begins to fade — *tranquilo.*

A low stone and cedar-clad building near the beach building houses a public washroom with separate facilities for both men and women. Reflecting the homes in Carmel, even the washrooms are striking and architecturally designed. Outside the facility is the water fountain that became the primary source of fresh water for Robert's cooking, drinking, and laundry: the same fountain he used on his first trip into town for water and food. He possessed two, two-gallon jugs, with handles, and a flexible bladder that held one gallon: all well used after years of camping duty. Each day, he collapsed the jugs and stuffed them into his knapsack before heading to the facility. Inside the men's facility is a pedestal sink, one stand-up urinal, and two enclosed toilets that feature stainless steel toilet seats. Beside the washbasin is a water tap threaded to accommodate a garden hose for the occasional bathroom "disaster" maintenance. City maintenance usually removes the spigot knob after they are done with it, presumably to ensure nobody uses the tap as a tool for vandalism. Robert brought pliers in his knapsack to defeat their precaution and to access the water he needed.

A trip to the facility — a twenty-minute walk — became part of Robert's daily routine. It was open every day of the year and, as it was a frequently busy public facility, his arrival went largely unnoticed. That said, he was sensitive to his own appearance and chose to make the pilgrimage his priority early each morning. On days when ground fog obscured his well-worn path, Robert would slow his pace to a shuffle — picking and feeling his way through the woods, lest he trip an fall. Anyone observing him from a distance would have seen little more than a disembodied torso and head gliding silently between he trees.

He'd arrive at the washrooms by seven o'clock: earlier in the summer months. The first order of daily business required a high degree of fortitude. *Who was the genius who'd decided that stainless steel would make an ideal material for a toilet seat in an unheated public bathroom?* Rob wondered. They probably thought of the hundreds of dollars the city would save in replacement costs compared to a plastic seat. Each day, Robert endured this medieval torture device by easing himself onto it slowly and gently, silently wincing as the shock of cold steel met his warm posterior. It took a minute or so for the seat to warm to his body temperature and become tolerable. After his morning constitutional, he'd peek out of the front entrance to see if anyone, the local police in particular, were approaching. He'd wet a microfiber cloth with water and some liquid soap and rapidly concentrate his attention on his face, underarms, neck, shoulders, and chest. Rob had the personal hygiene equation timed to the second: covering it all in about three minutes flat. Checking the front once again, he ducked back in and use paper towel or a J-Cloth to focus a good cleaning of his genitals and anus, then threw the cloth into the garbage receptacle. Twice every week, he would shave in the sink. He'd then fill his jugs and cram the flexible bladder of water into his pack. Finally, he brushed his teeth. The entire practice, washing, shaving and all, took seven minutes. The routine required military precision, moving from one hygiene chore to the next. Given the human traffic in the facility and beachgoers engaging in similar drinking, washing, changing and peeing, his routine did not look entirely out of place. Robert's sensitivity and embarrassment about the exercise was largely self-generated — one of the many burdens he had to shoulder.

Weeks later, to his delight, Robert discovered a brand new, second public facility on the south end of the beach. If the facility at the end of Ocean Avenue could be compared to a Marriott, the south-end facility was most assuredly the Ritz-Carlton. This facility, architecturally designed as well, featured two completely self-contained and separated bathrooms with lockable doors. It had reportedly cost $750,000 to build. They proved to be the nicest public restrooms Robert had ever used. While access to them required an extra three-quarters-of-a-mile walk, this facility became his default bathroom — unless nature demanded a closer drop zone. The stylish facility boasts an actual living roof with native flora, and solid mahogany doors that take two hands to persuade open. Artfully crafted stone walls help it blend in with the adjacent bluff. From the intersection of Santa Lucia Avenue and Scenic Road, you wouldn't know it was there had the City of Carmel not added signage. Each of the two bathrooms is like an open-concept Manhattan apartment and sized similarly — maybe 150 square feet. The floors are finished in quality ceramic tile and neat white tiles adorn the walls. The sink, toilet, and wall urinal are, predictably, stainless steel — but in this place, it gives it an industrial-chic look. The bathroom was larger than Robert's entire cabin, well lit, and conveniently private. The solid door and stone walls provided for sound insulation in the bathroom, and outside. No longer would he have to rush through or conceal his morning routine. This was luxury. This became Robert's ensuite bath.

It was early March and the sun had yet to rise over the eastern hills. Nobody could be seen walking Scenic Road, let alone accessing the public facility. Robert had come to know the schedule of the city maintenance crew. They were unlikely to empty garbage receptacles and replenish toilet tissue before nine, so Robert decided on a leisurely shave. Shaving was one of the few things that made him feel human, even civilized, and reminded him of his previous life. The bi-weekly shave was also the only time he glimpsed his own image. His body was slowly but assuredly transforming.

After washing and shaving, he paused and stared at his reflection, inspecting himself from head to waist. Robert had become almost unrecognizable. He had lost a lot of weight. Years sitting at a desk, four business lunches every week, and the output of a spouse whose cooking prowess was legendary had added a good thirty pounds on his waist. His frame was lean and his skin as weather-beaten and roughened as the cedar siding on his cabin.

Looking at his midriff now, he could see that the paunch he had been carrying had given way to a slim waist. The weight loss had required him to sew a little pinch-gather in the pants he had brought. He'd have to find pants at the thrift store with a 31-inch waist, down from a 34. He was also developing a six-pack after eight months of daily hikes ranging from five to ten miles, often carting food, water, *found* building supplies, furniture, and repatriated clothes. Tromping through the undulating terrain of the woods, navigating fallen trees and rotting stumps, was physically challenging and would whip anyone into shape. Looking at his chest, he noted that the "man boobs" that had previously adorned his chest were now muscular, firm, and much flatter. Daily trips to the gym could not have generated better results, no matter how often he might have gone. His arms were muscled, tanned, and sharply defined.

His face showed the greatest changes, though. The wildness of the woods had somehow transposed itself into his eyes. When you look at the big cat or wolf in a zoo or a documentary, they seem to have a detached and purposeful look to them. There's never emotion behind them — no hurt, jealousy, fear, happiness, or compassion. The eyes are a tool for sight only and offer no window into their owner's soul. Juliana had told him many times that he had "kind eyes." Now they looked wild, distant, and resolute.

Robert attempted to put on a smile and failed terribly. It looked more like the smirk of a gunslinger preparing for a shootout, completely confident in his abilities to outdraw the other. The only thing missing was a little head bob. He took a breath and opened his eyes, squinting at himself, trying to get a better look. The double chin that had been developing had given way to a firm, square jaw. It looked completely out of place on the face he had once known. He had never considered his fitness but arrived at the conclusion that he was possibly in the best shape of his life — an unintended consequence of the lifestyle that he had imposed on himself. It occurred to him that he could probably enter one of the marathons organized in the area every year and place well. Jules would have been proud of him.

chapter **22**

The cabin completed and his routines in place, Robert found himself all too frequently sitting in his cabin, staring at the walls or wandering the quieter sections of the woods. Creating his shelter had been a Herculean task, and now that it was finished, he had time on his hands. Growing tired of his self-denial, Robert allowed himself to consider pleasure, and quickly thought of golf. When camped out with a backyard bounded by a dozen of some of California's best courses, what else would you do? His obsession with the sport was revitalized, at first, by simply observing golfers playing on his favorite courses. It proved to be a low-risk option. He enjoyed the game vicariously at first. Remaining hidden in the shadows of the trees, he could watch a game on any of the courses and derive as much pleasure as he would by watching the PGA Tour on HDTV. He could follow a specific foursome through any portion of a course bordered by forest — stalking from hole to hole — or remain in place, seated inside the forest border, and enjoy a procession of golfers play through a single hole. On any given day, he'd slip through the forest undetected, using the trails that he had come to know so well. His knowledge of the woods became so well-honed, he could travel to Poppy Hills in complete darkness, if so inclined. Robert knew at exactly which tree he should turn left, where best to cross the street, and how many steps were required to arrive at the sixteenth hole at Spyglass. He had mapped out a specific path from the woods, through the Morse Botanical Reserve, to the fourth hole at the Monterey Peninsula Dunes course. Emboldened by his stealth capabilities, he even made it to Pebble Beach and Cypress Point — both considerably more exposed and largely denuded of bordering forest coverage. The Monterey Peninsula soon became his own personal Golf Channel. Robert enjoyed a front row seat of sorts.

Observing golfers for entertainment became woven into Robert's daily routine. While reading occupied the evening hours in the cabin and on long winter days, his surveillance and quiet critique of other golfers became rather a preoccupation. It also turned out to be an unexpected catalyst for Robert to partake in the fine game once again. His increasingly honed skills as a master of salvage, recovery, reclamation, and recycling came in handy. Every hermit needs a set of golf clubs after all.

As Robert discovered, golfers occasionally and absent-mindedly left behind clubs after either teeing off, following up with fairway shot, and putting out at the green. We've all done it at least once. After months of quiet observation and unscientific statistical analysis, Robert roughly calculated that one in fifty golfers inadvertently left *something* on the course, including golf clubs, sunglasses, sweaters, hats, and jackets — or less costly accessories like a golf towel, umbrella, water bottle, or glove. Robert assumed that many of the golfers on the Monterey Peninsula were tourists who included playing these courses on their golf-based bucket lists. After rationalizing that errant golf gear would likely be picked up and kept by following golfers, or remain unclaimed in lost-and-found limbo, Robert disregarded the ethical dilemmas that used to plague his conscience. If he found something on a course on his morning forays, Robert would claim it — clubs, jackets, sweaters, sunglasses, and all. And then there were the hundreds of golf balls he plucked from the bordering forest like so many low-bush blueberries, picking them at will and stuffing them into his pockets. There were more than a few times when, sitting statue-still in the forest, Robert would watch a drive as it arced toward him, striking an adjacent tree with a tremendous knock. For the lucky golfer, that ball bounced back into the fairway. Many an unlucky golfer unwilling to accept loss of a ball would go search the woods, despite course regulations prohibiting it. That proved to be an inconvenience for Robert, often forcing him to relocate to avoid detection. If he was feeling playful and was certain he couldn't be seen, Robert would toss a ball driven into the woods back onto the fairway. It was more protective than altruistic. Each time, the look on the face of a golfer was replaced by elation when they determined that their ball had bounced back into play. That stunt never got old. In fact, after the first time he pulled this, he had to cover his mouth to stifle laughter. It was a rare "joyous" moment for the hermit golfer.

Over time, Robert's collection of golf balls grew, as did his fine collection of mismatched golf clubs and lightly used golf wear — some of which almost fit him. On one of his many missions to Poppy Hills, Robert watched an older foursome of men, aged sixty or so, putting out on the eighth hole — one of Robert's favorite safe places to observe play. Their golf carts hummed as they crossed the path leading to the tee boxes on the ninth hole. One of the foursome had carelessly left his putter on the edge of the green while patiently waiting for the others to putt out. Robert's eyes locked on the club like a fox watching a chick who ventured outside its henhouse. He counted out six-ty seconds. *Fifty-seven, fifty-eight, fifty-nine…sixty.* Convinced the foursome was gone, Robert sprang from the shadows and snatched the club, returning to the woods within seconds. Rob-ert had barely reached cover when the man, realizing he had forgotten his club, doubled back to retrieve it. If he'd been thirty seconds earlier, Robert would have been busted. The putter was, of course, nowhere to be found. The grey-haired golfer circled the apron of the putting green twice looking for it. The club had, mind-bogglingly, vanished. Gone. Perplexed, frustrated, and exasperated, the now club-less duffer threw his hat on the ground (rather pointlessly), picked it back up, and returned to his group at the next hole, matching each footstep with an audible curse: "Fuck! Fuck! Fuck! Fuck! Fuck!"

Robert felt horrible. It was one thing to pick up lost, forgotten, damaged, and discarded clubs. Admittedly, he enjoyed an adrenaline rush by pushing the boundaries once in a while. But, he had crossed the line this time. He needed to make it right — if only to assuage his feeling of guilt. An analytical man, Robert hastily considered his options. It took him a few seconds at most. He leapt from his hiding place, bounded through the woods and passed behind the golfers, at the tee boxes on the ninth hole. Startled by a sound in the woods, one of the golfers turned toward the trees and squinted.

"Did you guys hear something?"

"A deer, no doubt."

"A bear, maybe?"

Robert ran as fast as he could, curling around the far end of the driving range, headed to the tenth hole. The fairway at the ninth hole led right up the clubhouse. He couldn't get anywhere near there, so he sprinted directly as he could through the thick woods and over the undulating forest floor toward the tenth. At Poppy, the tenth hole lies a considerable distance from the green at the eighth. Robert held tight the putter as he sprinted, weaving in and out of trees, while trying to control his pace and breathing. His lungs ached from the effort. For a moment, he imagined how his obituary might read if he had a heart attack and died right then and there, in the woods, grasping a stolen putter. Passing the parking lot, he crossed Lopez Road and re-entered the woods, on his way to the next hole. It would take

Robert a solid ten minutes at a steady run to make it to his target. He looked at his watch and tried to judge the time it might take them to finish out the ninth. He was grateful it was a long par five. Robert understood that he had to make his move before the golfers arrived at the tee box at the tenth. They had carts and that worried him most. He prayed that the gents would grab a sandwich or have a beer after the ninth hole, buying him a little time to get out ahead of them. Robert had to stop twice to catch his breath, his chest heaving, before setting off again. The forest cover ends on the right, east side of the tenth, about 120 yards before the green and the cup. He'd be exposed and could potentially encounter other golfers on the adjacent eleventh hole. It was a risk he was willing to accept.

As the trees thinned, Robert slowed his pace to a jog and increased vigilance. He peeked through the trees to judge the situation. There was nobody playing the tenth, and a foursome had just left the eleventh. He was damn lucky. And drenched. He mopped the sweat from his forehead and face with the tail of his shirt. Taking a deep breath, he jaunted out of the forest cover, and speed-walked the remaining distance to the green on the tenth, glancing over each shoulder. If anyone did spot him, it might look less suspicious if he were not running. Nobody runs in golf.

After that episode, it might have seemed prudent for our lovable club thief to head home, lesson learned. He didn't. Robert needed to be certain that he had redeemed himself and gotten back to at least a Karma-neutral place in the universe. He lay prone in the woods a hundred yards away, on the right side of the eleventh. It was a relief to lie down, frankly. His breathing returned to normal. Robert watched intently as the foursome approached the green on the tenth. A par five, 514-yard hole, it took the foursome each three or four strokes to fetch the green. One of them delayed the group by searching for his ball in the woods — unsurprisingly. "Stop searching for the lost ball," Robert whispered, citing course rules. Robert rolled his eyes but waited patiently, enjoying the breeze blowing through the thin tree cover.

He observed each player take their turn. They pitched onto the green. The closest to the cup walked up to mark his ball and noticed something odd about the flag shaft. It looked split in two. He squinted, walked closer, and, to his astonishment, noticed a putter, shaft down, standing in the cup. He pulled it out and held it aloft.

"Danny, I know this probably sounds crazy, but isn't this your Ping?"

"What the…?"

chapter 23

It is a rare person who can indulge in an obsession merely through observation. Collectors, enthusiasts, fans, fanatics, aficionados, and devotees with any passion — be it for sports, watches, stamps, cigars, wine, antiques, art, tea spoons, Ferraris, travelling, food, or Royal Doulton figurines — commence their fixation by *reading* and *learning*; move on to visually *engaging* and enjoying, from a distance; and eventually, graduate to *doing*: that is, obtaining, collecting, owning, holding, consuming, and experiencing. It was predictable that Robert would eventually tire of merely observing other golfers, from his safe zone inside the woods. Golf is not an interest that one can truly appreciate vicariously. Robert had long since graduated to *doing* and was, despite the risk, determined he would play the game once again. After amassing a ragtag set of clubs, he began to sneak out to play a hole — and just one — before sunrise. At first, he'd pop out of the woods, often mid-fairway, to strike and simply feel the pleasure of connecting club and golf ball. He'd abandon the ball where it fell and duck back into the woods, exhilarated by the experience and the risk of getting caught — like a kid egging a house and running. There *would* be consequences to getting caught, he thought, although it was unclear to him exactly what those might be.

"What is the charge, officer?" Robert imagined asking authorities as handcuffs were placed on him, again.

Um…theft of a green fee. Illegal play before the course is open. Inappropriate footwear. Possession of stolen golf equipment. We'll think of something. Name and address, please. Do you have identification, sir?"

"Oh shit. Not again."

Robert had no desire to be uncovered, the hermit he was, squatting in the woods of Carmel. Nonetheless, he progressed to playing a full hole, from tee to cup, before retreating to safety in the cover of trees. With his rediscovery of the sport, Robert also began to appreciate the work of the groundskeepers at the many courses on the peninsula. They are truly the unsung heroes of the sport. Their hard work goes unappreciated by the hundreds of golfers who play every day of the year, in this part of the world. The watered, tended, cut and manicured fairways and greens are the output of true craftsmen. They are no less talented and committed than the painters, carpenters, writers, and sculptors that comprise the local artist community and make the peninsula their home. Robert reveled in the early morning sounds and smell of the course and the feeling of walking on a freshly cut fairway. He marveled at the way it gave ever so gently under his weight. It was more comfortable underfoot than the plushest carpet money could buy. He appreciated the simple beauty of what he called a dew-print. In the morning, when the light is low on the horizon, and the grass still moist, you can look back and see your own footprints in the short, finely cut and dense grass.

As summer and his first anniversary of living in the woods approached, Robert increased both the frequency of his play and the variety of holes and courses he would dare tackle in the early hours. One June morning, after a quick pee behind a tree and in advance of his more detailed hygiene routine, Robert set out to sneak in as many holes as prudent. Reaching out in the early morning darkness of the cabin, he felt for his blue, lady's golf bag (don't ask) propped up in the corner closest to the door.

They weren't much, but he valued the hodgepodge of clubs poking out of the bag, both ladies' and men's, by a variety of golf gear manufacturers: Titleist, Nike, TaylorMade, Callaway, Ping, and Adams. Robert bestowed upon his aggregated collection of clubs and golf bag an affectionate nickname: '*Mulligan*'.

The term *Mulligan*, as golfers know, signifies a do-over — an informal and strictly against-the-rules chance to take another swing or hit after flubbing the first. Mulligan stew, as fewer people may be aware, is a dish prepared and popularized by American hobos (as homeless, travelling workers were known) in temporary camps, in the early 1900's. The stew consisted of a contribution of whatever food each person had, to make a collective stew, for their shared meal. Both references seemed to be altogether apropos and Robert adopted the moniker. Robert's unmatched and mixed assortment was a true Mulligan stew of clubs. But he was proud of it. Other than the watch, that never left his wrist, the club set was Robert's most valuable material possession.

At most golf courses in the area, even in the busiest season, the groundskeepers, administrative staff, course marshals, and pro shop staff rarely arrived before sunrise. That time varied between months and seasons, of course. They'd get there earlier in the late spring and summer to accommodate morning bookings, which might be allowed as early as 6:30. Golfers can't play in the early morning darkness from October to February though. These months proved to be among Robert's favorite, and he'd sneak in the greatest number of holes over the cool, wet Carmel winter.

Before the morning course inspection by the grounds manager, and tee off by the day's first foursome, all the courses on the peninsula proved to be little more than well-manicured parks — quiet and still save for the wildlife that lived on or around the greens, the rough, and the surrounding woods. The local fauna knew the course schedule as well as any groundskeeper or caddy. The most shy and elusive among them usually retreated at first sight of a golfer on the tee box. Squirrels were oblivious to golfers. The occasional cheeky fox would bound around the edge of the greens, hoping to initiate a game of catch-me-if-you-can. Years ago, there was a brazen kit who would pick up and carry away balls in play, often while still rolling, after a drive or a chip. That little guy mysteriously disappeared one day and a private animal control contractor was seen driving away shortly thereafter. One must acknowledge the pricey courses in the area are but exceedingly attractive, well-kept, and costly recreational parks. There are strict rules for golfers and animals alike. Break those rules and there will be repercussions.

This morning, the sun was still below the horizon. The first sliver of light promised to join Robert in thirty or forty minutes. Despite his empty and growling stomach, he decided to forgoe the crackers he'd unboxed the previous evening, that tempted him from their resting spot on his makeshift dining table. He downed a glass of room-temperature water instead and pocketed an apple.

"Got to get going," he whispered. "Might miss my tee-off time."

Robert hurriedly dressed in golf slacks and a V-neck sweater, slung Mulligan over his right shoulder, closed the door to his cabin, and began walking along one of many established routes he had memorized by sight and feel. Remaining in the gulley, he took careful and calculated steps through the pitch black and headed due north. His shadowy silhouette was noted by a raccoon tiptoeing home after a long night as both passed each other while crossing Costanilla Way. Robert was certain that the raccoon gave him a knowing and friendly nod. He responded with a wave. After Costanilla, Robert hung a sharp left and paralleled Ronda Road a safe twenty feet inside the tree line, until he arrived at the most southerly green on Poppy Hills.

The crickets were still in full chirp as Robert stepped onto the green. He peered into the dim first light. Poppy was closest to his home, easiest to get to, and featured the most perimeter tree coverage, among the local courses. It became his "home" club. Robert had even managed to scavenge a golf shirt with a Poppy Hill logo, in case he got caught out on the course. He hadn't been — yet.

Poppy Hills is a lovely course. Robert always maintained that it was one of the finest public courses he had ever played. All the courses on the Monterey Peninsula, public or private, are pristine. Poppy is no exception. It can lull a cocky golfer into playing an aggressive game and then chastise him or her for doing so. The sloping greens and prolific bunkers guard its holes possessively. Poppy Hills doesn't enjoy the attention it deserves. Sure, it doesn't offer holes that overlook the roiling surf, or craggy cypress trees perched on a precarious rock outcrop. And, while it doesn't enjoy ocean views, it remains resplendent with gorgeous scenery and upkeep that is uncharacteristic for public links.

Poppy might have been Robert's favorite, but even home-bodies like to travel now and then. There were other courses he was still itching to surreptitiously play. Stealing playtime became a source of entertainment for Robert — as stimulating an exercise as the game itself. Sneaking in a few holes at Pebble Beach was his Holy Grail. Although Robert had played at Pebble Beach Golf Links many years ago, he had not done so since establishing his home in the woods, though it was, as the crow flies, the closest of the neighboring courses. Among the links on the peninsula, it proved by far the most exposed, and therefore riskiest for him to creep onto — let alone play a hole or two. Every hole at the Beach was in direct line of sight of one of the multimillion dollar homes that bordered it. Its location, and associated prestige, along with the views of the course, alone, might represent 50 percent of the market value of an adjacent home, Robert presumed. The views over Carmel Bay and smaller Stillwater Cove, anchored by Pescadero Point; the holes running out to the tip of Arrowhead Point; and the cliffs that slide into Carmel Beach, all add to the magnificence and mystique of the course. There is a good reason why Pebble Beach remains number one on the bucket list of so many golf enthusiasts.

Another course on which Robert had successfully slipped in a few holes was Spyglass. Spyglass Hill Golf Course features incredible greens, certainly, but failed the security test. That is, it offered minimal tree protection and had no useable egress points on its southern end. Only a thin slice of the Del Monte borders it, on the eastern edge. Robert was agitated by Spyglass and its immediate neighborhood because it represented the excessive residential density that plagued the peninsula and crowded out the Del Monte. And, because he could play only four holes with sufficient privacy there.

Except for a couple of sequestered holes, Monterey Peninsula Dunes and the adjacent Links at Spanish Bay were out of the question. Each was surrounded by the most tightly packed homes and condos in the vicinity, supplemented by almost constant tourist traffic — each car passenger gawking at every foot of 17-Mile Drive in slow motion.

Cypress Point Club certainly rivals Pebble Beach for its beauty: with its natural sand dunes complementing the man-made versions, and the scarred coast conceding to the sea at Cypress Point Rock. Few would argue that the seventeenth hole at Cypress is one of the most spectacular and inspiring holes in golf. Its greens lead to the very precipice of the adjacent cliffs. Robert played Cypress only once. It was too tempting not too. Just getting there ,unseen, was challenging — a covert, Army Ranger–level operation. But Robert had made it under cover of the pre-dawn. He imagined himself a sniper in a ghillie suit, focusing his breathing, taking his time in the stalk, controlling his fear and heart rate until he made it to his first green safely, ready to squeeze off a bullet of a drive. Of course, his ghillie suit happened to be brightly colored and made by a golf brand. No matter. Holes five, six, seven, ten, and eleven in the southeast quadrant of Cypress were the most secure holes. If he was feeling confident, or if the weather had scared away fair-weather golfers, he'd include holes eight and nine for good measure. Both holes are plopped down in the middle of natural sand dunes that are protected areas. They're quite private. Course maintenance at Cypress, Robert learned the hard way, is based in a cluster of buildings tucked in between holes four and five. That crew arrives before everybody else. With the sound of the first car, he'd slip back into the forest before making his way back home, his golf attire providing what he liked to call *Carmel Camouflage*.

Robert tried to remain unseen, always, but nobody looks out of place in golf attire in public areas around Carmel. In the middle of the forest, however, one might look suspicious dressed in red slacks and carrying a golf bag. Once, while headed back to his ravine home, golf bag hung off his back, Robert almost ran headlong into an early morning walker. They both negotiated a sharp bend in the forest trail, from opposite sides, and found themselves face to face. Robert and the hiker stopped abruptly and stared at each other, wide-eyed, for a hanging moment. The meeting was unexpected and more than a little awkward. Robert could appreciate how out of place he must have looked. Without further hesitation, he offered the most spontaneous and immediately disarming comment that popped into his head.

"Excuse me. I'm searching for my ball. Feel free to play through."

The hiker laughed aloud and went about her way, any suspicions thoroughly eliminated. *That was one serious slice,* she might have thought.

Of course, this morning, at Poppy, Robert wore the only clean golf shirt he had at the time — a plus-sized ladies' Puma polo. Robert had "recycled" it after it was dropped (or unceremoniously thrown out) in the course parking lot just off Lopez Road where it borders the woods. It was fuchsia. Bright fuchsia. As a matter of fact, now that the dark was retreating, Robert began to seriously question his judgment. Fuchsia is not a stealthy color. He was certain he could be seen from five hundred yards away, even in the low light. Nonetheless, he teed his ball at the senior men's box on nine. The ball he was playing, for practical reasons, was not stealthy either. When you play at five am in the morning in the dimmest of light, you need an orange ball — as untraditional and gauche as they might be. He had a full bucket of them back at the cabin, that he'd found in the woods at the far end of the driving range at Poppy.

Robert's drive disappeared into the evergreen background as it became airborne. He squinted deeply, as though that would somehow help him track its path. It didn't. It was too dark. He usually defaulted to conservative play. Conservative, to Robert, did not mean playing the middle of the green or a shorter, more controlled game. It meant playing his ball as close to the forest as practical, walking along its edge rather than the established cart paths. That way, he could disappear into the woods in an instant. It's why he also carried Mulligan across his back, always — even when swinging the club. He had also learned how to play well in the near dark. Instinct more than anything enabled him to judge a drive's lie, based on departure speed, angle and trajectory, when playing in low light.

Robert proceeded along the periphery of the forest and found his ball. A good drive on nine brings you perilously close to the clubhouse. Seeking to limit his exposure, he picked up his ball and bounded through a thin line of trees, over to eight — the adjacent hole. Eight, he knew well. It was a lovely little dogleg right with forest lining both sides. From there, he'd slip over to four, and, though a little unorthodox, play it backwards. The green at eight is adjacent to the green at four. He'd drop the ball, enjoy a few practice putts, and then drive back *toward* the tee box. Of course, a gentleman would never drive off a putting green. He teed it up on the approach to the green, play it over the sand trap to the right — left if he were playing the correct direction — and onto the fairway, putting out an imaginary hole at the actual tee box.

The fourth hole is a monster at 629 yards: a challenging hand-full. Playing it backwards proved to be even more difficult. After a drive from the green, a player has to make a decision. *Do I try and drive the enormous complex of sand traps ahead of the women's tee box, or lay up?* On some days, when time and light allowed, Robert would drive a dozen balls from the same location on the fairway — just to play out the various options. It was a luxury that few golfers get to experience. He also enjoyed the fact that there were no marshals hassling him, and no foursomes ahead holding up play. If there is golf in heaven, he was certain it looked like this — only better lit.

This day, Robert played on through three and chipped away at the diminutive 202-yard second hole. He should have back-tracked up to seventeen — perhaps the most private hole on the course, shrouded as it is by Pinion Pines. Instead, he played on to the seventh with the intent to finish the morning on hole one — the end of which provided a convenient forest exit door. He didn't finish the first hole this morning.

They saw him, or perhaps his fuchsia golf shirt, a few seconds before he saw them. They had no idea who he was, of course, but if they had, Robert wouldn't have known. They surely knew that nobody should be on the course at six o'clock in the morning. Two of them simultaneously yelled "Hey!" — a short-form declaration, observed around the world and understood in nearly any language, for "Stop!" and, simultaneously, "What the fuck are you doing?" A third man was astride an idling John Deere 1600 wide-area mower, contemplating the hot cup of coffee in his hand. The alarm raised by the two others surprised him. He spilled his drink and cursed. Looking up to determine the source of the commotion, he too saw the man in fuchsia. He gunned the mower. Diesel smoke belched as he stamped the accelerator and drove purposefully down the path toward Robert. The other two looked at each other and wondered if they should provide back-up. With a shrug, they decided by unspoken agreement against it. They bore no responsibility for course security. And they were enjoying their own fresh, hot coffee. The man on the Deere, on the other hand, felt compelled to lay down the law. Though not conveyed by election or a badge, a position of moral superiority proves intoxicating to people of all stripes. The groundskeeper took it upon himself to be *the* authority that morning.

The turbo-charged Deere gained speed on the paved path leading to the seventh, and with a slight downhill slope helping it along, the mower gained on the errant golfer. Robert might have stayed put and played innocent, but his fight-or-flight instinct kicked in. He tensed, considered his options for a brief moment, and ran. Nine feet away, he stopped abruptly, realizing that he had left his clubs on the ground. It might have been the first time in all his surreptitious golfing that he'd bothered to lay his clubs down to putt. Robert returned to the green, grabbed the bag, and again headed in the direction of the nearest and most dense forest fringe. His prized Ping putter, unfortunately, did not make it to the lifeboat. It lay on the putting green where he'd dropped it.

"Stop!"

Robert ignored the command. Anyone who runs, when a person of apparent authority demands they stop, is inferred to be guilty, without uttering a word. It's another one of those universal principles. At least that's how it was interpreted by the man now chasing him. Robert was breaking a rule, sure, although he was certain that neither he nor the overzealous groundskeeper knew what the consequences would be if he were caught. It's quite possible that as the low-speed chase unfolded, the question crossed both of their minds. They might have felt quite silly about their respective roles in the affair, as it unfolded. I suspect dogs might ponder the same thing from time to time when giving chase to an innocent, yet accessible cat.

Why do I feel so compelled to chase after this feline? What is it that is hardwired in me to bolt after her, growling and gnashing my teeth, knowing full well that she will run up a tree and I will park myself at the base and bark, ineffectively, for ten minutes, before sauntering away whilst trying all the while to look victorious and heroic?

"Hey! Stop!" shouted the groundskeeper once again. He received no response. Nor did he likely expect one. The groundskeeper had the diesel mower wound out for all it was worth. He gained on the man he was pursuing. Robert enjoyed maybe a ten-yard head start. Like the proverbial dog, the groundskeeper might have pondered what he'd do if he actually caught the unauthorized early morning golfer adorned in fuchsia.

Robert increased his speed by increasing the length of his stride. He picked up a mile per hour. Over the last ten months, he had become the most fit he'd been since his early teens. He was still twenty yards from the forest's edge. The mower was almost upon him. The blades of the mower weren't engaged, but Robert didn't know. Subconsciously his fear, and thus his speed, was fuelled by thoughts of being run over and diced like a food processor — bits of bone and skin mixing with fuchsia polyester and sprayed across the otherwise pristine and manicured greens. I'm uncertain how that mess might be cleaned from a short green, to be honest. It wouldn't be easy.

Robert deftly executed an abrupt, ninety-degree turn that, while it slowed him, was well calculated to evade the mower driver. It provided him a much-needed gap and allowed Robert to make it safely to the forest fringe. The dodge worked. The groundskeeper attempted to duplicate Robert's turn and follow with his mower. While a fine piece of machinery, the Deere was not designed for ninety-degree turns at full speed. Distracted by his quarry's regained advantage, and too preoccupied to re-member the topography of this specific hole, the operator drove straight into and up a steep earthen berm. The hill bordered and contained a water hazard behind its bank. At full speed, and with the grass still wet with morning dew, the groundskeeper's radical adjustment of the steering wheel met with a negligible mechanical response. Hitting the berm at fifteen miles per hour, the mower — resplendent in its trademark John Deere green, black and yellow livery — became airborne: surprisingly so, con-sidering its four-thousand-pound gross weight.

The groundskeeper was astonished. His heart rushed to his mouth. In a frozen moment, he realized that the Deere had tak-en to low-level flight, and that he and the mower were headed to terrain that was "outside the operating parameters" of the ve-hicle. He had time to consider it for two very long seconds. The operator's focus alternated, in micro-seconds, between Robert's final leap into the woods and the disorienting sights surround-ing his immediate location, in mid-air. The magnificent machine arched over the pond's muddy edge, changed its horizontal mo-mentum to something more vertical, and plunged into the pre-viously mirror-calm surface of the pond.

Little-known fact: course designers frequently dig the artifi-cial water hazards on golf courses deep enough to dissuade golf-ers from wading in to attempt recovery of their balls. It is poor form to do so and holds up play, as everyone knows. Damned if golfers don't do it anyway. And some golfers carry those ridiculous aluminum poles with baskets on the end, designed to repatriate balls from those purposefully deep ponds that they shouldn't be fishing around in. But I digress.

The John Deere mower landed in roughly the centre of the pond and became completely submerged. Nothing could be seen but bubbles and a growing wave. The groundskeeper emerged first and, treading water, began to swear repeatedly in Spanish: "*Mierda! Mierda! Mierda!*"

A slick of leaking diesel and oil began to grow on the surface of the pond. If you count the expensive mower, there were, in fact, two fatalities. The groundskeeper hadn't noted it in the excitement of the moment. Neither had the victim in its decidedly unfortunate decision to swim directly under the arching path of the mower. The Deere landed atop the mallard drake, whose response to the crisis had been, to its detriment, all too nonchalant. It bobbed to the surface seconds later, dead as, well…a duck. The groundskeeper's wallet popped up to the surface last. Groundskeeper, deceased duck, and wallet all floated in different directions, carried by the concentric undulation of water caused by the splash. The groundskeeper struggled up the muddy bank of the pond. He retrieved both his wallet, and the bird. All three of them were the worse for wear. Clearly, the prognosis for the Deere was not positive. It remained uncertain what the employment prospects for the driver would be after this. He looked in the direction that he'd last seen the man and swore: "*Tu hijo de puta! Tu hijo de puta!*"

Given the church-like silence of the morning and the now silent mower, Robert heard the furious shouting while scurrying through the woods. He understood the Spanish and grinned a broad yet slightly guilty smile. The two other maintenance workers, witnesses to the whole affair, dropped their coffee cups and, in unison, also said, "*Hijo de puta*" — but in a more hushed tone. It remains unclear whether they were referencing the Hermit or their co-worker: who just destroyed a $35,000 commercial mower. All they'd seen, from their vantage point, was the mower become airborne and disappear — followed by the unmistakeable sound of a loud *splash*. They agreed with one another that they had nothing to do with the instigation of the chase, or the outcome.

"*Vamos a salir de aquí,*" *said one.*

"*Yeah, let's get out of here,*" *agreed the other.*

His heart pounding from the chase, Robert eventually slowed and adopted a more relaxed pace as he found a familiar path back to the gulley. He silently reviewed the valuable lesson he'd gained from that morning's outing: *1) Don't play golf too close to the clubhouse or maintenance facilities, even if I'm tempted by challenging and/or entertaining holes; 2) perhaps carry fewer clubs to reduce weight in the event of a forced retreat or foot/ vehicle pursuit; 3) consider talking my way out of an unanticipated encounter. Speaking calmly and kindly, even if in halting Spanish, might be sufficient to earn walk-away privileges when I encounter course staff just doing their job; 4) do not, under any circumstances, wear bright fuchsia, again. Ever!*

He removed the fluorescent polo and threw it under a low bush, continuing his return to the gulley sweaty and shirtless.

chapter 24

Approaching his second anniversary of camping in the woods, Robert awoke with the birds, as usual. It was still dark. First light was still a half hour away. A dream, still fresh but rapidly fading, brought a wry smile to his face. It was strange and somewhat erotic. By his vague recollection, it included a *ménage a trois* with Jules and a girl he knew from Stanford. It was an all-too-brief but enjoyable distraction. The dream faded as quickly as it had arrived. Robert sat up in his cot and drew his hands across his face. He lifted his legs over the cot and sat upright, massaging his sore back. The cot legs had given in some months ago and his bed was now supported by six wooden crates — purloined from the back of several restaurants and from Nielsen Brothers Market. The boxes were hard. The setup was not the least bit comfortable. Robert lit his camp light, fired by a one-pound propane cylinder, and sat down on the one chair that graced his hovel. The light was always a welcome respite from the pitch blackness of the cabin and the fire warmed even the coolest morning with its glow. Robert had gradually begun to relax his rules on covertness. He was comfortable enough, now, turning on a low light, in the early morning, so he could see his way around the cabin. It was a hell of a lot better than fumbling in the blackness, trying to get both dressed and eat.

This morning, Robert looked around the cabin and its contents as one might when selling one's home: deciding what might be improved to command the highest market value. Robert had, without conscious intention, embraced his own interpretation of *shabby chic* or *country cool*. The place didn't look half bad — for a hermit cabin. He now had a suite of rustic and eclectic furniture. It looked, frankly, like he had hired an interior decorator with a trade discount at Anthropologie. The bed was his only source of complaint. He had noted a variety of once-loved headboards, bedframes, and mattresses every time he did a midnight scouting run on garbage day. They were just too heavy for him to drag through the neighborhood and into the ravine. Even if they weren't cumbersome, the sight of him dragging furniture through the streets would have aroused suspicion and brought undesirable consequences.

Robert *had* upgraded his nightstand from a wooden box to table with an oval top and four legs that he'd found on Sunset Lane. It was a Scandinavian design from the mid-seventies, made of teak. Clearly, nobody had informed the owners that mid-seventies Scandinavian furniture was once again all the rage, and that original pieces were commanding top dollar. Or, perhaps when you own a five-million-dollar home, you just don't give a shit. Only one thing rested on the bedside table — an eight-by-ten-inch picture of Juliana, her bright smile and deep brown eyes filling the wood frame. Wear on the frame confirmed its daily handling over the previous two years. As he did every morning, Robert picked it up and stared fondly at his late wife. He placed it back down, adjusting it so that it could be seen from any angle in the cabin.

"I miss you, babe," he reminded her, or himself.

Robert could have upgraded his dining table too, except a table would also be just too heavy and awkward and conspicuous to heft back to his cabin. So, he was still using his original dining table — several stacked nesting wood crates topped by a road sign that read *Pacific Grove Gate, Visitor Entrance — 17-Mile Drive.* It resided roughly in the center of the cabin. Rather than being an homage to the 17-Mile Drive, his decision to rip the sign from its anchor posts reflected his utter contempt for the road and all it represented. And, of course, because he needed a nice flat tabletop about that size.

Comfort, Robert came to conclude, was underrated. The thing he truly desired was a recliner. The wooden kitchen chair wasn't cutting it for long evenings spent reading. He was certain he'd find a discarded easy chair, eventually. To get it home, he might fashion some fashion of dolly — a flat, strong board (perhaps another road sign) with four casters and a length of rope for a pull — to efficiently drag one. He could haul it back to the woods along surface roads, then remove the wheels to drag it through the forest to the cabin.

Robert's prized golf clubs rested in the corner of the cabin beside a wire bucket filled with golf balls. In the gaps of the cedar siding, Robert had jammed several sticks that served as coat hooks to tether a Gortex camping parka, two bucket hats, two baseball-style golf hats, a duckbill cap, two belts, and a tan-colored golf jacket with a little alligator on the breast. Robert had upgraded his clothing storage from duffel bags to an old but funky steamer trunk complete with leather straps, brass hinges, and a locking clasp. The trunk might have been the largest thing that he'd dragged from a curb. It was open now and its colorful contents lit by the light of the propane torch. The trunk held Robert's entire wardrobe, consisting of two distinct categories of clothing: clothes he had brought with him, which were now well-worn and a little tattered, although clean; and the collection of golf attire he had "found" around his neighborhood courses. One pair of very bright pants stuck out like a beacon. He would have never purchased them, even at the height of his obsession with the sport. Yet, there they were. Red slacks.

Maybe if Jules had bought them for my birthday, Robert thought, *I might have worn them, to spare her feelings*. The slacks, bold as they were, told their own story. He chuckled to himself as he recalled the circumstances behind their acquisition.

Stop me if you've heard this story. It's legendary around the Carmel and Monterey area. It has never, however, been attributed to or associated with the hermit — until recently. Nonetheless, it's a story that has been told and embellished a thousand times, at every golf course lounge, dining room, and coffee shop, within a hundred miles. Even the victim himself tells the story to howls of laughter and delight. Three other witnesses to the event have debunked the claims, by some, that the story is a gross fabrication. Let me frame the story. Two months previous, Robert made his way over to Cypress Point to watch some play. He set up viewing from his favorite vantage point on the steep, wooded embankment overlooking the fifth hole. It's a great hole — a par five, 491 yards with a gentle dogleg to the left. Robert had played it a few times and watched many an amateur from his forest gallery.

The clubhouse at Cypress lies nestled in a nook, at the cliffs where holes one and eighteen converge. Before you tee off at the first hole, you're advised to stop at the bathroom facilities. By the time you hit the fifth hole, the farthest from the clubhouse, you are a *long* way from any toilet. It was about eight thirty that morning when a foursome played through the fourth hole and teed off at five. Robert had just taken his station. After the last golfer took his second stroke off the fairway, he deviated to the right, in the direction of the woods. This confused Robert, given that the man had hooked the ball to the left. The golfer headed directly toward Robert's hiding place. Hypersensitive to his potential exposure, he rose to his feet and prepared for flight. The man continued directly toward Robert, picking up his pace from a walk to a trot. Robert stood, backed away slowly, and shifted ten feet to his left — to protect his position and remain hidden. The man, wearing bright red golf slacks, continued his now rather awkward gait with a curious but definitive sense of urgency. As the golfer came closer, Robert heard what he was shouting to his mates. What Robert had mistakenly interpreted as a potential confrontation turned out to be nothing more than one man's unrelenting biological need.

"I've got to shit right this second or I am going to ruin these pants!" he shouted. "Sorry, but I *cannot* wait! Play ahead!" The other three chuckled awkwardly. Anyone who has played the game for a while will confess to the occasional emergency pee, or worse, in the woods. A well-prepared golfer might even carry some baby wipes in their golf bag, just in case. "I should not have eaten that jalapeno breakfast burrito!" he exclaimed as he entered the fringe of the woods. "What was I thinking?" His golf partners patiently waited for him on the fairway.

To ensure his privacy, the golfer in red pants waded deeper into the trees. He was following an invisible path, unbeknownst to him, directly toward Robert. The man was now almost on top of him. Thankfully, the golfer was distracted, undoing his belt while simultaneously tugging his zipper down. He was less than eight feet from the Hermit when, unexpectedly, he pulled his pants completely down and off — presumably to ensure that he didn't soil his pants when he squatted. The golfer was literally shitting while Robert was figuratively doing the same. Robert grimaced and turned away at the sight. Knowing his discovery by the diarrheal golfer would lead to awkward questions, Robert became understandably anxious. He began to panic. Robert remembered his late-night confrontation, with an aggressive black bear dining on garbage, that evidently mistook him for competition. The bear had growled, huffed, and bluff-charged Robert. It scared him so badly that he ran non-stop back to his cabin, where he pushed the dining table against the door for good measure.

Robert did what any normal hermit who had just been confronted by a hapless golfer with an uncontrollable colon would do. From behind a tree, he launched into an entirely convincing imitation of an angry black bear. Robert knew what one sounded like, for certain. He started with a low, deep growl and graduated to several louder huffing sounds. For added impact, he shook the waist-high bush beside the tree. The convincing sounds, paired with the visual effect, achieved the desired result. The golfer, minus his red slacks, shouted at the top of his lungs as he ran out of the woods, full bore, waving his hands and screaming, convinced he was escaping an imminent bear attack — and thoughtfully warning his partners. His actions got their attention. Each of his golf buddies, stricken with fright, involuntarily dropped their golf club and readied to flee for their life. After a twenty-yard run, and in the absence of an actual bear at their heels, they eventually slowed to a halt. Their composure turned to hilarity at the sight of their friend — standing in the middle of the fairway, wearing nothing but a collared golf shirt, striped boxer shorts, knee-high socks, and golf cleats.

The golfer at first remained oblivious to the source of their laugher. He considered it cruel and unsympathetic, given his brush with death at the hands (or claws as it were) of a ferocious bear. Then, he looked down. His face turned the color of his now absent pants. It was hard to tell from his position, but Robert was certain that two of the other golfers wet their pants, they were laughing so hard. All in all, it was a biologically messy affair. Robert cupped his hand over his mouth to muffle his own laughter at the sight and at his unexpected success in mimicking a bear. The boxer-clad golfer grabbed a jacket out of his golf bag. He wrapped it around his waist like a skirt, and the four golfers agreed to drive back to the clubhouse for a stiff drink — or two. In the meantime, Robert considered the fine pair of slacks left at the site to be officially lost and abandoned. He helped himself: rolling them up and tucking them under his shirt for the safe trip back home.

chapter 25

One homeowner cast-off that Robert did take the trouble to heft back to the cabin was an ornate, waist-height cabinet, vaguely Spanish-style, with two doors and four wheels. He assumed it to have been a bar cabinet or a small buffet in its previous life. It was quite a lovely piece. On the top of the cabinet, Robert kept a small basin, used variously for washing dishes and his face, and for brushing his teeth. Beside it lay a toothbrush and half a tube of toothpaste. After years of pestering by Jules, he'd finally adopted and maintained the habit of rolling it from the bottom, as it emptied. Behind a door, the cabinet featured two fixed shelves. While once it might have held a crystal decanter of brandy, it now held dried food; salt and pepper; a bottle of olive oil; a limited selection of cutlery; plates; two cups; two coffee mugs; a camp thermos; and several pans and pots. The largest of the pots was, at the time, filled with golf balls. Robert had nowhere else to contain his growing collection. The cabinet was well-worn. He imagined it had spent many years collecting dust in a far corner of someone's garage. Very possibly, it had become victim to a spousal demand to "clean up the garage" — its presumed final resting place, at the curb, on garbage day.

As a means to purge, garage sales around Carmel are considered socially unacceptable. Anything that isn't passed down to the kids is unceremoniously kicked to the curb for disposal. More often than not, the community's refuse never makes it to the garbage trucks. Much of it is picked up by scores of nocturnal scrappers who scour the neighborhood in cars and pickup trucks. They have all come to know Carmel as a priority neighborhood for high-quality curb picking.

The cabin and its weathered cedar walls remained unadorned. His intention to address that oversight had yet to be fulfilled. Unfortunately, Robert had left a collection of paintings and drawings neatly stowed in the back of the Volvo — now resting somewhere in Salinas. He wondered he'd ever see the car again, and if so, whether the art would be where he'd left it, two years prior.

There must be at least twenty retail galleries in Carmel that featured the work of local artists. The best deals can usually be found at the artist cooperative — the Carmel Art Association. Robert committed to buy a painting someday for his cabin wall. In the meantime, the only thing that did garnish the warped board wall was a rectangular mirror with a crack, running diagonally across the entire pane. It hung just above the washbasin. Robert walked to the cabinet, tossed some water over his face, dried off with a hand towel, and stared at his reflection. He looked gaunt, but his eyes remain sharp and his look purposeful and focused, albeit fatigued by the hard life he lived. Robert was now sporting longer hair that had clearly been "self-managed" — not the sixty-dollar haircuts he was used to. He looked perhaps ten years older than he had before crafting his home in the woods.

Robert left the forest later than usual for his morning hygiene and water collection routine. As he neared the end of Ocean Avenue, he took the less populated beach route and walked its length to get to the facilities, at the south end of the beach. He could tell, even in the low light of the morning, it would be another glorious August day on the peninsula. The Highlands had released the sun from its captivity and its beams created a halo effect over Jack's Peak. Several early risers were already on the beach walking their jubilant dogs. Fit and slim, Robert looked much like any other fitness buff getting in an early morning walk before break-fast if you ignored his knapsack. He covered the thousand yards between Ocean Avenue and the southern end of the beach effi-ciently and without breaking a sweat. As he approached the stairs that wound up to Scenic Road and the entrance to the public re-stroom, Robert was startled. A woman, at first unseen, sat tucked in behind a rock retaining wall that lay at the bottom of the cliff. She was astride the canvas seat of a folding stool. A portable ea-sel sat perched in the sand in front of her. The easel cradled a canvas stretched over a frame. A paintbrush projecting from her mouth looked like a colorful cigarillo. She was staring pensively at the canvas — like she might chastise it at any moment. Robert couldn't see what she was painting but assumed it was the beach and jagged rocks that marked this end of the beach. While he certainly noticed her, his intent to pass unseen failed terribly.

"Good morning. I've seen you before somewhere," she said out of nowhere. Her eyes remained fixed on the canvas, at first. She turned to look at Robert directly. "You must live here…at least seasonally." She was not the least bit shy.

He slowed, almost to a stop, and turned toward her. "Good morning."

"You do live here, don't you?" she asked. "Unless you're just a tourist who comes here often…are you?"

Robert stopped walking. "A tourist? No. I live here," Robert said, hoping to limit the dialogue without being rude.

"Where do you live?" She was direct and unabashed in her questioning.

"Here. In Carmel."

"I knew it. I've seen you walking the beach before. Sorry. I tend to notice people. It's a gift. I've got a photographic memory of sorts. You didn't answer my question. Where do you live? Like, in what street?"

Robert hesitated. This woman was not going to let him go. He wasn't certain that he objected at that moment. "Forest Road," he replied.

She furrowed her brow gently and looked at him as though struggling to remember where exactly that street was. Robert's head wanted to avoid further dialogue. But, he suddenly found his heart was dominating the encounter. He hadn't spoken to many people since settling in the woods. She had started a tennis match, and he felt compelled to return the volley.

"If you had a photographic memory, then I suppose you wouldn't need to sit at the beach to reference a scene. You'd paint from the memory or picture you have in your head," Robert said.

He meant it in a playful, teasing way, rather than sarcastically or maliciously.

She smiled and nodded her head, confirming she perceived it as the former.

"I come to the beach to paint once a week, mostly because I love just sitting at the beach. I can't paint for shit. And," she added, "because you just never know what strange men you might run into."

"Strange men?" Robert asked, somewhat defensively.

"I was teasing you back. You've got a healthy vacation beard going," she said playfully, drawing her hands across her own face and chin, adding body language to her description of his scruff. She spoke with her hands often. Actually, as it turned out, all the time.

"I'm on vacation now, yes. Very observant of you."

"You're in my photographic memory album now, scruff and all. I don't want to sound too forward," she said quite forwardly, "but I'm starving. Would you like to join me for breakfast? I was going to just leave for a place in town that has the best eggs benny. I hate to eat alone."

She brushed her long blonde hair, blown by a morning wisp, away from her freckled face. She raised her gaze from the canvas to check his response — words or body language.

Robert shook his head no, with entirely unconvincing body language. "Perhaps some other time." He wanted to sound sincere and meant it to be perceived as such. He offered a hesitant smiled as he passed her. Their eyes met one last time as he continued his progress, starting up the stone stairway, toward the landing and men's restroom.

She shouted to be heard over the background noise of the wind and crashing waves, as he left: "I always eat at the Forge in the Forest. It's my favorite restaurant in town!"

He took a quick look back and saw she was still watching him intently.

"Mine too. That...um...forest place. So long." He paused and added, "see you again, I'm sure."

The painter didn't return his salutation. She simply smiled as she continued stroking the canvas with deft hand, but questionable artistic talent. It wasn't a snub. She knew that she would see him again. Robert bounded up the stairs and disappeared into the men's washroom. He didn't shave this time, speculating that maybe she liked the scruff. After concluding his hygiene routine, Robert let the heavy mahogany door swing closed behind him and did a quick 180-degree survey to see if he had been spied. He strode west up Scenic Road to avoid the artist on the beach. It most certainly would have aroused suspicion and triggered more questions if he had taken the beach path with his water jugs in hand. She was rather an attractive woman and, as much as he enjoyed the brief interaction, he feared further questioning. *How would I explain the water jugs?* he wondered. *Broken plumbing? That would be an unconvincing bluff.*

Still, Robert found himself thinking of her as he walked away. He was intrigued. He was attracted. He was conflicted. Robert felt an unfamiliar pang in his heart, but knew exactly what was ailing him. He missed the company of a woman, for the first time since his wife died. And this woman had taken him off guard. She had looked directly and unblinkingly into his eyes when she spoke. She was direct. She was bold. She was assertive. He hadn't seen that look since the day he met Jules. The feeling was powerful enough to make him stop again. He peered over the edge of the cliff down to the beach, hoping he might spot her from above. The cliff and bushes that grew on its banks hid the little corner of the beach where she was perched. He let out a sigh and continued his return trip home, disappointed he hadn't at least asked her name.

To avoid the morning walkers, who typically hugged the path alongside Scenic Road, Robert walked a block east, parallel to the beach, on San Antonio. As he made his way back to the woods, an airliner passed overhead with a thick, puffy contrail behind it. He stopped and stared at it for a minute. It occurred to him that he missed travelling just then too. *What the hell is happening?* He felt the pull of the real world — his old world — and it was aggravating him. Robert felt he needed to let a little of the real world back into his life but was at odds with the concept. He was, perhaps, feeling a little sorry for himself too.

No women. No cars. No planes. No travel. You can't be a part-time hermit. Back to the woods where you belong, he reluctantly resolved.

He focused on the street ahead. Twenty minutes later, nearing his forest entry point, he spied a police car headed in his direction, a block away. He once again exercised his carefully honed disappearing act. In seconds, he slipped unnoticed into a narrow beach access path between the streets. He stepped stealthily through the backyard of a home he knew to be currently unoccupied, and made his way north to an entry point for the woods just south of the Carmel Gate tollbooth. He disappeared into the thicket. Like the deer with whom he shared the woods, his daily routine led him to wander into civilization and chance engagement with people. Like the deer, he knew he needed to retreat and hide to be assured of safety.

Back at the cabin, Robert made breakfast — oatmeal, an apple, and the remains of a loaf of French bread with jam spread — and swept a week's worth of dirt out of the place. He felt disinclined to watch golfers from the forest today. He'd already replaced the dead and browning branches on the cabin roof with fresh pine boughs. He also had sufficient food in the cabinet; enough drinking and washing water for two days; a clean and tidy cabin; and clean laundry that he'd plunger-washed earlier that week. The clothes typically took two days to dry in the dark and still air of the cabin. Now that they were dry, he folded each article and stored his underwear, socks, shorts, and pair of jeans in the steamer trunk.

Chores completed, Robert sat at his table and stared out the window — the former tollbooth window. As the sun climbed higher in the sky, it brightened the gulley and the interior of the cabin. It occurred to him that, perhaps for the first time, he felt bored. Boredom is a bad thing for an inadvertent hermit. It forced Robert to think about his circumstances and motivation for remaining in the woods. And think he did. All day. After Juliana's death, Robert's goal had just been to get away — to deal with the grief and depression that had consumed him. His decision to sell or give away the bulk of his material belongings was somewhat impulsive, he acknowledged. But, the act did have a foundation in his sincere desire to embrace simplicity — a concept that had distracted him for years previous. The loss of Jules; the shedding all the unnecessary "stuff" from his life; going simple; the decision to camp out in the Carmel Woods; and the eventual commitment to building a cabin, were an accidental nexus of events, emotions and thoughts. Robert was a smart man though. He had learned over the last two years that simplicity couldn't be discovered or imposed by voluntary poverty any more than it could in the wealth he had previously earned. We all complicate our lives unnecessarily. A life lived simply is merely one grounded in a pursuit of what is important. He regretted not figuring that out while he had shared a life with Jules. It had taken two long, hard years in the forest to achieve this revelation. *Revelation* makes it sound like it had been sudden. It wasn't. It had been quietly creeping up on him over the months, like a presence trailing him in the forest — except this spirit was benevolent.

Robert had, little by little, prepared himself, allowed and awarded himself the entitlement to be human again. He had granted himself the permission to feel and to at least to engage the world, observing and living vicariously, even if not permitting anyone to come too close. Humans are social creatures, however, and cannot survive forever in isolation. Castaways on deserted islands, even when afforded all the resources necessary to live a healthy life — food, shelter, and clothing — will always try to build a boat or raft to reach civilization. People need people.

I'm inclined to believe that solitary confinement is the worst form of torture inflicted by humanity. Humans justify their actions by claiming to reserve that fate for the worst offenders yet inflicts the same torture on animals he purports to love, in things he calls "zoos". There, frequently, one specimen is held captive, with no mate, no sibling, and no family with whom to share their life — only the strange bipedal species that arrives daily to watch or feed them. Solitary confinement breaks the hardest man or beast. Sentient beings need social contact so fundamentally that even a visiting mouse or cockroach to a man in *"the hole"* can become welcome company and source of small joy.

Robert had done his time in the hole and found himself close to an emotional breaking point. He could no longer rationalize his self-imposed imprisonment. He had, quite literally, developed cabin fever. We can only sequester ourselves physically and emotionally for so long. And so it began: Robert's slow progress toward rebuilding his mental and emotional health. His self-rehabilitation. He hadn't committed any crime, but he'd certainly earned himself a day pass.

chapter 26

Late that day, Robert put on his cleanest clothes, walked out of the woods, and headed to the beach. He felt a rare source of joy just watching people and their dogs enjoy the beach, as the sun set. Robert also secretly hoped that he might run into that attractive, assertive artist again. *Call Triple A*, he thought. It was a lame joke, but a joke nonetheless. He hadn't thought of one for some time.

Lamentably, Robert didn't spot her. But, he enjoyed his evening. Sure, he had gone to the beach many times. In the past, he chose to remain far from direct contact with people. This time, rather than watching the activity from a distance, he plopped himself down on a sun-bleached log, half-buried in the sand, close to the most trafficked section of the beach. He wondered if it would be possible for him to live some form of *dual* life — to continue dwelling in his forest cabin but also blend in and socialize with the residents of Carmel. As if on cue, a dog ran up to him to introduce herself and identify Robert with a series of sniffs.

"Sorry, sorry. She's gentle and won't bite," said her human companion.

"I can see that. I wasn't worried," said Robert. "I live with a lot of animals."

He gave the retriever a good rub on the side of her neck, eliciting some nuzzling and a lick from the dog. As suddenly as she arrived, the dog was off again, to discover and inspect the next human or canine whose path she might cross, on this gloriously free night at the beach. The beach seemed alive with life, as he had never appreciated it before.

Robert reveled in the sight of shorebirds that came winging in as the human crowd began to thin. A hundred yards offshore, several dolphins breached the surface for the brief second it took them to exhale and inhale a lungful of air. He imagined what life swirled below the kelp beds offshore and wished he could scuba dive among them once again. He thought he glimpsed a sea otter surface, but then decided it must have been the light playing off the surface of the ocean and swaying kelp tops. He heard a rustling in the coastal sage scrub behind him and spun around — too late to uncover the tiny beach hermit who had evaded detection. A small flock of brown pelicans in fighter-jet formation passed low over the ocean, just past the surf line. And the gulls…there must have been thousands of them. Robert considered himself a knowledgeable naturalist, but had no idea where gulls went at night. *Do they roost like other birds? Do they even have nests? They must*, he thought, *commute from the suburbs to the city every day to do their gull work.* Every evening at dusk, the sky over the coast along the peninsula becomes a veritable one-way, five-lane thoroughfare of seabirds all headed to, apparently, the same place. If you listen, you can hear them impatiently honking at the slower birds ahead of them who are going too slowly, or who have the nerve to change lanes without warning. Depending on your perspective, their shrill is either an obnoxious cacophony or one of nature's great symphonies. It's a sound that rarely evokes neutrality of opinion. Robert envisioned an off-ramp invisible to humans near a seagull neighborhood, and a large parking lot with orderly, diagonal lines of graceful birds, their heads turned, and bills inserted into their tail feathers, as they called it a day. The skyway eventually goes quiet once the sun sets, save for the stragglers who were working late to curry favor with the boss, in the hope of a promotion.

Robert had appreciated his day. It had been the most enjoyable of the last two years. He likened it to one of those mornings we have all experienced after suffering through a bad flu and a high fever for days. One awakens, completely cured and feeling one hundred percent better than the day before. Robert's fever, he felt, had broken.

As darkness fell, Robert broke from his perch on the log and contemplated his trip back to the dark forest — this time reluctantly. He remembered a magnet with an inspirational quote that Jules had bought and affixed to the fridge, a quote from Kristen Butler: *"Sunsets are proof that no matter what happens, every day can end beautifully."*

Robert followed his usual path down San Antonio to Carmel Way, on his way back to the ravine. The flashing amber lights of a tow truck punctuated the now dark sky, its beams bouncing off the shrubs, walls, and homes as it cautiously threaded its way slowly down the narrow street. As it came toward him, Robert could see the form of a car strapped down to its flatbed. As the trucked passed him, Robert noted the black Bentley Flying Spur with vanity plates it was escorting away. Inconveniently for its owners it had four completely flat tires. *No wonder it needed a tow*, Robert observed. *No car comes with four spare tires.*

It was the best day ever.

chapter 27

As his grief subsided and depression receded, life for Robert became pleasurable again. He appreciated everything more, even those tasks that his impulsive lifestyle decision had imposed upon him — peeing in the woods; shitting, washing, shampooing, and shaving in public bathrooms; hauling food from a grocery store two miles away; washing clothes in a bucket; cutting his own hair; cooking with a propane stove; eating and reading by camp light — all seemed more enjoyable. It sounds terribly cliché, but even the air smelled better. Robert shook off the dark cloud of pain and sorrow that had paced his every move for two years.

Robert couldn't get that artist off his mind, but felt remorseful for it, just the same. Juliana was but a thought away — always. Yet here he was, contemplating another. Rob felt guilty of infidelity. He wondered if every widow or widower experienced the same conflict after having romantic (or sexual) feelings for someone new. Robert began incorporating an amble through town every day, hoping to find out where she lived. *It's not stalking*, he assured himself. *It's proactively trying to advance another chance meeting.*

She couldn't have lived too far, Robert presumed, if she hauled her easel and canvas down to the beach weekly. He hadn't recalled seeing a car parked up on Scenic Road near the stairs to the beach that morning. *She must live near the beach.* It was a reasonable assumption. *Be patient*, he thought. *Just let it happen.* Besides, his newly embraced decision to socialize required him to spend more time in Carmel and around its population. Robert even started to visit coffee shops, sit for a while, and occasionally even speak to people. In some regards, he thought of himself as a living social experiment — albeit one managed by an entirely unqualified practitioner.

On the third morning of his newly adopted routine, Robert took the beach path to the south end facilities. He had dispensed with the water run on this morning, and, after washing in the bathroom, walked the lattice of streets east of the facilities, between 10th Avenue and Santa Lucia. The walk and the review of the fine homes and cottages in this area is entertainment enough for anyone who appreciates unique architecture. Robert regarded each home he walked past with just a tinge of envy. He'd have considered owning any one of them had he the budget to do so. It's an attractive yet pricy neighborhood.

Turning from Santa Lucia onto Carmelo, he continued his grid search, with faint hope he'd see the woman from the beach. Down the street, a unique car parked in a driveway caught his eye. It was a butter yellow Mercedes Benz 300D, from the early 1980s — the same model car his late father had driven in that era. It had been the first car Robert knew and remembered from his boyhood. And, it held special meaning for him. He'd learned to drive behind the wheel of that 300D. Among old Benzes, it has a cult following. Today, they are much sought after for restoration. The "D" stands for diesel. The 300Ds are known to be tough and unbreakable, with many clocking five hundred thousand miles or more and still going strong. They're built like tanks! Robert smiled as he approached the car, standing to stare and appreciate it for a moment.

"You're either a vintage Mercedes enthusiast or a car thief scouting the neighborhood," said an oddly familiar voice. The source of the voice had been kneeling below low bushes, in the front yard of the home, tending a lovely flower garden. She always did so early, before the sun forced her back into the comfort of her air-conditioned home. Robert had, once again, been caught off guard. He looked toward the gardener and recognized her immediately.

She stood, and Robert got a much better look at the artist — for the first time since their meeting at the beach. He was surprised by how tall she was. She had been sitting in a chair the last time he saw her. Now he estimated her height at five-foot ten inches. She was lithe, graceful, and well kept. This woman had the healthy glow one would surely achieve by daily walks on the beach. Her eyes were brilliant blue and framed by wrinkles — experience lines — that dipped when she smiled, which she did every time she spoke. Long dirty-blond hair framed a slim face covered in freckles and hung perhaps eight inches below her shoulders. Her hair was straight and parted in the middle, forcing her to move it out of her face and occasionally tuck it behind her delightfully well-shaped ears. Robert assumed Scandinavian heritage given her fair skin and hair. She didn't wear makeup as far as he could see and was the most naturally beautiful woman he had met — since Jules.

Robert struggled to maintain his composure and hide his enthusiasm. The chance meeting transported him emotionally to another time in his life. He reverted to age sixteen again, and quite magically, became Rob — at least when near her. *Of course, the beautiful, assertive artist would have to own a car that I love!* He struggled to respond and counter her sardonic comment with something equally clever. His retort was weak. "Nice car."

She raised her eyebrows and pushed her hair away from her face and behind her ears. She looked unimpressed. "That's the best you've got?" she offered, with rich sarcasm. "No, Good morning, Kate?"

"Sorry. I don't…I didn't know your name, so I couldn't have said that. Good morning, Kate. I do like your car, though…and your home…and the garden." He was going overboard now. *Shut up and calm down.*

"Well, it's actually Katherine until you get to know me; then you can use 'Kate.'"

"Okay, Katherine, it's nice to meet you once again."

"You know me now. Please. Call me Kate."

The comment made Rob smile broadly. *This woman is unique*, he thought.

"So, I guess you don't live that far away, if you're on Forest Road. Turns out, you're only a few blocks away. That might be too close for comfort," she said teasingly. "I don't know anyone on that street, though. Are you going to tell me your name?"

"Sorry. It's Robert Das. Friends call me Rob. You can call me Robert."

"Touché," she volleyed. "Well played. Are you coming in to admire my hard work, or not?"

Rob silently accepted the invitation, opened the green wrought-iron gate to her garden, and walked in. He was getting nervous now. His stomach churned and he had to check his natural tendency to talk too much when he found himself attracted to a beautiful woman.

Kate's home was exquisite, at least from what he saw on the outside. It was designed in the Tudor style, the exterior walls finished in stucco and painted a pale pink. The house was framed by forest green window frames and front door, and featured delightfully appropriate carriage-style garage doors. Its classic look was accentuated by salt air-weathered cedar shingles on the roof. A large stucco-covered chimney dominated the face of the home. Robert imagined a superb fireplace in a great room just behind it. The yard was meticulously landscaped and featured a variety of trees and bushes, a mature

Yucca, and a wide variety of wildflowers that she tended with expert care. The yard, and her entire home, appeared well ordered. *She has superb taste*, he thought. The fact that she was out doing the gardening herself told Rob that this was one resident who didn't outsource all the hard work to professional landscapers. He was impressed, on all levels.

"What's your house number on Forest?" she pried.

Rob attempted, again, to deflect any questions related to his residency.

"It's a nice package," Rob said, looking directly at Kate.

"Excuse me? That's rather cheeky."

"No, I didn't mean it like it sounded. What I mean to say is that everything — your home, the garden, the car, and all… go together so well. You obviously appreciate and value vintage and classic things."

"Are you saying that I'm old?"

"No, no. Crap. Look, it was nice to run into you again. I should be going." He felt like the exchange wasn't going as well as he had hoped. A well-timed sought escape seemed to be the best tactic.

"Slow down, cowboy. I was messing with you. Thank you. I graciously accept your awkward compliment. The house is complements of my ex-husband. Spoils of war, so to speak. We owned it together for ten years before we split. The car, I bought a few years ago from an elderly neighbor, who had to quit driving. She owned it from new, I think. I do like it, though, Robert. I never thought about it, but you're right, it does go with the house quite nicely. It's a classic for sure — like me. I should paint it to coordinate with the house."

"Rob, please. Call me Rob. Don't paint the car. I love the color. Mercedes named it Maple Yellow, by the way. My father's Benz was a rich maroon with tan leather interior. It was Orient Red."

"Stay for a little, won't you? I don't get many strange men

in my yard. There's something about your terrible awkwardness that I find adorable."

"I'm out of practice," Rob said, apologetically.

"I couldn't tell," she said, sarcastically. "Recently divorced?"

"Widowed."

"I'm sorry for your loss. Me and my big mouth. How long ago?"

"A little more than two years now."

Conscious of his visible discomfort with the subject, Kate deftly redirected. You'd have thought she was a lawyer. "Speaking of classic, I love your watch. My ex-husband used to collect fine watches and had a few Rolexes. I learned to appreciate a good-quality mechanical watch. Funny, he never bought one for me. Only his mistress."

"Thank you. It was a gift from my late wife. Sorry about the mistress."

"She had impeccable taste!"

"Indeed," agreed Rob. "You meant my wife, right, not the mistress?"

"Funny guy. Yes, I meant your late wife. May I ask what you do for a living, Rob?" she continued her questioning.

"I'm retired now."

"Really? What did you do *before* you retired?"

"I was a lawyer."

"How unfortunate," she said, mischievously. "You must have been a successful lawyer to retire at such a young age and live here."

"Looks can be deceiving."

She furrowed her brow at the comment, not understanding precisely what he meant by it. It might have been perceived as a comment designed to end the line of questioning. She changed the subject again. "Do you like gardening at all?"

"I like plants and flowers and trees, yes. You might say that they surround me. I don't like the work it takes to care for them, though."

"You maintain a garden yourself?"

"My own garden is rather…un-manicured. Very wild. Left to grow in its natural state."

"Ahhh…A natural garden. That makes sense around here, especially if you travel a lot. Plus, water is so scarce here in Carmel. I have water barrels on my downspouts to collect water and I water a little every morning. It keeps things nice and green." She motioned to the water barrel at the corner of her house.

"I get around, but never that far," Robert said. "I don't mean to be rude, but I must be going now."

He became more nervous, fearing additional questions about his home. *What shit luck*, he thought, *that my attempt to be clever, and reference to a fake residence, on Forest Road, turned out to be a real street, and close by.* Robert needed to figure out a strategy before he engaged Kate again, lest he screw it up completely.

"Hope to see you by another time. It's a small town; I'm sure I will. Maybe we can meet for a tea sometime."

"I would like that, Kate. Now that I know where you live, I'll drop by sometime."

"Aren't you going to ask for my number?"

"I'm old-fashioned," he said, struggling to hide the fact that he didn't own a phone. That would seem odd for just about anyone these days. That said, he was genuinely old-fashioned. He added, "Plus, there's a certain charm in a serendipitous meeting, don't you think?"

She appeared a little flabbergasted by the remark and didn't respond. Rob opened the gate and started to walk away. He stopped himself and turned back to her. "It was very nice meeting you, again, Kate."

"Goodbye, Rob."

Old-fashioned? Rob thought. *What a stupid comment!* He was quite certain that she must have been thinking the same thing. What Robert didn't realize was that there was something disarmingly charming about him and his clumsiness. Many women, including Jules, found his awkwardness an attractive quality — it made him less threatening than an intelligent, handsome, and well-spoken man like him might otherwise be. And it likely didn't hurt that Kate thought he was well off enough to have retired early. A home in Carmel indeed. Single people seeking a new mate tend to be somewhat cautious when it comes to the motive of new suitors. It's a gross generalization, but I expect that's why people of the same socio-economic class and comparable net worth tend to partner, after a failed first, or second, marriage.

As soon as Robert disappeared from view, down Carmelo, Kate rushed into her house, sat down, turned on her computer, and launched a browser. She typed Robert's name to do a quick background check. She was curious, more than anything, now that she knew his name. But, it wasn't entirely unwarranted and a prudent thing for a single woman to do — especially one with a high net worth. Social media and an internet query, concluded in minutes, have replaced hours of phone calls to friends and grocery store gab among singles to screen, investigate, and scrutinize a potential date. There's got to be an app for that.

There he was — right on the screen. He was real. *Robert Das — Stanford Law, 2000.* Check. *Called to the California bar in 2002.* Check. *Law firm partnership announcement in* LA Times *in 2008.* Check. *A reference to Robert as the surviving spouse in an obituary for Juliana Das.* Check. *Previous home address in Los Angeles.* Check. He was legit. Oddly, there were no references to an address in Carmel found. He *had* said he'd lived in town for two years. The next morning, she jumped in her Benz and drove up and down Forest Road, to try and determine which house might be his. There were two homes under apparent renovation, so Kate remained uncertain exactly where he lived. She considered it, but chose not to knock on the door of either, or both.

Rob kicked himself as he walked away. *This is never going to work,* he fumed, critiquing his own ungainly performance and the seemingly insurmountable challenges. Hiding his true living situation would not be simple. He had no idea what to do next. As the day ended and the sun began to set, he lay in his cot, closed his eyes and sulked. It was probably an appropriate response for someone who felt completely out of his element, and league. Robert soon felt sleep wash over him like the tide gaining ground on a beach. He wondered if the wise owl might offer some advice tonight. This time the owl answered. *Go get a real haircut.* Or at least that what he imagined, as sleep overcame him.

chapter 28

It was very early — still a few minutes before six in the morning. The surf was still and the beach empty. The first dogs of the day were still nose-deep in their chow dishes before dragging their human companions out the door for their twice daily walk. Kate too was up earlier than usual, having lolled in bed since before the sun considered its daily responsibility. Finally accepting she wouldn't fall back asleep, she surrendered to the sunrise, got up and dressed. Yoga pants, a form-fitting hoodie, and runners were her morning wardrobe. Pulling her hair up in a ponytail, she grabbed her water bottle and house keys and was out the door for her morning power walk.

The beach at Carmel is a mile long, with rock faces that impose a natural boundary at each end, north and south. Occasionally and admittedly savant in her necessity for order and repetition, Kate felt a compulsion to touch the southernmost rock wall, walk the beach with purpose and momentum, and touch the rocks on the most northerly point of the beach. She'd then turn, walk back, and touch the southern rocks once more, ending the routine with a run up the stone staircase, to the path overlooking the beach. Regardless of your level of fitness, you'd be certain to work up a sweat after that workout. The difficulty of the beach route can be tempered by the pace and location of path you follow. At the surf line, the sand is tamped hard by the wave and water action. The surface is hard to differentiate from asphalt, other than being cold and wet. The farther away you walk from the high-tide mark, the deeper and drier the sand gets. Your feet sink in the sand with each step, and it can feel as though you're carrying five-pound weights on each leg. Two miles of that, and I can guarantee heavy perspiration and the desire for a hearty breakfast.

Kate's route to the beach from her home, three blocks away, followed a gentle downhill slope — the only civilized way for a forty-something woman to warm up. Assuming her regular route and athletic stride and incorporating a strong-arm pump to prompt her heart into action, Kate headed west down Santa Lucia Avenue; crossed Camino Real; then Carmel Street and San Antonio, before arriving at the fork formed where Santa Lucia meets Scenic Road. Scenic Road is appropriately if un-creatively named. Parallel to Scenic Road is a narrow, well-worn dirt path, the Bluff Path, just above the beach proper. Walkers not wishing or able to venture onto the beach can enjoy the view from a higher vantage point, on the path. There, Kate accessed the stairs closest to the southern end of the beach — one of numerous sets that provide visitors beach access.

There is a reward for daily walkers who arrive at the beach first. "First on the beach" carries little by way of glamour or even bragging rights — but it brings self-satisfaction, and enough gratification to evoke an inner smile. When passing a friend in town later that day, one might be tempted to smile and say, "first on the beach today," and earn a knowing nod from a previous trophy holder. Out the door at six o'clock today, a weekday, Kate anticipated being a contender for the award. As she skipped across the Bluff Path to the top of the beach stairs, she realized that she would be silver medalist today — the first loser, as some might taunt.

A dark figure emerged from the mist as the first light of the morning kissed the sand. Her heart jumped. It was Rob.

He was easily recognizable to her, even from a distance, by his slim, muscular build and purposeful stride. It's fascinating the way that you can recognize someone a hundred or more feet away, well before you can make out their facial features. The way we carry ourselves, the way we move, the way we walk and swing our arms, and the way our head cocks to one side or another, are all visual clues. It doesn't even matter if the person is headed toward us or away from us. Those movements are as distinct as a fingerprint.

Kate shouted to Rob and waved one arm, trying to capture his attention. "Hey. Hi! Hey!"

If he had heard her, he didn't acknowledge it. She was sure it was Rob, but, situated upwind, her voice got stopped short — bullied by the building offshore breeze. She walked at first and then initiated a trot down the stone stairs. At the bottom, she vaulted onto the sand. Kate strode purposefully, arms pumping rhythmically, in a trajectory she calculated would intersect precisely with his. He too appeared to have picked up his pace. She increased her pace, initiating a jog but stopping short of a full-on sprint. She wanted to catch him and talk to him again but didn't want to appear desperate, or, God forbid, look like a stalker. She remembered a movie from the early 1970s, *Play Misty for Me*. The film starred notable local resident Clint Eastwood and was filmed in Carmel as well as nearby Pacific Grove, Seaside, and Monterey. It was about a woman who becomes obsessed with Eastwood's character and stalked him. When her advances were rejected, she wished him harm. I won't give the rest of the plot away. A mischievous smile formed on Kate's lips. She might have been thinking about the flick. Kate promptly stopped running and resumed a more innocent pace.

"Hey Rob!" she shouted, from fifty yards away. This time, she caught his attention. He turned to see her waving. Rob tried his best to be cool and composed. Of course, their meeting wasn't the least bit accidental. Each of them had set out that morning hoping with all their hearts they'd intersect.

"Kate. Hi. I was just out for some exercise. Fancy meeting you here."

"You're full of shit. But I'm glad you are. How have you been?"

"Good, thank you. How about you?"

"Right now, I'm beat."

Two days before, Robert braved Carmel society, walked into town had had his first haircut by an actual stylist in over two years. He looked like the old Rob, but slimmer and more fit. He looked good. And, he looked considerably less despondent.

"Nice haircut. I hope you fired your last hairdresser," she quipped. Kate was less than subtle.

"With extreme prejudice," he stated. He was becoming used to her outspoken nature.

"Want to grab a tea this time — my place, perhaps?"

"Why don't we finish the workout by walking into town and get one there? I drink coffee, though."

"You might have to carry me the last block, but okay. Let's hoof it."

They exchanged pleasantries and frequent eye contact as they walked together to the north end of the beach and then headed toward town and its multitude of cafés. They huffed up the Ocean Avenue hill to the heart of the commercial center of Carmel. Each time he brushed against Kate, Rob felt an electrical charge. Rob was tempted to grab for her hand, but resisted, convinced that this whole "thing" with Kate was likely to be fleeting, at best. He walked gingerly over that tightrope between optimism and pessimism. He really had no expectation of what might develop.

At the café, one drink turned into three with no awkward moments in between. They took turns ordering and paying for drinks — she drank tea and he, black coffee — while the other anxiously waited. Both carried the conversation, and, as if by unspoken agreement, they avoided all discussion about their former partners. Even the occasional silences didn't feel uncomfortable. Kate launched her predictable salvo of questions in her genuine interest to learn more about this slightly mysterious man. Robert expertly deflected the questions he was uncomfortable with. Kate was consistent in her assertive and frequently sarcastic approach. The exchange might have compared to a tennis match between fierce competitors who both liked and respected one another. Coffee ended with a tie. The game resumed and match extended with relocation to a nearby restaurant for lunch.

"So, tell me about your place on Forest," Kate said. "How long have you been there? How come I haven't seen you at social functions around town? You said you love art. Are you a patron of the Carmel Art Association? There's a show there this week. Would you like to be my date?"

"That's quite the volley of questions," Robert said. "I've been on Forest for two years and a bit. After Jules's death. I've kept a low profile since then. Been a bit of a hermit, to be honest."

"I can understand that, given what happened to you."

"I had been thinking lately of going to the Art Association gallery, and even buying something new for my place. So, yes, perhaps we could arrange to meet for the next show."

"Oh goody!" Kate exclaimed. "A real date. And art", she added.

"Is *this* a date or another chance meeting? Is there a difference?" asked Rob.

"Yes and no?"

It was eleven-thirty and they had been talking, almost without break, for some five hours. It had been a marathon of a first date, but both enjoyed themselves. It was Rob's first time at The Forge. In fact, it was his first time at a restaurant in quite a while. He ordered an appetizer, two cold beers, a huge lunch, and something he had missed perhaps above all — ice cream —

for dessert. He thoroughly appreciated a real, chef-prepared hot, and cold, meal. Kate had a salad. When the server returned to check their progress, she reached in to take the plates. Rob's included some uneaten food. "Have you surrendered to the portions sir?" she asked with a grin.

"Yes, but can I get this packed up — to go?" he said.

"Of course. I'll be right back with it. Is there anything else I can get for you?"

"Uh huh. Can I get another burger? And can you wrap it in tin foil please?" She smiled and nodded. The bill, and her tip, just expanded. Rob looked at Kate. "Uh, I don't cook much for myself. This will be dinner tonight, or lunch tomorrow."

"That's a healthy appetite. You must have an amazing metabolic system or work out a lot. Or both. You eat very, um, well, but you don't have an ounce of fat on you. I'm envious!"

"I keep physically active. It's a lifestyle choice," he said, cryptically.

"You've seen my house now. When do I get to see yours?"

Rob froze. He'd known this was likely to happen and yet hadn't figured out a good way to deflect or avoid it. His fallback strategy was to end any progression of the relationship, if that's what was developing. There was no way that she would understand and accept who and what he was, he was convinced. Given that truth was not an option, he came up with what he thought was a convincing lie. "I'd love to show you around, but to be honest, the place is a shambles! It's under renovation, and even I have trouble getting to it — what with the equipment and fencing and doors boarded up. Total interior makeover. It was a complete shack, trust me. You'd have thought a hobo lived there. Please, let me show it to you when it's done. Okay?"

"That's crazy, Rob. I've renovated my home and had my friends through, to show them the progress. We are friends, aren't we? C'mon. Let's go see it."

"No, Kate. Seriously. I'd fear for your safety. I'm thinking of moving out myself for a while. At least until it's finished. Really. Think I'll shack up at a motel or something. I'd like to show you when it's done. A grand unveiling."

Kate pursued her lips, holding back any further comment or argument, as much as she wanted to argue, and ultimately get her way. She conceded, nodded and they finished their drinks: ending an otherwise perfectly good date. Ever the gentleman, Rob walked her home, and she offered a gentle kiss on the cheek in thanks. The to-go burger did not survive the trip back to the cabin. Rob wiped the juice from his mouth, on his sleeve, just before easing himself down into the ravine.

chapter **29**

Anyone who has spent even minimal time in a forest, wooded park, or their own back forty will have learned that sound takes on some strange qualities there. It's muffled, attenuated, and dispersed by the trees. It bounces around like a pinball and it's hard to determine exactly where it's coming from. Sound seems to come from nowhere and everywhere at once. It encircles you, tickles you, pokes at you, and then runs away. This makes it both delightfully fun and frustrating when you're playing hide and seek. Someone hiding can tease a searcher by shouting out, *"I'm over here!"* Usually the seeker remains confused and spins around, desperately trying to locate the source of the voice.

After two years, Robert sure knew his way around the forest, but he hadn't become any more skilled at pinpointing voices that rebounded off the surrounding pines and cypress. He could judge distance well by volume, but location remained hard to nail down. He had likewise learned where most people walked and eventually discovered that most of the time, they remained on the trails. This knowledge made him less anxious when he heard voices in his neck of the woods. There had never yet been a time when he felt the need to flee, or, God forbid, abandon the hut that he had spent so much time building. He had a plan. That plan was founded on concealment. He assumed that if he maintained his living roof coverage, didn't leave any equipment or supplies lying around outside the cabin, only used his stove inside the cabin, and employed his lamp sparingly, his home would continue to go undiscovered.

He had his multiple exit routes, but other than that, Robert didn't know what exactly he'd do if he or his cabin were ultimately uncovered. He had run across people many times over two years while walking in the Carmel Woods, but never in the gulley. Some eyed him with what seemed like a look of suspicion or concern. Other times, he passed hikers without incident. Some offered a polite "Hello," or, "Gorgeous morning to be in the woods." He'd nod his head or return the greeting but would never stop to engage.

He'd had a few awkward occurrences when he'd run into people in the depth of the woods while dressed in golf attire and Mulligan slung over his shoulder. He was certain that these encounters amounted to nothing more than a few stories shared among friends and neighbours that heightened the mystique and mythology of the "Hermit of Carmel." Robert grew to be somewhat amused by that, though he never thought of himself as such. Of course, they might have just considered him an eccentric golfer who lived nearby and frequently employed a shortcut to his favourite course. Maybe he was just "that weird guy." Everything would be fine for everyone involved if they didn't dig deeper, investigate, follow him, or find his cabin.

Robert's first real scare arrived in the form of two young and fearless boys. I suspect that ten-year-olds are the same everywhere in the world: irresponsible, adventurous, and curious. Every abandoned factory, every dark forest, every highway underpass, every deserted and derelict old house, to a ten-year-old, represents uncharted territory to be explored and discovered. That recklessness is magnified many times when you put two or more together. They feed off each other and dares are reinforced by double-dares.

Robert had returned to his cabin after his first dinner date at Kate's home. It was eight in the evening and the sun was already low. Rather than his usual ingress point south of the Carmel tollbooth, he continued on to 17-Mile Drive and entered the ravine from the southeast side. It was a far easier route than his typical one through the woods. Robert had been feeling less cautious — a by-product, perhaps, of his more positive perspective on life and optimism for the future. Perhaps, he was just getting sloppy.

It might have been an error in judgement to let down his guard, or just more shit luck. As he got closer to his camouflaged home, he could hear voices. Rather distinct voices. Not grown men's voices, but definitively male. Not able to gauge the exact location, Robert paced himself more cautiously as he entered the ravine — maintaining a 360-degree perspective by stopping and doing a little spin, every fifty feet. The voices were near, and that startled him, given his experiences of the past. He knew precisely the volume of speech used by walkers on the trails above the ravine. They were always muted. He could hear them but never understand specific words. *These* voices were much louder, and thus much closer. He could also understand the occasional word. The voices, quite suddenly, became muffled and then died off altogether. That confused Robert. He breathed a sigh of relief, concluding that the sound pattern was likely a trick of the trees and gently swirling wind. The site and the cabin exterior appeared normal, as he arrived, unlatched the door, and swung it open. Inside, it was a different story.

There they were: two boys who looked to be about ten years old. For several seconds, the two boys and Robert remained frozen — staring at each other, mouths agape. The wild of Robert's eyes, directed at the children, pierced the shadows of the poorly lit cabin. Abject fear filled the boys' hearts as they stood there, motionless and speechless. Robert was furious but didn't know what to do. He remained unmoving — an angry statue. The boys knew differently. The boys knew exactly what to do. They screamed. Screamed as though they were facing pure evil, intent on murder. Their screaming filled the cabin and, Robert was certain, all of Monterey County. It was deafening and echoed in his head for what seemed forever. The boys ran directly at Robert. Or so it seemed to him. In fact, they were trying to get past him, and out the door. It would be necessary, they might have thought, to save themselves from inevitable torture and death at the hands of the Madman of the Carmel Woods as he might have been named, by the boys, thereafter. They had *found* him, but had come to regret it — deeply.

Robert, wanting to avoid physical confrontation at all costs, rolled back on his heels defensively and promptly fell off the stoop at the cabin door. He landed hard on his back as the boys bowled him over on their way to safety. The fall knocked the wind out of him. The commotion and noise of the incident and its outcome seemed altogether one-sided. He still had not said a word. As he lay on the damp ground, trying to regain his breath, he could hear the boys yelling excitedly as they climbed the banks of the gulley to reach the plain above and, Robert assumed, take whatever path through the woods that brought them there.

Between his shock at being found, his surprise at the discovery of two kids literally inside his cabin, and now, not being able to breathe, Robert considered the event to be an altogether dismal way to end the day. They scared the shit out of him. Now that they were gone, he became even more fearful. *What's going to happen now? Try to think like a ten-year-old boy. It wasn't that long ago that you did the same thing, looking for adventure and trouble. Think!*

He picked himself up off the forest floor, and, brushing off his red golf slacks, noticed they'd split — a fatal tear, right in the worst place possible. After the momentary distraction, Robert began to panic as he pondered the worst-case scenario — regarding the boys, not the pants. But as the minutes passed, he began to settle and apply logic to the problem. He imagined one of two potential scenarios unfolding right about then. In the first, the boys would arrive back at their respective homes and immediately relate the incident and location of the cabin to their parents, who would promptly call the police to report it. In that scenario, he was screwed. He ought to grab what personal items he could carry in a knapsack and bail without delay. The police could arrive any minute. In the second scenario, he could stay put. When ten-year-old boys find themselves at the wrong end of a be-careful-what-you-wish-for moment, they clam up. They keep whatever they did, found or stole, and wherever they trespassed, secret. These adventures often form the foundation for lifelong bonds and friendships between boys. Adult golfers, who run from bears in their boxer shorts, don't always maintain a commitment to secrecy. In some ways, ten-year-old boys have a greater sense of discretion and can maintain secrets better than grown men. At that moment, Robert hoped with all his heart that the boys were exchanging pinkie swears or blood oaths to never mention what had just transpired to anyone — ever.

Robert hoped for the latter but decided that he needed to be more cautious. He changed his pants, grabbed his duffel and knapsack and quickly left the cabin. There was no telling what the outcome might be, or when or whether a parent or the police might visit. He had a couple of well-hidden "safe boxes" in the forest beyond the gulley. Some time ago, he had dug holes large enough to accommodate a plastic storage tote up to its lid. He had placed a two-inch-thick layer of moss over each sealed bin. In one tote, he had left some survival supplies (energy bars, a bottle of water, some toilet paper, a flashlight, a sweater, and his old bivy sack) for potential emergency situations like this. The other safe box remained empty, to accommodate anything that he might want to safely hide in the future.

Robert's imagination got the better of him and he opted to not spend the night in the forest. He envisioned a posse of wealthy and angry Carmel Woods residents with pitchforks and torches making their way through the woods, hunting down the freak who tried to kill their youngsters. He envisioned a police dragnet, complete with bloodhounds baying and straining their leashes as they picked up his scent. He feared shotgun-wielding police sergeants shouting out orders to "spread out and maintain formation." Robert's imagination proved as vivid as any ten-year-old's.

Darkness had overtaken the Carmel Woods, and Robert felt that his only viable option was to leave the forest and lie low to determine what, if anything, might happen next. If the police did come, he reasoned that they'd take the 17-Mile route to get to his cabin. He chose the alternative route and had to stumble through the dark forest until he exited near Carmel Way, headed down San Antonio. There, he enjoyed some degree of anonymity — just another walker out for an evening stroll. It was getting cool out and he realized that, in his haste to get out of the ravine, he had left his coat in the cabin. As he found himself getting closer to Kate's home on Carmelo, he felt a pull — both romantic and practical. He was cold and tired and needed the comfort and company of someone who cared for him. Rob continued directly to Kate's home. He tucked the duffel and knapsack on the outside of the garage side of her home, mounted the front step, and knocked on the heavy green door. The muffled sound of footsteps on the tile foyer floor inside triggered a sudden feeling of apprehension. He wondered if Kate might have company already. The door swung open. Robert had spent the last few hours in the dark, and the bright light of the foyer made him squint. He was relieved to see Kate standing there, smiling.

"Rob. Hi. Um, what a pleasant surprise. I didn't expect you. Got to get you onto those new things we call cell phones soon. But come in."

Rob looked to the street behind him to see if he had been followed, then stepped through the doorway. "Hey, Kate. I'm sorry to come here unannounced. To be honest, I enjoyed myself so much today, I wanted to see you again. I hope this isn't inappropriate."

"Of course. How sweet. I was just thinking about you too." Kate poked her head out and looked around before closing the front door.

"Where's your car?" she asked.

"I walked." In fact, he was still panting from his escape from the woods.

"Come to think of it, I haven't seen your car. What do you drive? Don't tell me, I'm sure it's something classic, like a vintage Porsche."

"Well, no. I *had* a Volvo. It was recently stolen, though, so I'm on foot. I should have mentioned it before. It's a bit of an inconvenience. I haven't bothered to go shopping for another yet."

"That's terrible. Stolen here in Carmel? There's been a rash of thefts, apparently — outsiders, no doubt. I want to go car shopping with you. C'mon in, silly."

They moved from the foyer to the great room. Kate had just started to pile kindling and some newspaper in the fireplace. Robert conducted a visual 360 of the living room. The choice of furniture and the décor is usually an accurate reflection of a person's life and style. This home's overall theme, or at least what he could see of it, was country cottage — appropriate for Carmel. The oak, cedar, stone, and leather gave the place a very woodsy feel that made Robert feel instantly comfortable. Kate's furniture was casual and relaxed. He felt he could replace his cot with Kate's sofa and be forever content. Original paintings, mostly oil and featuring land and seascapes of the area, drew Robert's attention. He wanted to believe that it was Kate who was the art aficionado, not her ex-husband. The stone fireplace was a work of art itself. Photos of Kate and her one child, a daughter, who attended college on the east coast, adorned the mantle and sideboard, on the adjoining wall. A grandfather clock in the foyer leading to the living room marked out the time in the otherwise quiet house with its gentle tick tock. Kate's calico cat entered the room and made a beeline for Robert's leg. It rubbed up against him like he was a lifelong friend.

Robert wasn't a cat guy but gave the feline a gentle pat anyway. On cue, the cat started purring like a John Deere mower. Kate could tell from watching him that Rob wasn't a cat lover. "You'd think I'd have a dog. This is a dog town. Everyone has a freakin' dog! I appreciate the subtleties of cats, though. They offset my own brashness and calm me," said Kate.

She crouched over the fireplace hearth and finished piling kindling. "It's getting cool, and I thought a fire would be nice. Now that you're back, it completes the picture, don't you think?" Kate stood and dusted the ashes off her hands.

Robert moved toward her, pulled her to his body, and kissed her full on the lips for the first time. Kate offered no resistance and responded by returning the favour. She upped the ante with an open mouth. He called her hand and added tongue and groping hands to the wager. All bets were off by then and they showed their cards. Inhibitions and clothing fell rapidly.

The fire never did get lit that evening. As every great relationship eventually does, Rob and Kate's connection ascended to another, more physical level. Two years of abstinence and sexual frustration were released that night too. The nickname *Wild Man* was adopted and uttered more than a few times. Kate, of course, had no idea how accurate she was. She, as it turned out, was unlike Jules — at least in bed. Robert thought about it and struggled to think of terms that defined how sex had been with Jules. The best he could come up with was *democratic* and *subdued*. It was good sex and deep, on an emotional and romantic level — just tame. Sex with Kate proved to be the opposite: authoritarian and wild. He was surprised and felt the slightest bit guilty about how much he enjoyed the difference. Kate told him everything she wanted, and demanded Rob tell her what he needed. If nothing else, this woman was a great sexual communicator.

Rob volunteered to make breakfast the next morning. Kate purred at the gesture. Her ex-husband, she informed him, had never made her breakfast. Rob hadn't used a real stove for a while and fumbled with the gas controls. After whipping up eggs for an omelette, he turned on the radio in the kitchen. Rob tuned into the local news to learn of anything that might have reflected his worst fears. Kate nuzzled him and whispered in his ear, suggesting he postpone the eggs and come back to bed to finish what he'd started. Just the act of offering to make breakfast was an aphrodisiac to her. He complied. His performance, however, suffered from distraction. Rob put back on his shorts and walked to the window, parted the heavy curtains, and gazed at the backyard garden.

"Something on your mind, lover?"

"Feeling just the slightest bit guilty, even though she's gone," he said. In fact, while he had had a few guilty thoughts about Jules, his true concern was about what might have happened, or might be happening, in the woods.

"I understand. Should I assume that I'm your first?"

He turned to her and offered a reassuring smile. "Yes. You are. I have no complaints whatsoever."

"Perhaps you should just come back to bed, lie back, and let court resume. The Honourable Judge Katherine Garvey presiding. Please take a seat, counsellor. Are you giving notice of objection?"

It was a cute metaphor. He took his best shot at playing the game. "If it pleases the court," he dutifully replied.

"Approach the bench, counsellor."

Rob returned, as instructed, to the side of the four-post, king-sized bed. "Requesting a sidebar with the judge." He kissed her deeply. "Objection?"

"Overruled," she said, catching her breath. "Will the defendant please rise," Kate instructed.

"I think I already have, Your Honour," Robert stated, quite accurately, as he looked down at his boxers.

chapter 30

After leaving the bedroom again, at one in the afternoon, Robert fulfilled his breakfast duties and served up some warm scrambled eggs and toast, chased with more coffee. Kate had to run to a monthly hair appointment and firmly kissed Robert goodbye.

"You're welcome to stay, Rob. You don't have to do any gardening, but I might when I return."

"I think I'll run home and see what damage they've done today," Robert said — the only one between them who understood the entendre.

"Toodles," said Kate as she dashed out the door to the 300D. The colour of the car matched her honey-blond hair perfectly.

Robert waited for the car to turn the corner. He dashed away, intent on returning to his cabin to check on its status. As he got close to his home site, he approached warily, listening carefully for danger. All appeared quiet in the woods. There weren't even any hikers, or, thank goodness, wayward boys. He could hear the occasional car pass on 17-Mile Drive, to the east of his camp in the gulley. He decided that the prudent thing to do was to conduct a full recce of the ravine. Forty-five minutes later, he returned to the cabin and checked, for the first time, to see if anything was missing.

Did the little buggers steal anything or take a souvenir?

Everything seemed to be in its place. After Robert had first heard them, the boys must have entered the cottage perhaps no more than a minute before he found them. Had he seen them go in, he might have hidden patiently and waited for their departure.

The outcome wouldn't have been any better — or worse, Robert convinced himself. If they hadn't been terrified by the unexpected meeting with the Evil Hermit, face-to-face, in the dark, they would have likely returned. The second time, they might have brought a cadre of other boys to show off their discovery — or, worse yet, brought parents… or police. The fact that all seemed so quiet, suggested to Robert that the boys had been scared to death by the encounter. Rather than feel guilty, Robert was relieved. He felt certain he had inadvertently spawned a blood brotherhood between the kids. Twenty years from now, over beers, they'd be telling their story of the Hermit and discovery of his cabin — filled with stolen jewels and the bones of young boys that came before them, exactly as they remembered it.

Robert felt cautiously optimistic that his secret home would remain so, at least for the time being. His enthusiasm for developments with Kate had begun to distract him too. He began to pay less and less attention to his cabin. It needed a good cleaning and some of his food had gone bad. It smelled, no doubt adding to the mythology Robert imagined the boys would construct — reinforcing a notion that bodies of dead children lay buried under the cabin's foundation. Robert had also become more lackadaisical about how, when, and where he entered and traversed the forest and ravine. It's hard to say, but maybe he had simply been emboldened by his own capabilities of stealth. Or, perhaps he was convinced of the apathy that residents might have had for his presence in the woods. He might have otherwise just become preoccupied by his budding relationship. It's also quite possible that Robert had already, by that time, made up his mind that he was ready to leave — to end a private and lonely existence to re-engage in society and live a more conventional life. Likely, it was a combination of all.

Robert was certain of Kate. He had fallen for her after their second, not-so-chance meeting. She was different from Juliana in so many ways. But, she also had some of the same qualities that he'd so valued in Jules: warmth, compassion, intelligence, and a very sharp sense of humour. Kate exuded a sexiness that Robert found intoxicating. She might have displayed a little pretension related to her wealth; her place in the pecking order and social strata in Carmel; and perhaps, even her own intelligence. But, she had never once behaved as if she knew she was undeniably and quite naturally beautiful. This was a relationship in which Robert wanted to invest, to ensure its momentum and success. He knew that he might have given her cause for suspicion or concern. After all, he had no car and had successfully deflected all efforts to prove ownership of a home in Carmel. The relationship was developing quickly. He felt an appropriate level of concern that he might get busted.

The first thing I need to do, Robert thought, *is get myself a cell phone. Everyone over the age of fourteen has one and I can't fake my way out of that for too long.* He grabbed his knapsack and wallet and tromped his way out of the woods and into the center of town — an exercise he had repeated many times before. He found a little shop that sold phones with a pre-paid option and enjoyed cell functionality within thirty minutes. *When did cell phones get so big?* He'd witnessed them go from small and light and then back to big again in the space of two and a half years. *Go figure.*

The first thing he did with the phone was to make a very difficult call to his mother and his sister. Tears ran down his cheeks as he dialled the numbers he'd memorized years ago. He knew how badly he must have hurt them. They might have thought he had died. He found a private corner in Devendorf Park, in

Carmel's downtown core, and sat on a bench. He shared his long and complicated story with his mother, whose tears likely matched Robert's drop for drop. She offered him sage advice. "Grieving requires work, Robert. Do the work."

"I thought I was."

"No, you've been running away from it," she said, from experience.

"It's been so hard Mom. I can't tell all I've been through."

"You know and love nature Rob, so I'll try a metaphor. Life can be seen like the growth rings on a tree. Each year in life is a ring. In good years, the ring is wide. In tough times, the annular ring is thin. But the tree grows regardless. A tree with thin rings grows the strongest. They're tough and resilient. You've had a couple of difficult years. I guarantee, though, that you've grown, and you will survive. Your roots. Your trunk, are sturdy."

Rob laughed. "That was the metaphor of all metaphors Mom. But thank you. Can't wait to see you again."

His call to his sister mirrored the previous call, tears and all. She offered to pick him up in Carmel. He politely declined but promised she'd be his first stop once he was back home. It was an emotionally draining morning on many levels — and for all.

Depleted, Robert found a diner in town, ate lunch, and fortified himself with more coffee. He agonized over what he might tell Kate, other than *prove* to her that he did, in fact, have a cell phone. Notwithstanding her compassion, he harboured uncertainty that she would accept the real Rob — the man who had lived in the forest for the last two years, eschewing most possessions, including a car. He now had a cell phone, so that was at least something *normal* he could confirm owning.

Disclosure might be best managed in small chunks. Robert called Kate on her cell. He had memorized the number, even if he had never called it. Kate answered. "Have you finished getting beautiful yet?" he teased.

Never having heard his voice on the phone, she failed to recognize Rob. "Who is this calling, please?"

"It's me. Rob. I found my phone. It had somehow fallen under my bed. I combed the entire house and finally found it. Hi."

"Welcome to the twenty-first century, mister. Now I can actually call you to check up on you. Now, we just need to get you a big-boy car."

"I'm not convinced I need a car. I did mention, didn't I, that I was an environmental lawyer? We tree-huggers advocate for public transportation use."

"Booooo. You need a car, Rob. How's your house coming along anyway? What's left to do? You're showing it to me this week. I insist!"

"I was just there. Everything looked like it was coming together. There were no, um...scares. The place is still a mess though. Meet back at your place for dinner or shall we eat out? I can cook if you want."

"Oh, let's eat out. You can pick the restaurant."

"Great. I've got some things to look after and we can connect later."

Kate and Robert's relationship continued to develop. They spent increasing time together, walking the beach, dining in town, attending a showing at the Carmel Art Co-op — all the things that adults do when they are early in a relationship, enjoying each other's company and figuring each other out. Their time together was spent either in town, or at Kate's house. Some nights, Robert would stay over, and other nights, he'd excuse himself and walk back to the cabin. He successfully maintained his secret life for a couple of weeks. At least he thought the act was convincing. With the cell phone, one small suspicion had, at least, been allayed. He was now available and able to communicate with Kate whenever she wanted.

Like in any budding relationship, the most awkward moment inevitably arose for Kate and Robert. I'm uncertain exactly when, conventionally, it should be laid bare, or, if a dating etiquette delineates the timing. Eventually, the dirty deed must be done.

"Rob, you've never talked about your family. Been very cagey about it. Do you have siblings? Parents? What gives? Do you hate them? Seriously. It's okay. I hate mine."

"I have a sister in Los Angeles."

"Now we're getting somewhere," Kate teased. "Tell me more. Are your parents still alive?"

"My mother is, yes. Yours?"

"Funny you should ask." She had set him up. "You're going to hate me. I've asked my parents to come for dinner tonight. I'd like for you to meet them. I know they'll like you. The truth is, they just *demanded* to come for dinner. I did *not* have a choice, so *you* do not have a choice. I've already told them about you, anyway. Just a little."

The trap was sprung. Robert stood, catatonic, as a man might having just heard the diagnosis — a terminal illness — from his trusted physician. Three words were all he could manage. "Your…parents? Tonight?"

Kate's hands could have done all the talking, but she continued. "They are overbearing bores. But they're my parents, for better or worse. The better part is my trust fund. The worse part will unveil itself tonight. If you do this, babe, I will play judge again tonight. I promise to find you guilty and dole out an appropriate punishment."

"Isn't dinner with your parents punishment enough?"

Somehow, he had gone from being a hermit in the woods to being an up-and-coming member of Carmel society — in mere weeks. It was surreal. He wasn't certain he was quite ready for it all. At the moment, he secretly wished to be back in his cabin, door locked, in the dark: a Pacific cyclone, thrown in for good measure, might have been acceptable. Meeting the parents of someone you are dating, no matter your age, might be the most stressful part of any developing relationship. *I'd rather tell her I live in a cabin in the woods than meet the parents.* He hadn't met anyone's parents since being introduced to Jules's some fifteen years earlier. It was one thing to hoodwink Kate about his fabricated life and fake home. Introducing two more people to the equation sounded like a recipe for disaster.

"I can't," Robert hastily and unequivocally stated. "I have to go to my daughter's piano recital."

"You don't have a daughter! That was pathetic. Surely you're a better liar than that."

"Indeed."

"They will be here at six. Gordon and Katherine. Yes, I am named after my mother. I am still Kate, the little girl. She is *Katherine.* Do *not* call her anything other than that. Please. She hates it. He is *Mr. Garvey.*"

"I'm thirty-six years old, Kate. Surely I can call him Gordon."

"You're only thirty-six? Holy crap, I'm robbing the cradle. I thought you were, like, mid-forties. Sorry. That came out wrong. Sorry."

"Well, how old are you?"

"A gentleman would never ask a woman that."

"I think you already answered my question."

"You're walking a very fine line, mister."

"I will require some serious fortification for tonight, Kate. Do you have any wine?"

"Is Gordon Garvey a misogynist? Yes, of course. In the fridge for white. The cabinet over there has a few bottles of red."

"Great," Robert said sardonically. "Where do they live?"

"Right here in Carmel. They have a home overlooking Pebble Beach. They moved here when they retired, to be closer to me. And, I'm sure, to exact their plan for perpetual torture. Trust me, I wanted some distance between us — a lot of distance."

"Really? What luck! Parents that live just around the corner," Robert said sarcastically. *I'm screwed*, he thought.

"Oh yes, I should warn you. He's also anti-Semitic. Hates Jews. You're not Jewish, are you? Shit. I'm sorry. That came out wrong. It doesn't matter if you are. It's my parents. They fluster me even when they're not here."

"No. I'm not Jewish. My grandfather, on my father's side, was Hindi. I'm not religious at all, really. Don't practice anything. I went to mass a few times every year, with Juliana. She was raised Catholic. Pour me a very large glass of sacramental wine please. Why does he hate Jewish people?"

Jules poured the wine to a level defined by etiquette and dodged the question. He knew it to be a rhetorical question anyway.

Rob motioned for a better pour. "No, no. That's not quite full. More, please. To the top. I'm not going to like him, am I?"

"No. You're not. Tell him you're a lawyer, though. He might like you better. Everything he cares about ends with a double-e: *degree, pedigree, admittee, trustee, licensee, invitee, vestee…*"

Robert jumped in to play along. "*Disagree…*"

"*Soiree*," Kate added, trying to end it on a positive note.

"*Arrestee?*"

"Okay, okay. That's enough. Daddy plays golf too. Talk about golf."

Robert and Kate both got mildly drunk as they prepared dinner together and playfully told embarrassing family stories. Rob, however, had to dig deep to find any negative things to say about his parents. He missed his mother deeply right then. The wine wasn't helping his emotional state much either. As the appointed hour of terror approached, Kate asked Rob to make a fire in the great room fireplace. He went to access the wood stacked outside on the far side of the garage. Picking out a selection of large logs, medium-sized sticks, and kindling, he cradled the pile of wood in his arms. He walked along the side of garage to cross the driveway, intent on going back in the front door — the shortest route to the great room. The cat had followed him out the front door and sat, dutifully, in front of the garage, watching him.

Looking up, Rob noticed a car rolling slowly down the road, directly toward Kate's house. It was immediately recognizable — a black Bentley without so much as a speck of dirt or a water spot. The obnoxious vanity plate confirmed it. He could read it as the car slowed to a stop and started a lazy turn into Kate's driveway. Rob's legs nearly buckled, his heart choked his throat, and this time, the flight instinct took over. He promptly dropped the armload of wood on the driveway. Backing away, he fled to the safety of the side yard by the garage as if escaping an angry black bear. At the sight of the car, the cat too wailed and ran for her life. She leaped the fence and disappearing into the bushes of the adjacent home. He wasn't certain if they had seen him or not, but Rob was sure it was them: the coiffed couple who had almost killed him. *They must have seen me*, he convinced himself. *Did they see me? What the hell do I do now?*

Kate's words rang in his ears. They hadn't even gotten out of the car and the *worse* part had already been unveiled. *If there is a God, they are not Kate's parents. Just use the driveway to turn around and go back the other direction…If they are her parents, and they don't recognize me, I will go to mass every Sunday! Please, God.* Robert had, once again, found religion. We all do, in the toughest times. This was arguably tough.

The sound of the heavy Bentley doors closing were felt as much as heard — *thunk, thunk.* From his vantage, pressed up against the side of the garage, knee-deep in the bushes, he listened. He heard men's dress shoes and women's heels click up the driveway and pause.

"What the hell is all this wood doing here? It looks atrocious!" he heard Gordon…*Mr. Garvey*…bellow.

The sound of the front door opening, and Kate's less than sincere but cheerful greeting made Robert tremble.

"What's all that firewood doing on the driveway?" Kate said, repeating Mr. Garvey's question almost verbatim. "Robert? Where are you? Mother and Father are here. Robert?"

Robert gained sufficient composure to shuffle out from behind the garage, convinced that he couldn't avoid the inevitable forever. *Just pull the Band-Aid off quickly,* he told himself. It was then that he had an epiphany. *Tell them you're a Jew and the evening will end right here and now.*

Robert stepped out from behind the garage and waved his hand tentatively. "Hello. Um, the cat got caught in the fence and I had to go rescue him. Thought he was a goner. I'll meet you inside in a moment." He waited a terrifying moment for Mr. and Mrs. Garvey to recognize him. But Kate, Katherine, and Mr. Garvey simply walked into the house and left the door open for Robert to follow. He was tempted to light the Bentley on fire with the sticks, but prudence demanded another, subtler tactic. "Let me pick up this wood and I'll be right in."

Rob collected then dropped the logs and kindling at the fireplace, brushed of his hands and stood, waiting for the awkward introduction.

"Mother, Father, I'd like you to meet a very special friend. This is Robert."

The Garveys approached Robert tentatively.

"Hello," said Katherine, as she held out a limp hand — one of those terrible, half-hand, doll-like shakes that some people offer. Her grey hair had been covered up by abundant salon colour and pulled back in a tight ponytail. She looked to have once been a striking woman. Unwilling to give in to age gracefully, she had chosen to embrace the unpredictable outcomes of multiple plastic surgery procedures. It showed. Now she looked gaunt and stretched. Katherine Garvey said nothing more.

"Katherine, don't monopolize the man's time. Go fetch me a drink." He turned to Rob. "I am Gordon. You can call me Mr. Garvey."

Garvey was barrel-chested, and although in his seventies, still intimidating. He appeared taller than he seemed during their first interaction. Garvey could have been cast in any war movie as the tough, retired, decorated General. Robert was grateful there hadn't been a physical confrontation. Like Mrs. Garvey's, his hair appeared to be coloured. It had a most unappealing tint of yellow. His skin lacked pigment. He was ghostly white. If Garvey hadn't been conscious, and speaking, Robert might have mistaken him for a cadaver in an open casket funeral. Kate's father also wore a perpetually perturbed look on his face, making him appear altogether unapproachable. I expect he had friends. If so, they must have grown accustomed to his persona or seen something more likeable in him. Garvey inspected Robert with squinted eyes for some time, as one might a used car, and finally thrust his hand toward him. Robert tried his best to hold his shit together but fulfilled the obligatory, manly double-pump. *I think he recognizes me. How do I shut this down? Should I? Do I dare?*

"Shalom. Pleased to meet you. I'm Robert Goldstein," said Robert, doing his best to maintain a serious face.

The look on Garvey's face was priceless. He abruptly dropped Robert's hand and donned a grim scowl. It was obvious. The man had no subtleties — or filters.

Kate interjected quickly. "He's kidding, Daddy. He's got such a great sense of humour. A real comedian he is." She shot Rob a look.

"His last name is *Das*. That's Indian, right? He's a lawyer, Daddy. Or, was a lawyer, I should say. He's retired already. How about that?" Kate was struggling. Rob shouldn't have done that to her. But the temptation had been just too great.

"You don't look like an Indian. What tribe are you from?" questioned Garvey.

"Tribe?"

"Yes. What Indian tribe?"

"Not native American Indian. India. The subcontinent. My grandfather on my Dad's side came from India. Punjab, specifically. My Grandmother was from the UK. Guess that makes me a half-breed."

"Hmmmm… indeed. A lawyer, you say. Well, well. I'm impressed. I am quite certain that we have met before, Robert. I can't place you, but I am sure of it." He shook his head gently, as if to shake the memory free. "It will come to me soon enough. Carmel is a small community. Perhaps golfing. You do golf, don't you?"

"Yes sir. I play here and there. Everywhere, actually."

"Well then, we must get out one day. I belong to Cypress Point. And you?"

"Kate, do we have more wine?" Robert shouted to Kate, who had abandoned him to check on dinner. "Kate!"

"I don't understand your attempt at humor, though." Gordon looked over his glasses at Robert and asked him, in a more hushed tone. "Do you like Jews?"

Robert, gaining some liquid confidence, gathered his breath and responded. "I like anyone, Mr. Garvey, of any gender, race, religion, or cultural persuasion, who doesn't advocate killing people who do not subscribe to their belief system. That's who I like." He added, "I am unaware of any Jews who have embraced suicide bombings, beheadings, vehicular attacks, or hijacking of commercial airliners to make a religious or political statement."

"Indeed," said Garvey. "They use the monetary and political system to achieve their insidious objectives."

Robert stared at him blankly for a few seconds and then said: "But idiots come in all shapes, sizes, races, and colors, Mr. Garvey. I don't give *any of them a pass on bad behavior.*"

Garvey produced a most unsettling scowl. It made him even more unattractive.

"I'm told you've enjoyed tremendous financial success in business, Mr. Garvey," Robert said in a valiant effort to change the subject and avoid a full-blown war. "Perhaps after dinner, you can detail for me your philanthropic contributions. I'd love to hear your position on the need to support and save our diminishing wildlife habitat, or, say, for solving homelessness."

"Why don't you two jaw about golf?" Kate shouted from the kitchen.

Garvey did that squinting thing again. Katherine entered the great room. Kate followed her and gave Rob the "*I'm so sorry*" look.

"Dinner is served," said Katherine softly.

"There you go again, woman, interrupting me as I was having a conversation. Jesus H. Christ!" bellowed Garvey.

Robert and Kate hung back for a moment as Katherine and Garvey shuffled to the dining room, Garvey still grumbling. Rob whispered into Kate's ear. "Please tell me you're adopted."

"I wish I were. I'm afraid to wade into my own gene pool."

"And what is with your mom?" Robert asked.

Kate looked suddenly sober. "I haven't figured out, yet, if I have inherited and adopted my father's loud and unfiltered voice, or if I'm simply speaking up on behalf of my mother. Both possibilities bother me."

She looked away. Her eyes were red and swollen with tears. She fought their release like a champ. A look of sadness over her long-term, emotional estrangement from her parents, remained painted on Kate's face. There was a chink in this tough, independent woman's armor and Robert had just found it. He knew better than to say anything more about her parents. Leaning in, he gave her a gentle kiss on the forehead — all she needed, right then.

Quickly regaining her composure, Kate announced, "Who is ready for some delicious pork roast?"

"You know I can't eat pork," declared Rob. "It's not kosher." It was an unnecessarily provocative comment, but he couldn't resist one last shot at Garvey.

Garvey looked up at the two in horror. Kate didn't know if she should stab Rob with the carving knife or laugh. She found a happy medium by punching him hard in the bicep, shaking her head, and offering a peacekeeper's smile.

chapter 31

Robert and his relationship with Kate survived her parents' visit — but only just. In dating terms, they hovered between life and death, at least for that one night. The next day was spent recovering emotionally and reconnecting. Robert, however, was forced, again, to defend his decision to delay a tour of his home. That evening, after a quiet, late dinner, Rob and Kate drove to the beach. It was not far, but they were both feeling lazy and it had been threatening rain all day. They hoped to get in a lap of the beach before the clouds opened. As anticipated, no more than ten minutes into their walk, it started to pour. They sprinted for Kate's vintage Mercedes Benz, parked on Ocean Avenue. Safely tucked inside, they kissed as the rain drummed on the car's roof.

Kate pulled away briefly. "Oh, I forgot, babe. I've got to get out early in the morning. I have to drive up to San Francisco to see my lawyer. Divorce stuff. You won't want to be there. Trust me. I don't want to be there! Don't hate me, but, can I just drop you off at your place?"

"Sure. I'll make it easy for you. I'm going to go grab a coffee in town anyway. I'll say goodbye here and we'll catch up later this week." It was the best excuse Rob could come up with to avoid the while house issue.

"What do you mean by later this week? And don't be silly. It's pouring out! Let me at least drop you off at the coffee house."

"I didn't want to presume that you were available all week, or that you wanted to see me every day. That's all. And thank you for the offer of a ride."

"Rob. Something's been bugging me, and I need to talk about it. Are we dating exclusively? Are you seeing someone else?"

The frequency and magnitude of Kate's hand gestures, Robert had discovered some time ago, were directly related to the level of passion she held for the topic of dialogue. Now, her body language and waving hands reflected the seriousness of her distress.

"No. I'm not seeing or dating anyone else. Yes, I'm seeing you exclusively. Is that what you want? Why do you ask?"

"I don't know. Well, no. I *do* know. I'm not beating around this any longer. I feel like you're hiding something from me. Not telling me the whole truth. I'm sorry, but that's how I feel. You won't even show me your home. How are we supposed to move forward if we maintain secrets? You've got to be honest with me. It's not fair."

Robert felt backed into a corner, with few options for escape. He chose the only one that had worked in the past — deferral. "I don't know what to say, exactly. I hate that you feel this way and that I've somehow given you reason to doubt. You're just on your way home now. Can we discuss this tomorrow, when you're back?"

"Sure," she said, sounding unconvinced. "I'll call you when I get back."

She drove up Ocean Avenue and stopped off in front of the café. They engaged in a tentative kiss goodbye. When he had one foot out the door, Kate grabbed him by his shirtsleeve and yanked him forcefully back into the car. His head hit the roof on his way in.

"Damn. Shit, that hurt. What?" he asked, rubbing his head.

"You're not listening to me, Rob," she shouted, quite unexpectedly. She was pissed. Her hands, gesticulating wildly, matched the intensity of her emotion. "Do *not* blow me off with that bullshit, passive-aggressive stay of execution! If you're not into this relationship, or if there's someone else, just say so right here and right now! I'm a big girl."

Rob was taken aback. He had limited experience in relationship fights. "Kate. I don't want this to end. I can't explain what's happening, right now. I swear. I will explain everything soon. It's complicated." He meant it, even if his defense was unconvincing.

Kate glowered at Rob. She looked like she wanted to punch him in the face. "Go then. Leave. Go do or see whomever you want in the coffee shop. I'll see you later. Fuck!"

Rob got out, fully and safely this time. He gingerly touched the growing goose egg on his head as he closed the car door. Kate drove off slowly, watching him out of the rear-view mirror as he entered the shop. Then, as Rob was waiting for a latte, she did something not entirely unexpected. She drove by a second time. Through the glass front of the shop, while distorted by the cascading rain, he saw her cruise past. The car was unmistakeable, her rationale obvious. Kate's suspicions had increased, even as their relationship had grown and an emotional bond had been cast. He felt horrible. It was his fault, not hers.

The coffee that evening, though hot, rich, and black, was unappealing. It turned cold as Rob alternated between staring at the cup and the rain on the window. The café was quiet; few people were braving the horrendous weather to fulfill their java fix. An online music service served up an acoustic playlist in the background. One song slapped Robert in the face: "*The Great Pretender*," by The Platters. It was disturbingly coincidental. The significance was, of course, lost on the other patrons remaining in the café.

Robert left an almost full cup of coffee and departed the café. Pulling the hood of the jacket up to shed the rain, he started back toward his cabin. His legs felt heavy, reflecting the weight of his concern as he continued the familiar route back to his home. There was no enthusiasm or resolution in his stride. He looked like a man headed to the gallows. To further his anguish, Robert had begun to truly and passionately dislike the cabin and the dank ravine in which he had made his home. He felt smothered by the forest and claustrophobic in the cabin. He had started to despise the cold and damp and resent the dark. After enjoying Kate's comfortable, king-sized bed and down comforter, he loathed the horribly uncomfortable camp cot propped up on wooded shipping boxes. Even the sound of rain pinging against his sheet steel roof, which he used to enjoy, irritated him and kept him awake. A taste of creature comforts had spoiled him in a matter of weeks, and that irritated Robert. He wished he were in bed with Kate at that very moment, the sound of a crackling fire emanating from the great room down the hall, the cat curled up at their feet. Real life. He missed real life.

Robert made his way, grudgingly, through the trail in the woods, and down the steep banks of the ravine — diagonally, so he wouldn't fall on the rain-slicked slope. He stopped twenty feet away from the cabin behind a thick tree and listened: his newly adopted protocol for safety. If he didn't hear anything for several minutes, he'd approach the site and enter his cabin. Everything appeared to be normal, so he proceeded. After removing his waterlogged jacket, Robert sat down hard on his cot and buried his face in his hands. Kate's behaviour had been unsettling, though he couldn't blame her.

I'm crazy, he thought. *This is crazy. Everything about me is crazy.*

Rob resolved then and there to move out of the woods. Kate had become just too important for him. He would move out and then tell her. She'd understand and forgive him for the lie about living on Forest Road, wouldn't she? It had been so hard to sustain the lie and it had been eating at him for weeks. He was certain it would catch up with him sooner than later. He had to come clean.

In the dim light from the propane lantern, Robert began to gather up the clothing that had lying about the cabin and hung from twig coat hooks. He jammed them all into the large duffel. He would find a motel at first light and check in. Having already told Kate about moving out, he'd have an excuse for doing so. Rob had already shared that "plan" with her — albeit as part of a greater deception that he had created. He'd figure out a way to tell her everything else later. He just needed to get the hell out of the shack in the woods and into someplace *normal*.

Out of the corner of his eye, he caught a glimpse of a light's flash through the one window in the cabin. At first, he thought it was lightning. Then it flashed again: too long to be lightning. It was a light — a flashlight. Someone had entered his ravine. They'd found him. *Those little bastards*, he thought, *ratted me out. What ever happened to the sanctity of the pinkie swear?* Truth was, Robert had no idea who might be headed his way — police, city officials, the parents of the boys. Robert sneaked toward the window and peeked out to see if he could estimate the number of men headed his way. The light bounced off the trees and presented a confusing target. It appeared to be just a single beam. *One person? You think one person can take me down?* He was slightly insulted.

Deep anxiety gripped Robert as he struggled to decide his move. *Do I bolt and run? Do I leave my stuff?* Determined to avoid another confrontation, he made the decision to bolt. He knew the woods better than anyone and could evade the most experienced and fleet police officer, under cover of darkness. As he moved rapidly to the door, he caught the bracelet of his Rolex on one of the clothes hooks he had jammed between planks. Distracted by the seriousness of the moment, he hadn't noticed. Rob's Rolex fell to the floor, clasp broken, the watch otherwise in one piece.

He was too late. As he opened the door, Robert found himself paralyzed by a single bright beam that fell directly on him, from close proximity. The light blinded him. He couldn't see who it was but recognized the voice instantly.

"Rob?" She said just one word but did so emphatically and resolutely. Never had a single word contained so much meaning and finality.

Rob stood in place, immobilized by the light. "Kate? Please, let me explain."

She held the light on him for another moment before turning and heading in the direction from which she had come.

"Kate!" Robert made one last attempt to get her attention. "There's a great story behind all this! A real story. Trust me."

The artificial light bounced, playing off the trees and branches, as Kate fled the forest. He sensed that the beam remained fixed and unmoving for a moment. Robert watched, hopeful and then, crestfallen. The light flickered again, faded, and then disappeared altogether as she headed south through the ravine. It seemed evident she had followed him through town and into the woods. Rob was numb. The loss was sudden and unexpected. It cut deeply.

chapter **32**

In the absence of someone who cared about him, Robert lost the positive psychological momentum that he seemed to have developed after meeting Kate. While he still planned to move out of the woods, it didn't feel as urgent. He felt miserable. Thankfully, he did find his Rolex, lying wounded on the cabin floor, the next morning. That was one small consolation. He picked it up and inspected the damage. It was minor — a broken clasp. The inscription on the back of the watch remained well defined and as meaningful as the day it was gifted. *Jules,* he thought, *never would have left me here. She would have understood and accepted me for what I am.* There was a watch repair shop in Carmel. He thought he might leave it with them, someday. In the meantime, he laid it carefully on his bedside table. It was the first time it left his wrist.

Robert's emotional state began to slip its clutch: it rolled backward. Maybe he was just acting like men do when they get dumped. He sulked. Frustrated, he paced in circles around his cabin, like an animal stuck in a cage. His disdain for the woods and growing nonchalance for maintaining secrecy manifested itself in odd ways. He dragged Mulligan and a bucket of orange range balls outside.

"Hey, anybody want to come play golf with me?" he exclaimed loudly. Every shot he set up — each chip and drive — he described and delivered audibly, in third person, with the tone and style of a television golf commentator.

"Welcome back to the Carmel Woods invitational. This is an interesting story, folks. Robert Das, back after a prolonged absence from the game — and by game, I mean real life — is tied for first. He's a local amateur and never considered a real challenger here. But the locals love him. Everyone loves the underdog. He steps to the box at the sixth. It's a short, dark, and technically challenging hole, blocked by almost complete tree coverage, with a thin wedge of open light through which players must carefully place their drive."

Robert dropped an orange ball on a flat section of open forest floor, close to his cabin.

"Well, this is unconventional. Das has chosen to try the long game. Looks like he's got a fairway driver. Most would choose an iron with loft: at least a 7, to clear the trees. Das is a gambler."

Robert drove a ball off the floor of the forest. The ball ricocheted off a tree with a tremendous *knock*. The sound echoed throughout the ravine. He struck another. It, too, failed to achieve orbit. His third ball miraculously threaded the needle of trees to find sky. It escaped the forest, sailing toward the neighbourhood beyond. The ball disappeared beyond his sightline.

"Fore!" Rob shouted, thoughtfully. "Fuck you all!" he added, less politely.

His cry got mixed up and muddled by the tree coverage and walls of the ravine. Only crows called back as they took to flight. Like submarine sonar, each strike of the club sent out a loud and distinct ping as Robert attempted to communicate his emotions though golf. Any amateur psychologist could have made the diagnosis. He felt isolated and didn't want to be a hermit anymore. Professionals call it autophobia — fear of being alone.

The bucket of balls drained, and tournament now finished, Robert sat on a fallen tree. He failed to place among the leaders and was out of the money. His lead had been squandered.

After a day, Robert settled. He also swallowed his pride and wrote, or, to be accurate, texted a long note to Kate. He did his best to explain what he had been through over the last couple years, and why he had lied to her. He admitted his struggle with mental health — depression, specifically. He copped to every falsehood, including the Volvo, which wasn't completely a lie. He told her that he had fallen desperately in love with her and wanted to remain in Carmel to be near her, somehow, some way. Otherwise, he said, he would return to Los Angeles to rebuild his life.

Rob never expected a reply and never received one. Satisfied that he had at least made the effort, he did his best to move on. He surprised himself with the emotional strength that he seemed to have conjured. The loss of Juliana had been survivable and he knew that, ultimately, he could endure this too.

In the meantime, Robert returned to his typical morning procedure. He chose to wash in the bathrooms at the end of Ocean Avenue. They were closer, but mostly he hoped to avoid an awkward encounter with Kate. He was certain that she would, likewise, seek to avoid a chance collision. That thought saddened him, as true as it likely was. His routine had once again become… routine. This morning, with a pack on his back and water jugs in hand, Robert started his tedious return to the Woods.

Halfway back, Robert instinctively cocked his wrist, to check the time, overlooking the fact that he was temporarily watch-less. The sun was gaining height. Robert was running late and wanted to get home to pack his duffel and knapsack with his few possessions. It was time to leave Carmel for good. He had investigated bus schedules the previous day. A bus, he learned, ran from San Francisco, with route stops in Monterey and Carmel, on its way to Los Angeles. That, or he could hitchhike. Other than tourists, nearly everyone heading south from the peninsula is destined for greater LA. There's not much between. The only thing that Robert wanted to accomplish, before he departed, was to get in one last hole or two at Poppy Hills. He had been waiting for a fair morning, and the impetus to get up at five a.m. *Tomorrow*, he thought, *will be the day.*

Picking up stride, and buoyed by thoughts of a new start, Robert chugged along his typical path, along North San Antonio. He was just about to enter the woods when the sound of an emergency vehicle siren split the tranquility of the forest fringe. The sound arrived suddenly. It surprised him, making him involuntarily flinch and drop his water jugs. The jugs split and their contents oozed across the blacktop. He spun to see a police car, lights blazing, no more than ten feet behind him. Robert recognized the overzealous, Ray-Ban-aviator-wearing cop behind the wheel at once. His previous experience had not been constructive and he had no expectations of a positive outcome this time. As soon as Torres exited the police vehicle and tore the sunglasses off his face, Das knew it was bound to be another long day. Torres had rage in his eyes as he strode aggressively toward the Hermit, one hand resting atop his holstered sidearm for added intimidation. This time, Robert initiated the exchange, hoping to defuse whatever might have set off the officer.

"Officer Torres, so pleased to see you again. I trust you are well."

"I knew you were trouble when you walked into this town."

"Big Taylor Swift fan, are you?"

"What? Don't you dare disrespect the law."

"You're a cliché, Officer Torres."

"And you are a parasite, Das. Everyone else in Carmel has worked hard to live here. You. You only take. I checked your LA address. You don't live there anymore. In fact, we could find no fixed address for you. You are just another homeless guy looking for a handout — to take from others."

"And in your tiny mind, anyone who has no fixed address is a criminal?" The comment, Robert realized seconds later, was more antagonistic than he intended. He wished he could retract it but braced for the reaction.

"In this case, yes," said Torres. "We received a complaint a few weeks ago about a man fitting your description, who vandalized a local resident's car. I'm taking you in, asshole." Torres was livid. The blush on his face reflected the rage that must have burned inside.

"*Asshole?* Who are you, Dirty Harry? What kind of police etiquette is that?"

The three options available to Robert were again open for consideration: take a car ride, lawyer his way out, or run. The ride, of course, would take him straight to the police station. The lawyer routine worked well last time. But he *had* deflated the tires on the Bentley, so it was quite possible the police had him dead to rights this time. He had briefly forgotten about that little adventure. The Garveys might have produced evidence in the form of home security video footage. He had no way of knowing. Running got the vote this time. Robert bolted, dropping his knapsack. Officer Torres anticipated his move to the safety of the forest and immediately placed himself in the path between the road and woods. Robert stopped instantly, weighing his alternatives. Torres and Das both froze, legs a-splay and arms hanging by their sides, staring at one another like gunslingers, waiting for the other to make a move.

Torres drew first. By that, I mean he blinked. Literally. He blinked several times in quick succession. The next scene played out in slow motion from Robert's perspective. Torres's right hand moved up to his mid-chest. It scared the hell out of Robert and he unconsciously flinched. For a second, he thought Torres had drawn his sidearm and was going to shoot him. Torres did not un-holster his gun. He might have been motioning to retrieve the remote microphone, integrated with the squad car radio, dangling below his neck. His right hand grabbed a handful of fabric in the front of his black, short-sleeved uniform. A look of fear and significant discomfort flooded Torres's face. The wince on his face spoke volumes. He was not well. Robert witnessed Torres's eyes roll back in his head and his head slump forward to his chest. Torres dropped, like a sack of rocks, onto the soft shoulder of the road where he had taken his stand. Torres hit the ground hard, on his side, and did not move. Robert heard a slight groan but that was all. The officer was still — possibly dead. He certainly looked dead.

"Holy shit!" Robert didn't whisper. It was more an involuntary shout — a normal reaction by anyone watching the event unfold.

Stunned, Robert spun around, thinking Torres had been shot — the sound of the crack muffled by the wind. If so, the shooter must have done it from behind. Robert turned in a slow circle, not certain what had just taken place or who else might have been witness. The street was silent. Robert stood, dumbfounded, staring at the police officer, not knowing what he should do next. Running seemed to be a reasonable option. He was, for all intents, free to do so. He had dodged likely arrest and could either hide in the woods or leave town immediately. The questions taunted Robert. *Did Torres call in the stop, or did he just roll up and jump out to make his big collar? Will I be accused of manslaughter? Should I stay? Should I run? Should I help Torres? What are the consequences of staying?*

Robert made his decision. He ran. He ran directly to where Torres was lying, in the grass, just beyond the shoulder of the road. With considerable effort, he turned the officer over on his back. The Ray-Bans that lay beneath him were bent. Robert checked to determine if Torres was breathing. The officer was, but with inconsistent, shallow breaths. *This man is dying*, Robert knew for certain. *I'm not a doctor. I'm a lawyer. What do I do?* On the edge of a panic attack, Robert's heart rate climbed as he struggled to gain enough composure to save the man.

He had no formal first aid training, but, like so many, had seen it in movies and television. *Okay*, Robert thought, *I think you check for blockage of the airway first.* He pried open the officer's mouth and peered in, not sure what to look for. He wasn't certain if he had swallowed it, but Torres's tongue appeared curled, deep at the back of his mouth. Robert reached in with two fingers and scooped it forward, as a precaution. He leaned in to listen again. Breathing was slow and shallow, still. He moved his hand down to Torres's wrist and checked for a pulse. It, too, was low and sporadic. *This man is having a heart attack*, Robert convinced himself. He grabbed the microphone hanging from Torres's uniform and keyed the button. The radio, he assumed, connected him to some disembodied voice at police headquarters.

"Hello. Hello. Can anyone hear me?"

He heard nothing. Realizing his thumb was still pressing the talk button, he repeated his call and left the button up.

"Christ! Somebody answer. Now!"

"Carmel Police dispatch."

"Hello. Please, I need help. Officer down." *That's what they say in the movies.* "Please send help now. Shit! Can anybody hear me?"

"Carmel Police dispatch. Please identify yourself and your location."

"My name is Das. I'm at the corner of San Antonio and Second Avenue. Police Officer Torres is down. I think he's had a heart attack. I'm right here with him. You need to send an ambulance right now. Hurry."

"Ten-four. I mean, affirmative. I acknowledge and will dispatch police and ambulance to the scene immediately. Is the officer breathing? Does he have a pulse?"

"Barely. Very lightly. A little gasping. I don't really know CPR, but I can try it. I think I know what to do. Should I try?"

"Affirmative. I can walk you through."

Robert ripped the officer's shirt open, sending the buttons flying in all directions. Below that, the ballistic vest frustrated his efforts to begin emergency aid. He had no idea how to get it off. Ripping the shirt further, Robert could see the Velcro straps attaching the vest at the shoulders and those holding it at the waist. He tore at them and peeled the vest away from Torres's chest area.

The dispatcher attempted to teach the basics of CPR over the radio. "Place two fingers on the spot where his ribs join, in the center of his chest. Use the heel of one hand with the other hand stacked on top of it. Lace your fingers together." She continued the instruction at a pace that Robert struggled with.

"Thirty compressions. Two breaths. Once second each. Got it." He stopped listening and focused on the job.

He leaned over Torres and started the resuscitation attempt. He pumped and delivered a life-saving breath into Torres's open mouth. Robert did his best to put fear aside to save Torres — at least until professionals arrived. It seemed to take forever.

Where the fuck are they? This guy is going to die if they don't get here soon.

Robert took a second to wipe the sweat from his stinging eyes. He continued CPR and mouth-to-mouth resuscitation in sequence at an unrelenting pace. Torres moved slightly beneath him, partly raising one arm, grasping at the invisible, before it dropped again. Robert leaned in, relieved to hear him breathing somewhat freely.

In the distance, Robert was reassured by the increasingly loud sounds of sirens zeroing in on them. Police, ambulance, fire — they would soon all be converging on his location momentarily, he anticipated. Once again, every instinct screamed, *Bail to the woods now!* He didn't. Robert waited and sat beside the officer, listening to his labored breathing and checking his pulse.

The sirens were deafening in the quiet of this corner of Carmel. A police car arrived first. It roared down the street and screeched to a halt, the siren tailing off and lights left flashing. An officer leapt from her car and raced to the grassy shoulder where Torres was laying, Das crouching beside him.

"What the hell happened here? Who are you?" she exclaimed. She looked as scared as Robert.

"Nobody, really. Um…Officer Torres stopped to say good morning. We were having a spirited conversation about, um… politics, when he collapsed. I called you guys immediately."

"Stand back, please, sir. And remain on site. Someone will need to get your statement shortly."

"I'm not going anywhere," Robert said. 'Let me know when you need me."

She was all business. No *"thank you, sir."* The police officer knelt beside Torres. He was unconscious but alive. She leaned in to listen as Torres struggled to breathe regularly. As she reached to check his pulse, EMS pulled up. Two first responders rushed to their side. Some sixty seconds later, a fire truck also arrived on scene. Two more police cars added to the increasingly chaotic site. With an officer of the Carmel Police Department down, all responders were focused on Torres. No one else said as much as a word to Robert. By that time, they might have assumed him to just be another among the group of residents who had started to gather, to investigate the commotion.

Robert shuffled slowly backward, foot-by-foot, and farther and farther away until, once again, he found himself positioned on the fringe of the forest. Convinced he'd done the right thing, but could offer no more, he made the decision to leave. Das disappeared into the woods with the subtlety of a skittish fawn. The last thing he heard was a paramedic yell, "Clear!" as they deployed the portable defibrillator. A hundred yards into the forest, he heard the ambulance siren begin to wail again. It was mobile and bound for the hospital. Officer Torres, he presumed but could never confirm, might survive to live another day. *Uncommon*, he thought, *that a man of that young age would have a heart attack. But he was a tense, tightly wound guy.*

chapter 33

As the sun rose, Robert lay in his cot, struggling to shake his torpor and rise. Insomnia left him with a hangover far worse than any induced by booze. His confrontation with Torres the previous day haunted him. The scene played in his head so many times. Snatching his Rolex from the nightstand, he watched the time pass throughout the night: 11:30, 1:42, 3:10, 3:55, 4:28, 5:16, 6:40. Sunrise.

While there was no love lost between Robert and the police officer, Robert had to acknowledge that he didn't really know the man. *He could be married and/or have children. He's someone's son. Somebody's brother, perhaps. The officer could have saved the lives of others — even the injured driver in a car wreck on the highway.* Torres's family and the local police fraternity were likely shaken by the medical emergency. Robert had been through it. They likely received an unexpected call and converged on the emergency department, anxiously awaiting the word of a kindly physician with some positive news. Rob had no way of knowing if Torres had survived. Hopefully, his young age and strength proved helpful. He wasn't looking for recognition, but Robert also wondered if Torres might ever find out who had come to his aid, assuming he survived and recuperated. Regardless, Robert was confident — even proud — he had done the right thing.

In the meantime, Robert focused on a strict adherence to a plan and schedule, despite his fatigue. Today, that plan included a final trip to Poppy Hills for a few holes before concluding arrangements for a return to Los Angeles. Robert donned his best gear (minus the red slacks) one last time before making his way to the course and sneaking in some early morning play. He shouldered Mulligan, secured the cabin, and assumed the now well-trodden trail through the Carmel Woods.

It was a glorious morning. Robert was certain that every crow and jay that cawed was wishing him a fond farewell. He sneaked in three holes and enjoyed some putting practice. The sound of cars rolling up Lopez signalled the arrival of the very first employees for another busy day serving enthusiastic and obsessed golfers. From the fringe of the woods, Robert took one last glance back at his home links — his favourite course — not knowing when he might grace its pristine greens again. A spanking new John Deere wide-area mower caught his attention. It was parked beside the south end of the clubhouse, beyond the driving range. He smiled and gave it a respectful nod as he slipped into the forest. Had he the means and the time, Robert would have chosen to play a "farewell round" on every course that dotted the peninsula. They were all worthy.

Fifty yards into the woods, Robert paused. He realized that he had unfinished business at Poppy and retraced his steps. Looking around to see if anyone was yet near, he crept past the driving range, over the practice putting green, and up to the John Deere. He hefted Mulligan off his shoulder and positioned the bag and clubs atop the driver's seat. There, the clubs could not be missed. Truth is, they were never Robert's clubs. Every one of them was technically stolen. As a lawyer, he could argue the legal case of abandonment, but he wanted to do something, if only symbolic, to earn himself some positive karma. While he had no idea if the groundskeeper who chased him was still employed, he wanted to offer a small gesture. He hoped that the man played golf, didn't have clubs of this quality, and didn't mind a mixed-brand, Mulligan stew of clubs.

"So long," he offered to the bag of clubs and wide-area mower.

The sound of voices and car doors closing confirmed that employees were near. Rob bounded into the woods, this time, with speed and agility afforded by the absence of a golf bag weighing him down.

Rob felt relieved. He acknowledged some degree of self-righteousness in returning the clubs. Beyond that, he was gratified to be leaving the woods, as much as he had come to love the place. He still had a bus ticket to purchase and would pack light, carrying only that which would fit in his duffel. It reminded him of his not-too-distant past. As a student at Stanford, he'd carry a duffel bag full of clothes, books, and CDs back home to Los Angeles at the end of each semester. It became a biannual family reunion. His dad would meet him at the bus station, in his maroon Benz, and they'd talk about plans for the summer on the drive home. The memory evoked a sense of happiness that now felt somehow less distant. He looked forward to returning home, even if his now deceased father would not be there to pick him up.

chapter 34

Ahead, on the trail, he saw a familiar face enjoying her morning walk. They had crossed paths on a few occasions, as Robert slipped back to the ravine after a playing a few holes. They were on a speaking basis, if not a first name one.

"Good morning. Surely you haven't finished a round already."

"No," said Rob. "I've absentmindedly forgotten my clubs. Just heading back to the house to fetch them. It's a lovely day. Enjoy your walk."

"And you, your golf," she said. "Best mind yourself. I just saw some Public Works trucks coming up the trail. Cutting up some fallen trees, I expect."

Her comment triggered concern. The thought of trucks in the woods was unsettling. Robert had never seen or heard them before. He listened but did not hear any. *They must have turned west, away from the ravine*, he assumed. He diverged from the most frequently used trail and trudged cautiously into and through the dense tree coverage. Robert climbed over logs and deadfall that lay between himself and the ravine. Before he could lay eyes on them, he heard the voices of men — many of them. *Is it Public Works and are they really out managing the forest today?* he wondered. If so, he hoped that's all they were doing. Alternatively, it might have just been a group of hikers who strayed near the gulley and were particularly vocal.

The Carmel Woods is a relatively small area and the tree coverage much more controlled and thinned out than in a true wilderness area. That coverage offered both advantages and disadvantages. Today, it was the latter. The voices of whomever had joined him this morning, hushed and garbled as they were, became increasingly clear as he stalked his own camp. Like the animals that he had observed so frequently, he made certain that there was always a tree between he and them, for security. The voices became louder as he approached. Robert couldn't make out the words but could soon discern between voices of numerous men, that were now surrounding his home. Those were joined disembodied voices on two-way radio — walkie-talkies or a VHF — he presumed. The conclusion was gut wrenching. They had found his camp. Robert's second thought: *It was the boys after all!*

"Shit!" he muttered softly. "Little fuckers!"

He wiped an unexpected tear from his eye. He knew he should just leave woods and immediately. Curiosity got the better of him. He wanted to know — needed to know — who they were and what they would do with his home and belongings. *Will they dismantle my home immediately or is this just a reconnaissance mission?* Best-case scenario, he could come back after dark to retrieve some belongings before they literally dismantled the foundation of his life. Worst-case scenario…

Hunched low and approaching slowly, he spied the large dark forms of two all-wheel-drive quad-cab pickup trucks on the low rise ten yards from his shack. As it lay in a small shallow beyond the earth berm, the cabin itself was obscured. He stopped short, just twenty yards from the site, and lay prone to obscure his form and shape. His chin and bare hands settled into the musty, decomposing leaves and sticks. For a moment, he felt like a hunter without a rifle. The irony was not lost on him. It was he who was being pursued, and he had narrowly escaped capture.

Upwind of the site, Robert realized they might hear him. Of course, had he known what would happen this morning, he might have planned a stealthy, downwind approach. The worst part of being upwind is that it made it infinitely more difficult to hear exactly what was being said. He could only imagine their conversation. It didn't matter. The sound of men's voices soon gave way to the agonizing sounds of sledgehammers and pry bars tearing his home into small, manageable pieces for removal and destruction.

It was heartbreaking to watch. The sound was worse. The cabin screamed like a living creature. He winced with each cry of weathered cedar boards. All his effort scavenging and jury-rigging a home would be demolished in the span of an hour or two. As he lay in the leaves, he remembered collecting the junk, carefully engineering the cabin, placing each stick, log, board, piece of corrugated metal, scavenged metal sign, and "borrowed" building supply that comprised it. Building the cabin had given him purpose. It had brought a joy that can only be experienced by people who discover, apply, and appreciate their newfound resourcefulness. The loss of something he built with his own hands proved to have a greater emotional impact than the sale of his and Jules's marital home. Robert had been immensely proud of what he assembled. His shack would have received praise from Bear Gryllis and "Survivorman" Les Stroud. It would have gained the admiration of every survivalist in America. It would have likewise earned him a goddamn Eagle Scout badge.

Robert harboured no ill will toward the men. He did, however, mutter, "*Hijos de puta,*" under his breath a few times as they tore into his walls and roof. It was understandable. They were just doing their job. He watched the men, municipal workers, he presumed, intently. Remaining at the site represented a risk and Robert knew it. It was a little like stopping on the highway to rubberneck an accident scene and catch a glimpse of the mangled steel and bodies strewn about. It was too personal to simply slink away.

One by one, men rose from below the berm to access the bed of the pickup trucks on the rise. Every time they emerged, they were hefting an armful of building materials — now refuse. Robert recognized each individual piece, its place in the cabin, and knew which adjacent piece they were likely to bring up next. Full sections of wall were unceremoniously heaved into the trucks, followed by the front door, torn from its garden-gate hinges; the tollbooth window, now broken; and the window frame. The walls alone filled one of the Ford F-150 double cabs. They tore at the carcass of the cabin like hyenas disembowelling a sickened wildebeest. Robert could hear the final audible cry of the metal roof as it collapsed, the structural support of the walls finally and permanently undermined.

Suddenly, it hit him. His watch. His Rolex — the most precious thing he owned — had been on the bedside table, next to the framed photo of Jules. The tears flowed as if he had just lost her all over again. His favourite photo of Jules and her wedding gift were gone. Or at least he presumed so. Either one of the men had filched the Rolex from the cabin or it was lying somewhere within the trucks — a footnote to the tattered heap that once was his home. Robert's sorrow at the loss turned at once to anger. He changed his mind. He *did* harbour ill will toward the men — enough ill will to take action.

He reached for a five-foot-long branch, almost three inches in diameter, which lay behind him. Fury permeated every part of him as he grasped it firmly and rose from a prone position to a low crouch. He was poised to strike and ready to defend his home. *Six against one*, he reasoned, *are not great odds*. An attack would result in an almost certain return trip to the Carmel Police Department lockup. Resigned, he lay back down behind the log and sobbed. Had the men not been making so much noise, they would have surely heard him in the silence of the ravine. Robert lay prone and motionless, waiting for it all to be over, and powerless to do anything more. The tears continued. He swept them away with dirty hands that transferred to his cheeks, leaving his face smudged by mud that looked like a sniper in camouflage paint. To his disappointment, he proved to be more pacifist than fighter.

Robert spent more than an hour mired in the dirt and leaves. The sound of four heavy doors closing and diesel trucks starting signalled that the party had concluded their demolition. The deed was done. Laden with the remains of Robert's home, the trucks threaded between the trees slowly and eased their way back through the woods. Once they reached the trail, they could turn either way to get back to paved roads and, Robert imagined, the local landfill. He considered going there at first light to search, hoping he might recover some of his belongings.

Everything is now gone now. Jules. The watch. The house in LA. My career. My relationship with Kate. My home in the Carmel Woods. All gone. Even after the trucks left, Robert lay on the forest floor. Robert had no idea where he would go, no idea what he would do or where he would sleep that evening. He was now genuinely and literally homeless.

The site was once again silent. Robert rose from his blind and shuffled toward his cabin site, afraid of what he knew he'd see. It was like an open-casket funeral. It bore no resemblance to the home he knew. The rock foundation was the only part of the cabin remaining. The rest was a horrific mess. Robert sifted through the few remains of wood splinters, screws, rope, and shards of road signs that endured. The City of Carmel, he assumed, had at least finally solved the mystery of the stolen road signs and tollbooth window. He wondered if the police might show up next as part of some formal criminal investigation.

He reached to his pocket for his new cell phone only to realize that it too had been in the cabin and now, likely among the demolished remains in the trucks. The only belongings he could find at the site were the aluminum cup that once served as receptacle for his French Press, one sock, and a couple of golf balls. He put one ball in his pants pocket and moved from the cabin to a location, some two hundred feet away. There he uncovered the buried safe box and removed the contents, and then he fled the woods. The site would likely attract additional authorities, and Robert wanted to get out as soon as possible. Once on the trail, he headed toward a familiar location — Poppy Hills. He knew the woods surrounding the course better than anyone and assumed that he could bivouac for the night in the forest fringe and enjoy relative security. If anyone initiated a search of the ravine and proximity, they'd be unlikely to poke around the golf course; the police would be sensitive to the concerns of the course manager, and a police dragnet might prove alarming to golfers. In the morning, Robert would have to leave town.

Robert spent his last night in the woods much as he had spent his first: fitful, uncomfortable, and largely sleepless. Tucked in a bivy sack, beneath a large pine, was wilderness camping at its best — and by that, I mean worst.

chapter 35

Life doesn't always deliver structured curricula. It had been a long and grueling semester, but Robert had learned something — mostly about himself. Self-directed learning often proves to be the most effective. It certainly proved so for him. Without Robert realizing it, grief's caustic smog had somehow softened the hard edges of lives he had experienced: that of well-paid professional and suburban homeowner, and of a hermit living in a shack in the woods. Robert had gone from having everything to having nothing. He had lost love, found love, and lost it again. His experiences had, however, brought him entirely unanticipated perspective. Resolution? Perhaps not. Personal growth? Certainly. Robert had wrestled with and beaten agonizing and debilitating grief, fought the dangerous black dog of depression and come out with a few wounds, scrapped with the biases of society and their perceptions of homelessness, and had brawled with the public authorities in Carmel — at least to a draw.

Two years in the forest had taken a physical toll on him too, but not all for the worse. His face might have looked older, but his body now reflected that of a more youthful man — a teenager, even. Robert had grown younger. His quest for simplicity had brought his soul closer to that of a ten-year-old boy than a thirty-six-year-old man. Headstrong. Defiant. Rebellious. It occurred to him that he had more in common with the boys he'd scared so badly than the golfers he watched so intently, Mr.

and Mrs. Garvey, the police officer who'd hassled him, and the men who so callously tore his home down without thought of circumstances or consequences.

Robert had always been passionate but life as a reluctant hermit had bestowed upon him additional qualities: compassion, empathy, and patience. Ironically, his time alone made him appreciate and long for meaningful social engagement, acceptance, and, of course, love.

After the immediate visceral and emotional impact of his latest losses — the cabin, his watch, Kate — had washed over him, Robert used his new perspective to rebalance. He was at peace. He had grieved the loss of Jules. He accepted that despite having left his career, he could and would work again. Robert conceded that he could find a home just about anywhere, and knew he'd be content living simply — in a makeshift cabin, in fact — if he had to. He could buy another car tomorrow if he wanted to. He had learned to live without one and was in remarkably better shape for it. He could buy another Rolex someday, and even match the engraving Jules had so thoughtfully added. He would find love again, he was certain.

With nothing but his clothes on his back and shoes on his feet, Rob left the woods and town that had hosted him unknowingly and involuntarily.

Before he left and returned to Los Angeles, there was one remaining thing to which Robert needed to tend. Given that Salinas was only twenty miles away, he took a cab. He arrived at the Salinas Police vehicle compound yard, the only one between Los Angeles and San Francisco. Upon arriving, Robert showed his identification (nobody noticed it had expired) and asked for access to his station wagon. The manager of the yard retrieved the requisite release forms. He led Robert through the bone yard of stolen, unclaimed, illegally parked, and retrieved-from-the-bottom-of-a-lake vehicles that lined the yard in someone's best attempt at an orderly grid.

The compound manager held a clipboard with a map of the yard. They identified each vehicle using some form of code they'd devised. They walked through the yard as the manager looked down at his map.

"Row C. Right this way," he said, gesturing to his left. "Here we are. One 2011 Volvo. This look like yours?"

"Yup. This is it, all right. It looks sad, lonely and dirty. The Hermit of the Compound."

"Huh?" grunted the manager. "Sure. Whatever."

"Never mind. Private joke."

Robert's Volvo was recognizable but camouflaged by the caked-on dust and muck that had accumulated. The rubber on the windshield wipers appeared dried and cracked, but the car looked otherwise none the worse for wear. He ran a finger across the hood and wiped the residue off on his pants. The paint was still silver underneath the brown-grey crust that encased the car. Robert had, for reasons he didn't comprehend, kept the keys in his backpack for two years. He rummaged through his pack, fished them out, and instinctively pushed a button to unlock the car. Nothing happened. The car battery was dead. Robert had no idea if the car would have started, regardless. Two years left alone in the sun can take its toll on cars as well as people.

"It's not locked," said the compound manager. "If we locked all the cars, we'd never be able to keep track of all the keys. Plus, it's a secure yard."

Robert opened the rear driver-side door. The air that escaped was searing but dry. The abandoned artwork remained stacked upright on the back seat. Next, he popped the tailgate and walked to the rear. More art and two boxes of books remained where they were left, hermetically sealed in the California sun — seemingly in good condition. Robert walked around to the front passenger door, opened it, and leaned in. He flipped the glove compartment open and reached in. He groped around and soon felt the cold, smooth silver links and pearls of one half of the wedding Lazo — a memento of his life with Jules — inadvertently left in the car. Robert snatched it, admired it momentarily, and slipped it into his right pants pocket. He closed the door and looked at the manager.

"Okay, I'm done here."

"Great. Just sign the release forms here and the car is all yours. It will be your responsibility to have it towed somewhere to get it running again."

"No, thanks. I don't need or want a car anymore."

"What do you mean? You have to take the car."

"You can have it," offered Rob.

"Sir, we auction cars that aren't claimed after two years. This has been here longer than that already. You got here just before our next auction. If you don't take it now, it will be sold. The state gets the money — not you!"

"That's okay. I don't want a car anymore. The State of California is insolvent. Hope they put the money to good use. Bye now." He tossed the key to the attendant and walked away

The manager looked perplexed, thought about debating the matter more, but abandoned his effort. He shrugged his shoulders, closed the doors to the Volvo, and walked back to his office at the entrance to the compound. It was too hot to argue. Robert exited the gated fence where the cab driver, as instructed, had remained, to take him back to Carmel. Sweat trickled down Robert's forehead. Grateful that the cabbie had left the car and air-conditioning running, he slid into the back seat and said just one word.

"Drive."

chapter 36

Back in Carmel and too impatient to wait for the next bus, scheduled for late that afternoon, Rob picked up a coffee and headed on foot toward Highway 1. Once there, he did something he hadn't dared since he was fifteen: he hitchhiked. Rob had a few days' growth on his face, but nothing about him screamed "serial killer." Nobody stopped to pick him up though. Evidently, perceptions about hitchhiking had changed over the last two decades. Few dared to stop for them anymore. A generation of paranoid horror tales and a few actual murders had long since given this form of carpooling a flat tire. Rob continued walking along the shoulder of the southbound lane, regretting his decision to not buy a bus ticket. The sun beat him down and, though he was protected by the bucket hat, the intense light forced him to squint. It got worse as the sun rose higher in the southern sky. He plodded on, occasionally walking backward to make eye contact with drivers while continuing southerly progress. It made Rob feel like a teenager again, despite his failure to attract a lift.

Two miles and an hour later, Rob passed the entrance to Point Lobos State Natural Reserve. Beyond that, he spotted a little store he knew well a hundred yards on the left: the Carmel Highlands General Store. You might never think of using the term "adorable" to describe a general store and gas station, but you would adopt it instantly if you saw this place. It looks like a cottage. It has stucco walls, authentic Spanish clay roof tiles, flowering vines and, outside, two slightly out of place but nonetheless charming British telephone booths. Campers at Lobos all patronize the place, because it's within walking distance of the park. If you happen to run out of the basics, like beer, it's convenient — particularly if you're not entirely sober. Rob decided to stop at the store. He needed to pee desperately, and eat something, slightly less so. Best-case scenario, he'd snag a ride with a southbound camper. After using the bathroom.

As Robert contemplated crossing the highway, a car passed him and pulled onto the shoulder just ahead, kicking up a cloud of dust that partly obscured it. It was hard to tell if the driver had responded to his thumbing or was just slowing to turn right at the next street. It came to a stop, fifty feet ahead of him and idled for a moment. Rob could see the rear lights turn from red to clear reversing. He was jubilant. It looked like he had a ride after all. He observed hitchhiking protocol and started the obligatory gentle jog — putting in the effort to meet the driver halfway. He squinted through the sun haze and halo of dust the vehicle kicked up. When he was thirty feet away, the cloud cleared. Rob could see the car clearly: a 1982 Maple Yellow Mercedes Benz sedan.

Robert's jog slowed to a slow walk and then stopped. The driver door opened as he approached the vehicle. Kate stepped out and stood, arms crossed defiantly, glaring at him. Any words she might have planned appeared frozen on her half-parted lips. Her face, Rob could see by now, showed a confused mix of concern, sympathy, anger, and love. She dropped her arms to her sides in surrender.

As he shuffled closer, Rob observed tears running down Kate's cheeks, wetting the wash of hair that the wind blew across her face. He dropped his duffel. The two stood there as traffic passed by, cars exhaling fumes and kicking up additional dust. It proved a decidedly unromantic setting. Robert and Kate stared at one another, engaged in a deep, complicated, and wordless conversation. Their respective body language and faces changed from looks of hurt and betrayal to forgiveness, relief, respect, and resolute love. The best pantomimes couldn't have staged a better performance.

Robert beamed and strode purposefully to the Mercedes. He hefted his duffel, walked it to the passenger side of the car, and tossed it in the back door. Once in, he sat for a moment, staring at the dashboard, not certain what to say. Kate broke the ice with a simple "hello stranger."

"Thank you for stopping," Robert finally said. He struggled to find the words he really wanted to say. "Did I ever tell you how much I love this car?"

"I was looking everywhere for you. I drove up and down this stretch of road four times today already. Five times yesterday! Where the hell were you?"

"My cabin…my home is gone. I had to go."

Kate softened. "I know. It wasn't me, Rob. I swear. Your cabin was there once when I went to find you, and the next day, there was nothing but rubble. I was scared for you."

Robert sighed. "I don't want to be a hermit anymore. Or at least not so, alone."

"You don't have to," said Kate. "The decision is yours though."

While neither made the statement, it was understood that both were offering unconditional apology, support and love. Robert paused and looked away — afraid to look her directly in the eye. But, he said what he had to. "I have to leave here now."

"I figured," she said solemnly.

"I'm headed to Los Angeles."

"Then so am I."

Robert managed a half-smile.

"Crap, I almost forgot," exclaimed Kate. She turned and leaned between the front seats to grab what appeared to be a grocery bag from the back. It was rolled up in a ball. Kate handed it to Rob like it was a Christmas present.

She winked as she added, "I retrieved these from your home on Forest Road. Fixed the rip in 'em, too."

Rob raised his eyebrows with puzzlement and unrolled the bag. A Cheshire grin filled Kate's freckled face. From the bag, Rob pulled out the now infamous, brilliant red golf slacks. Only Robert knew their rich history, but both were equally tickled. Laughter — the slightly nervous but relieved kind — filled the Benz. Kate punched the accelerator to coax the old Benz up to speed. Blue diesel smoke belched as they rolled south down the Pacific Coast Highway. Rob glanced at the bare wrist his watch had once adorned, and reached into his pants pocket.

"I'm afraid this is all I can give." He handed her a golf ball, recovered from the remains of his demolished cabin — the last artifact from his archeological dig.

She accepted the ball with a free hand and smiled. "Where in LA are you going? Would like to borrow my phone to call anyone?"

"Yes, thank you. I'm going to stop at my sister's home first I think. I should call ahead."

After his call, the small talk ground to an awkward halt. Kate tried to reignite the conversation. "You had quite the adventure Rob. Really. You should write a book about your experience. I suspect you've got something meaningful to say. It might be cathartic, if nothing else."

"Maybe," replied Rob. "I've got some time on my hands now. Maybe…"

His words tailed off. Rob became quiet again. Kate was hoping for a romantic confession, or at least a profound statement about his experiences as a golfing hermit. Her eyes fixed on the road, all she heard was soft breathing and the occasional snort. She looked over to see Rob sporting an involuntary smile as he leaned against the passenger door, head resting precariously on the window. He was sleeping like a man who had finished running a marathon and followed it by downing a handful of Lunesta. The potent combination of emotional fatigue and the hot California sun mugged him of his last dollar of energy. Kate drove south in silence. Five hours later, she jostled Rob to rouse him, as they approached Los Angeles.

"What exit do I take for your sister's home? I forgot already."

Rob woke but remained in a stupor, not knowing exactly where he was. He looked around, collected himself, and attempted to respond. "Um, hi. Sorry about that. Where are we? I wasn't much company, was I? Um, she's exit 148 — North Burbank. Have we passed it yet?"

"Not yet. We're near 170. Santa Clarita."

Both might have traded identical but unspoken thoughts as the next twenty exits passed. *Uncertainty. Indecision. Insecurity. Ambiguity. Hesitation. Anticipation.* Rob directed Kate's path in a tone and volume suitable for a funeral as they rolled into Burbank. The ride was coming to its end and there was no obvious resolution to the unspoken *them* question. Neither wanted to ask, lest the answer disappoint.

The diesel Mercedes rattled to an idle in front of Rob's sister and husband's rancher in Burbank. Rob recognized his mother's car in the driveway. They were all there, anticipating his arrival sometime that day or night. His heart swelled at the thought of seeing them again.

"Well," said Kate, "this is it. You're home." She looked hurt but resigned. "I love you, Rob, and wish the best for you. Guess this is goodbye."

Robert stared straight ahead — a confused, almost graven look on his face. Kate nudged him back into reality. "Rob, we're here. C'mon. Aren't you going in?"

"Sorry. My mind was elsewhere. What do you mean, good-bye? Don't tell me your daughter has a piano recital. It's payback time. You're going to meet my family now. But, I think you'll like them. Mom's going to love you — and your car. Put it in park and come in." The diesel gasped as the ignition shut off. As Kate pushed on the car door, Rob tugged her sleeve. "Were you planning on heading back to Carmel tonight?"

"It'll be late but yes, I was." She paused and added — "Why?"

"Would you take me back after dinner?"

"What? Back? To Carmel? Why?"

"I have to go back. I left something there."

Kate choked back tears, tucked her hair behind her ears, looked Rob in the eyes without blinking and shook her head. "Of course."

"The most beautiful people we have known are those who have known defeat, known suffering, known struggle, known loss, and have found their way out of the depths. These persons have an appreciation, a sensitivity, and an understanding of life that fills them with compassion, gentleness, and a deep loving concern. Beautiful people do not just happen."

Elisabeth Kübler-Ross